THE FORBIDDEN FRUIT

By: Khadijah

and

Carl Anderson

The FORBIDDEN FRUIT

This is the work of fiction. All characters , organizations, and events portrayed in this novel are either products of the author's imagination or are used fictitiously.

First Edition May 2014

All In Publishing, LLC

The Forbidden Fruit/ Ms. Khadijah and Carl Anderson- 1st ed.

1. Urban-Fiction 2. African American-Fiction. 3. Sexual orientation-Fiction.

4 Cincinnati 2(Ohio)-Fiction. All In Publishing, LLC

Edited by: 1st Choice Media

First and foremost, we want to give all the glory and praise to the Man above cause without Him none of this is possible…

Thank You God for not giving up on us!!!

TO our Mother's, who are truly made to be queens. To our Fathers, that are natural born hustlers. To our Sisters and Brothers, love is love always. To our sons and my daughter who give us our drive and inspiration to make a better us; for us!!!

Our Special Thanks goes out to the one person despite our procrastination and playing about getting this project finished.

Thank You for believing in us and our vision when at times we didn't believe in our selves…

Thank You Skeetee who is currently fighting a federal case…

Our shout outs to the men and women that are living that life and found themselves confined within the rims of those penitentiary walls rather it be state or feds, we salute ya'll !!!

Keep ya'll heads up. It's because of ya'll we write in order to take you out your present state of being if only for the moment you choose to pick up our novels and read.

We promise to give ya'll our all when we put our minds, our pens, and our creative ideas together…

(Believe Dat)

Now! Cincinnati stand da fuck up...Ohio, stand da fuck up...Two of yo very own are making it do what it do. Taking nothing away from the pioneers who paved the way before us. Just know it's a different breed and new blood on the block and we ain't going no where. From the bottom, to the top…

We wouldn't have it any other way!!!

Lastly but not forgotten, to our haters, life is too short for the bull-shit and if you spending all day hatin' on us, you missing out on the one thing that should matter the most, at the end of the day; which is self…

So to make a long story short and a short story sound better, Get Yo Mind Right.

THE MILLION DOLLAR STORY

In the Collaboration of the year, Khadijah and Carl Anderson have really out done themselves digging deep within their personal life experience's of sex, drugs, and money, to deliver a story of this magnitude...

From the beginning they waste no time captivating their readers throwing them head first into the pit of the fire where Black and his family find themselves suddenly awakened at gun point...

Forced without any other options, Black folds his hand giving the would be robbers what they want in hopes of seeing a better day, only to be betrayed and left for dead...

True to form, the forbidden fruit is a fast paced page turning novel full of surprises that will have you on the edge of your seat caught up in the web of lies, screaming out to the characters to watch out only to realize it's only you and the novel. If you think Eve tricked Adam to eat from the forbidden tree? Wait until you get a bit of THE FORBIDDEN FRUIT...

CHAPTER 1

SMACK! SMACK! SMACK!

"Get yo bitch ass up, you ain't dreaming dis shit's real." Face yelled looking down on Black watching him come to life with the realization that shit was actually real and not just a bad nightmare. Somehow through the pain and shock of being suddenly awaken, Black found his voice.

"Don't hurt my family, just take whatever you want and let us be." "Yea right, bitch ass nigga." Face responded snatching Blacks ass out of the bed, meeting his face with the butt of his glock 40 sending him to a state of total darkness.

While Face secured Black's hands and feet, he was looking over his shoulder at Black's wife hoping she wouldn't do or try anything stupid. Once he felt Black was good and secure, Face turned and told wifey, "Bring your ass over here."

At the same time, Mello entered the room with Black's lil-girl, she ran to her mother who was now next to her tied up husband. Face looked at his right hand man, his partner in crime. "Tie these bitches up.'"

Not waiting on a response Face turned his attention back to Black, unzipping his pants pulling out his dick and began to piss into Black's open mouth and up his nose bringing him back to his present state of being.

"What the fuck!" Black screamed opening his eyes, only to see a man standing over him with his dick in his hand, and to add insult to injury, Face bent down and smacked the shit out of him.

"I told you this shit is real and not a dream", Face said smiling while zipping up his pants. Black couldn't believe that this man had disrespected him, he felt helpless that he not only found himself tied up, but his wife and lil girl as well.

"Please don't hurt us, I got 50 kilos behind a fake wall behind the mini bar down stairs." Black just knew that would be enough to see another day.

Once Mello went to retrieve the goods, Face stood watching Black's half-naked wife smiling a devilish smile. "Damn, I bet baby girl head game is off the chain, especially with lips like those."

Mello returned letting Face know everything was good, but for some strange reason Face wasn't responding let alone, moving to Mello words. Then all of a sudden Face turned to Black and kicked the shit out of him, taking Black and the whole room by surprise.

"Bitch ass nigga where the rest of dat shit at! And I'm not talkin about no drugs either." Bending down in front of Black yelling, and to get his point across Face smacked his ass again.

Black couldn't believe his ears that his intruders were not happy with the 50 kilo's but wanted some money too. "I don't have any money, I just reupped." And before Black could continue Face smacked him kicked him and screamed.

" What! You think I am a pussy and you can fuck me without a condom. I know you got some loot around here somewhere and I'm not leaving until I get it or I'm going to turn this 211 into an ambulance pickup. The choice is yours. Now once again where is the rest of dat shit at?" face yelled lookin at Black waiting on the million dollar answer. "

"I-I don't have any money." Black replied hoping his intruders would believe him this time. "Wrong answer, bitch ass nigga. "Turning to Black's wife and baby girl. "Mello, untie wifey ass and bring dat bitch over here."

Mello, did as he was told and fell back into position by the door way. Face took in his surroundings looking at Black's lil-girl, his partner in crime then back at Black before looking down on Black's wife with tears running down her face shaking uncontrollable.

Face looked deep into Black's wife eyes knowing the eyes tell the true story and by the looks of things, Black's wife was terrified of not knowing, her own fate, let alone, her baby girl.

"Look bitch, if you do what I tell you to do, you and your baby girl will be spared, but if your husband don't play fair, well dats another story with in itself." Face unzipped his pants allowing his member to be exposed. As if she knew what was being asked of her, Black's wife went into survivor mode.

" If this nigga want his dick sucked in order to save me any my baby girl, I'm going to suck his dick better than that song I hear my baby girl singing from time-to-time." I know a girl name super heard she gives super-head just moved in the building and gave the super-head."

Black's wife took him into her mouth slowly allowing Face to feel the wetness and heat of her tongue until they caught a rhythm. She closed her eyes to avoid looking at her husband while she allowed herself to be violated. Mello didn't like what was taking place, but now was not the time nor place to say so. Black couldn't believe his eyes that she was actually enjoying the shit.

"Hell the bitch didn't even suck my shit like dat." her husband mumble under his breath. Face knew looking down at shorty giving him head dat the shit was going to be off the chain.

"Yea bitch, take this dick." Face said in between the ooh's and ha's pumping his dick in and out her mouth. Right before he was about to bust, he snatch his dick from her wet hot mouth only to turn around and shoot his load into Black's face. " What the fuck!" was all Black could say while trying to elude the fire works coming out the head of Face bell-head.

"Now bitch ass nigga, where my money at?" Black being in his feeling after being pissed on and now a nigga shoot his load in his face responded a little aggressive. "I told you, I don't have no money." Sticking to his story. "Wrong answer." Face said, turning on his heels rising his 40 Cal on Black's wife (POP-POP) straight head shots sending her to another place. "Damn, shorty head game was one in million, but the bitch had to go to prove a point."

Everybody in the room was in shock. Black began to cry out about the murder of his wife until Face smacked the shit out of him saying, "man up nigga! You know the deal." Then turning to look at Black' s lil-girl and how she was taking it cause the lil-bitch haven't said nothing or shed one tear. If looks could kill, Face knew he would be dead looking at the way she was looking at him.

Face turned back to Black. "I'm going to ask you one more time ,where dat loot at,. The wrong answer again will be the cause of me putting this dick. (Holding his dick in his hand) in your lil-girl and then I'm going to lay her ass to rest over there next to her mom.

" Okay- okay, you win. Look in my daughters room in the closet, pull back the carpet and pop the floor broad, their should be close to million dollars in there just take everything and let us be."

Seeing the mother of his only child, his wife, his better half being violated and murdered right in front of his very own eyes and not being able to help, let alone, protect her was enough to throw in the towel and to think his baby girl would be next was unthinkable.

From the location of Black's daughter room closet, Mello spoke to Face threw their wireless walkie-talkie. "Wrap the present and let's ride."

Face received the message loud and clear and a devilish smile appeared and now everything was in order. Face quickly went to Black's position without a word being spoken put him straight to rest, two to the head. Now he had to do the lil-girl, not that he cared, but the lil-bitch was a witness and she had to go. As he turned to finish his B.I, he was taken back by the words she spoke. "Before you kill me, can I see your face?"

Face was fucked up off dat, he had to entertain her conversation. "Why the fuck you want to see my face when it will be the last face you'll see in this life time?" "I was always taught you look a person in the eyes before you kill'em and I want to give you dat opportunity, plus to see the face I need to look for once you cross over to the other side on judgment day, so I can revenge the murder of my mother, my father and myself."

Face couldn't believe the words being spoken, that someone dat young could be so gangta. That he had to grant shorty her wish by taking off his ski-mask looking directly into her eyes before lying the lil-bitch to rest.

POP-POP!!!!

"See yo ass on the other side." Face quietly told himself before existing the room to retrieve the cans of gasoline to set this bitch ablaze because never could Face leave any physical evidence behind...

CHAPTER 2

Coming Of Age

Face and Mello were from Evanston better known as E-Town. They lived in the Notorious ST-Léger's Projects. While one (Mello) learning the ways of the world looking out his P.J's windows, the other (Face) was out there living dat shit. Even doe, the projects they lived in wasn't the biggest one in the city, but big enough to hold its own. People from all walks of life out of Citi, Ohio, respected them boy's from E-town.

Face was 15 years older than Mello and being dat the projects was pretty small everybody knew everybody and everybody's business. With that known, Face knew the struggle Mello and his ill-sister Cheri was going threw being dat their mother was one of the hoods prostitute and married to the Glass Dick. She would leave her children for days and weeks at a time, chasing her pimp or her next high whichever comes first, if not both.

"Mello I'm hungry." "I know baby girl." Mello replied to his ill-sister "I'm tired of eating wish sandwiches, we ate them all day yesterday." Mellow lil-sister continued.

Mello being frustrated about their current situation only could say, "I know baby girl, but to day will be our last day we ever eat another wish sandwich" looking out the window trying to put his plan and thoughts together.

That day was the beginning of young Mellow coming of age. Mello hit the projects with a sense of urgency knowing it was time to grow up and stop depending on the one person who gave him life and nothing else. The one person who was out for self and only self, not caring one way or the other if her children ate or not. Mello not knowing how to get in where he fit in, just stood around watching everything around him, while the hoe's hoe'in, the pimps pimp'in, to the players playin, and the hustlers hustling, shit was off the chain.

Face was taking a break from the dice game when he notice young Mello standing no more than 10 yards away from the crowd. "Young Mello, let me holler at you" Face yelled!

Upon hearing his name called, Mello took off toward Face like he was Carl Lewis trying out for the Olympic team. "Damn young solider, slow your ass down before you run somebody over." Face said smiling at how quick young Mello got there. "What you doing out here anyway."

"I'm just trying to make something happen for me and my lil-sister can eat" Mello honestly stated. "That's all, young Mello," Face said going into his pocket to break bread with the young solider, but before he could count out a few bills Mello told him.

"Nawl, I'm not looking for no handouts, I'm trying to work for mines."

Face stopped counting his loot to look at young Mello and recognize the fact dat the young buck was trying to get his hustle on and not a free ride. "I tell you what young Mello, I like dat in you, and for that and dat alone, I'm going to put you up on game, but for right now put this in your pocket and get at me tomorrow."

Mello accepted what was given to him with thoughts of what's to come and what tomorrow will bring for him as he headed up the street to IKE'S B.B.Q. when Mello return home with two rib dinners, Cheri couldn't believe her eyes dat big bra came threw because little did he know shit was about to get real ugly if he didn't.

"Thanks big bra" running to Mello trying to give him hugs and kisses. "I told you we'll never eat another wish sandwich," Mello said with much pride in his voice putting the dinners on the table. "You lucky your ass came threw." "And why is dat lil-sis?" "Because believe it or not, if you came threw dat door empty handed, you right! Wasn't going to be no more wish sandwiches going on around here because I was going to hit your ass over the head and put your slim butt in one of those pots and make me some Mello gumbo," Cheri said laughing so hard tears were running down her face. "You crazy lil-sis." Mello said trying to put a hurting on that rib dinner.

The next day Mello went in search of Face, only not to find him. He still had 50 of the 70 dollars Face gave him and without thinking Mello stepped to one of the hustlers he knew out on the block.

"Dirt Bert, what can I get for this money," Mello said exposing the 2-20 and 1-10. But before Dirt Bert could answer Face appeared out of nowhere. "I got dat Dirt Bret" Face said waving for Mello.

"First thing first, Young Mello. Patients is a virtue" and before

Face could continue Mello Jumped in. "It might be so, but not for me and my 11 year old sister who don't know where out next meal is coming from."

"You don't have to worry about dat no more, I'm going to put you on." "I told you I'm not looking for no hand outs." "This aint no hand out Young Mello, this is an investment" Face said, leading Mello around back of the P.J's. Mello was lost in his thoughts about what Face had said. Once they hit the back of the P.J's Face lead them to the candy lady in the projects named Max.

"Max what's good baby girl" Face playfully said knowing Max who was in her late 60's but acted like she was in her early 30's had something slick to say in response. "I got your baby girl alright, if I was 20 years younger or if you was 10 years older I put this thang on you, dat 80's way" Turning around poking her but out.

"You just to much Max" Face stated passing Max in the door way before playfully smacking on the butt. Face and Mello went straight to the kitchen where they sat Until Max made her way to where they were.

"Face ,what are you doing with Young Mello?" "I'm trying to put him on his feet, you already know his situation", Face said. Max stood there thinking about Mello mother and how she was running around the P.J's like a chicken with her head cut off. Face interrupted Max's thoughts saying, "Give Young Mello one of those oz's cut up in pieces". "What's an oz?" Mello asked. Max and Face looked at each other and burst out laughing dat Young Mello was so green to the game.

"Don't worry young solider I'm going to give you a crash course on hustlin 101." Face said taking the oz from Maz and opening the plastic bag, taking what looked like broken up pieces of soap, placing a couple of rocks in front of Mello.

"These are 20's and if someone want something for 10, just break it in half or if someone got 30 or 35 just give them 2 of these. It's just dat simple. Now pay attention to the size of these rocks because your next pack will be one solid piece and you'll have to cut the shit down yourself." Face said looking at Young Mello to make sure he was understanding everything. "So who I'm going to sell this shit to" Mello asked looking all wide eye's.

"I'm going to turn you onto a couple of dope fiends that's about their hustle and nothing else. For every three sells they bring you give them a 20 rock. Now, I'm charging you 600 for this oz and everything else is yours" Face said putting the rocks back into the plastic bag.

"So how much am I going to make out the deal?" Mello asked. "That's up to you and your ability to not only learn the game, but to master the game as well. But there is 1300 in rocks in here so you do the math" Face stated getting up from the table.

That day Face introduced Mello to Wannett and Jackie, they was the Thelma and Louise of the projects. If you played fair with them they would play fair in return, but if not your ass was shit out of luck without a pot to piss in or a window to throw it out. Within a couple of days Mello had made close to 1200 and was able to pay Face and buy his own pack.

"Mello, keep yo money. Every time you pay me just go get another pack from Max" .Face said counting his money. "That's cool, but I rather pay for mine just in case anything happens, it's on me, not you!" "Now dat's what up" Face yelled smiling at his young solider.

In the weeks to come Mello was buying 4 oz's and stacking his paper, making sure lil- sister had the things she needed and wanted, as well as himself. Wannett and Jackie was beginning to love Young Mello because instead of cutting 1300 out of a oz he was cutting 1000 making his rocks bigger than everybody else.

With dat, the nigga's became jealous and jealousy breeds envy and envy cause nigga to reach out and touch nigga unexpectedly. During these times Mello mother Louis began to hear and see things concerning her baby who was no longer a baby, but a young man in the making, that she started to watch young Mello in hopes she could find his stash. Son or not she had to have it!!!

//

"What's up baby-girl" Face said walking threw the P.J's. "I need to speak with you" Max, replied.

Instantly Face felt something wasn't right and headed toward Max's without saying good-bye. Once he made it to her back door, he let himself in with gun in hand, only to be surprised by Max . "Boy put dat thing away before you get somebody killed." "I'm sorry baby-girl, but the way you sounded I just had to be prepared," Face said still looking for something or someone to appear .

"We need to talk about Young Mello, he got the P.J's off the hook. He's buying 9 oz's at a time and people are beginning to talk, and not only dat, have you seen those rock's the young boy is slanging? "I know baby-girl, I'm going to have to pull his coat tail about dat." "Don't you do dat, he's playing the game how its supposed to be played he's making these nigga's step their game up" Max strongly stated. "But what I'm talking about is you pulling his coat-tail about protecting what's his."

"OH, I see where you coming from baby-girl and you right, I've been so busy doing me I let my young solider run wild without guidance." "My point exactly", Max said pointing her index finger at Face.

//

Things were finally looking up for Young Mello, He was doing what he always wanted to do, being his own man and taking care of his lil- sister Cheri.

"Mello, I want to go to King Island" Cheri said while watching a commercial advertising the amusement park. "Girl what you know about Kings Island", Mello said trying to play his lil- sister short. "Nothing really, other than what I've seen on T.V." "So why you trying to go somewhere?"

Before Mello could finish Cheri interrupted him with what was really on her heart because she knew her brother was trying to play her short.

"It's like ever since you been working we don't spend no time together, I love the things you do for me, but I like it better when you use to rock me to sleep at night when we were hungry."

Mello was so shocked dat he was tongue tied thinking about what his young sister was saying and true enough he couldn't deny the fact she was right. He tries to substitute his time with gifts when all she wanted was his time and attention.

"You know what lil-sis", breaking his train of thought," Go get your shit we going to Kings Island." Cheri couldn't believe her ears, but didn't waste no time going to get her shit only to return singin, " We going to Kings Island, we going to Kings Island."

Mello had two stash spots in their apartment, one in his room and the other in his sister room where he kept mostly everything being dat his mother was a bonafide dope fiend. His reason if she ever tried to rob him, she'll most likely look in his room first, so he only left a couple of OZ's and a couple of stacks in his room to satisfy her cravings hoping she think that's everything and stop searching.

Melllo went into his room pulled back the mattress and placed the little amount of crack he had on him next to the couple of oz's that was already there and picked up a band to go alone with what he already had in his pocket to make sure lil-sis enjoyed her self to the fullest. Once he returned to the living room Cheri was still singing," We going to Kings Island we going to Kings Island."

Mello looked at his lil-sister and smiled for the first time that day knowing he made the right decision to spend some time with her , instead of hugging the block making moves with thugs and taking penitentiary chances.

CHAPTER 3

Momma Gone

Kings Island was everything and then some, especially for a 14 year old boy and 11 year old lil-girl, who never been anywhere, let alone, travel outside the confinement of their neighborhood. Mello and Cheri enjoyed everything Kings Island had to offer, from the rides, to the games, to the food, and even the water park. They took the time to ride everything they could and the ones they couldn't because of Cheri not being tall enough, big bra made it happen by hitting the person in charge with a little something-something to look the other way while they got their ride on.

Mello was on natural high seeing Cheri having the time of her life, he never wanted this feeling to end. Seeing the sparkle in her eyes and hearing the joy in her voice was enough for Mello to make a silent promise to himself dat he'll always take a day or two out the week to be with his lil-sister because as sure as the day is bright and the sky is blue, Cheri won't always be lil-Cheri.

It was midnight when Cheri and Mello returned from Kings Island, even doe it was way pass Cheri bed time, she was still wide awake from the excitement of being at Kings Island and experiencing something she'd only seen on T.V.

"Thanks, big bra" Cheri said entering their three bed room apartment. "It's all good" Mello replied while throwing the many teddy bears and souvenirs on the love seat in the living room, shooting straight to his room to get his pack to hit the block, only to be surprised. "What the fuck"!!!

Cheri hearing her brothers outburst came running to see what the outburst was about, only to be surprised her damn self of how her brother room had been turned upside down. "What happen" Was all she was able to get out before reality set in dat cause Mello to turn and race down the hall way to his lil-sister room. Once their Mello realize everything he preplan for had finally came full-circle.

"Mello what's going on? and what happen to your room? and why are you standing in the middle of my room?"

With Cheri, coming at Mello with all type of question, Mello had to think quickly because the last thing he wanted to do was scare her or take away her joy from going to Kings- Island. "I'm just making sure Moms didn't tear up your room too, for me not taking the garbage out and cleaning the house up like she told me to. "Why she be trippin like dat?" "Who knows" Mello said turning around heading to his room.

 Dat whole night Mello laid in his bed thinking and wondering what was going through is mother head, while she plotted and stole from her first born, as if he was some trick on the street her pimp sent her after.

What Mello discovered the next morning hurt him even more, when he went to his mother room not to find her there, wasn't at all surprising under the circumstances, but to see her closet empty and all her belongings gone. That shit brought a ton of emotions, and feelings to his head. "I cant believe this bitch, she not only stole from me she packed all her shit and left without leaving a fucking note. ANIT THIS ABOUT A BICTH!!!

Mello really had to step his game up not only be big bra, but Mamma and Daddy too. In the coming weeks, Mello did just dat. He cleaned the house, cooked meals, and took his lil-sister to school every day while attending school as well. Everything was good until it was time to pay the bills for the month. It wasn't like Mello didn't have the money to pay, he just didn't know where to go or who to pay. Not knowing what to do, Mello went about his hustle with dat one look on his face, that one look dat said, (I woke up this morning screaming fuck the world).

When Face and Mello crossed paths dat day, Face could tell some-thing wasn't right. "What's good young soldier? " Face said trying to spark a conversation to see where young Mello's head was at. Without crossing dat line by being too noisy. "Nothing much" .

"Come on now young Mello, what's really good", not 'allowing' Mello to play him short. "Just wish my morns were around to answer a couple of questions" Mello replied looking up and down the streets as if his mother was going to appear. "Maybe I can be of help and answer some of those questions you look like you " so badly need answers to".

"Why you say dat"? "Because I can see dat look in your eyes and tell something ain't right". "OH, you Mr. Cleo now". "Naw young soldier it's bigger than dat and for what it's worth, I got your best interest at heart."

Mello looked at Face wanting to believe, but could he reveal his hand and take the chance of Face calling child services on him and his lil- sister or will he continue living in the dark waiting on the land lord to come an evict them. Decisions-Decisions, I NEED TO MAKE A DECISION!!!!!

"Peep game Face, I got a lot of shit on my plate right now and I really need some answers about some personal things that are going on in my life, but not at the cost of being taken away from my lil-sister," Mello honestly stated . After standing their listening to Mello shoot his spill, Face couldn't believe someone that young could sound like they had the weight of the world on their shoulder.

"Mello whatever it is, I'll never be the one to cause you to be separated from your sister, word is bond"! Face said looking Mello directly into his eyes. All of sudden the weight of the world seem to be lifted, to the point, Mello was able to tell Face his dilemma without fearing the repercussions of his story. After Mello finished his spill, Face told him not to worry about a thing and dat everything was going to be alright.

The following day when Mello and Cheri made it home from school, the lights were on with a note from Face inviting them out to eat. Mello smiled, not knowing why, but he felt good about his current situation now that he had someone to turn to in the time of need. After Mello finished his homework and helped Cheri with hers, they prepared to leave to meet Face for dinner.

"So young Mello where you trying to eat at?" "It doesn't really matter as long as my lil-sister can eat some good ass fish, I'm good.

Face recognized how everything was about his lil-sister and how her well being meant more to him than his own.

"Don't worry young Mello, I know a place where the fish is so good and the line is so long" it's like they serving crack heads out dat bitch, that the government is sending spy's in trying to get the recipe."

After sharing a laugh or two Face order three fish dinners from the FAMOUS ALABAMAI'S located down town on the corner of Liberty and Race ST. Once Face picked their order up, they headed to Jackson Hill Park in MT. Auburn so they could enjoy' the weather and allow Cheri to play while they discussed the turning events in young Mello life.

"Mello, I respect your gangta and there is not to many 14 year olds I know that would've stepped their game up, in order to survive in this mean and unpredictable world, when the person dat brought you in this world left you to fend, not only for yourself, but for your lil-sister as well."

"Yeah Face, she left me out there." "I know, and I know the unknown is scary, but with me by your side and my guidance, my wisdom, and my understanding about life and this game, you gonna make it." "I damn sure hope so." Mello said looking to the sky.

After dat day Mello and Cheri didn't have to worry about a thing. Mello still kept his apartment, even doe Face asked them to move in with him, but Mello wanted to keep his independence plus have some where for his mother to go, if and when she ever decided to come back ,her key will always have somewhere to fit.

Over the next three years Mello became the new student of the school of HARD KNOCK. Face had his work cut out for him dealing with a young boy that so far held his own and grew up over night, in order to stay above water and take care not only himself, but his lil-sister too.

The first thing Face did was gave young Mello the basic rules of life and the law of the land dealing with people out here in these streets because shit out here was real and not fairy-tale dat some of these nig-gas make it out to be.

"The things I'm about to share with you, you need to take to the heart I don't claim to know everything, but the little I do know I'm willing to share, in hopes you don't make the same mistakes I made "...

#1. Keep your friends close, but keep your enemies closer.

#2. Never be to quick to talk or respond, always listen because a person can only hide behind their words for so long before true them reveal its self.

#3. Always try to see a person for who they are and not what they betray to be.

#4. If you ever get caught up, keep your mouth shut.

#5. Don't make the mistake of trying to talk your way out of a case and end up talking your damn ass into a case.

#6. Let your lawyer do their job and under no circumstances do you snitch on the next man to set yourself free.

#7. Understand what you're doing out here and know the consequences of your actions.

#8. Never let the right hand know what the left hand is doing.

#9. Never trust no anyone.

#10. A dead man can't talk.

Face taught Mello all the different types of hustling, from selling drugs, to pimpin hoe's, to long and short con, to the paper game, to being a robbery boy. Telling Mello, it's better to know a little about a lot, than to know a lot about a little. Face even got young Mello his first piece of pussy and afterward explained and broke down every aspect about sex and dealing with females, letting him know they are the most conning people on this earth, even going back to the beginning of time when Eve tricked Adam to part-take in eating the Forbidden Fruit, so be aware!!!!!

Mello took what Face said, to heart and put everything into perspective knowing things could be worse, but life is good and his lil-sister is growing up, dat she stop a long time ago asking about their mother. She finally realized that it's only me and her, me and her against the world.

CHAPTER 4

The Come Up

As Face and Mello drove down 1-75, they allowed the music to be the only words being spoken between them. In order to gather their thoughts and reflect on what just transpired. (Three dead bodies and a burning house). Face was the first, to break the silence.

"Yea playboy, we made off real good with this one." "Yeah, just like you said we would, but Face I need you to promise me something." "Anything for you young Mello, we're family." "If anything ever happens to me, please Face, take care of my baby-sitter. She's all I got in this world besides you." Face turned and looked Mello directly into his eyes and told him, "That goes without saying".

Mello took the Dana exit off 1-71 with thoughts about his last statement he made to Face. Upon stopping at the stop light, Mello looked directly across the street into the cemetery thinking about his life, his sisters life and the lifeless bodies he left behind, that he never noticed the light turn green until Face called out to him, "Mello-Mello" "Oh, my bad. I just got caught up in my thoughts, thinking how I'm going to spend all this loot, not counting these birds I'm going to fly through the hoodz and before Mello could continue Face cut him off.

"Naw, Mello, dat's not how dat go! Never do you wake up the dead …about your new found riches because the streets are watching and if they see something out of the norm, the streets will talk. Then people will start connecting the dots and have your dumb ass sitting on death row somewhere." "Damn Face, I never looked at things that way." "I know Mello that's why I'm here to keep you on top of your toes and make you aware of your surroundings because there's a lot of wolves dressed, in sheep's clothing waiting on you to slip up, so they can expose their true identity and be the wolves they so badly are."

Mello turned in the back of ST. Ledgers to avoid a lot of eyes, even doe the back of the P.J's had eyes of its own, they were willing to take their chances this way rather than to pull around on front street and be put on stage. Face and Mello exited the Yukon quickly with bags in hand making their way to the staircase to the third floor where

Face stayed.

The night of darkness was their cover allowing them the advantage to go unseen, but Face knew in his heart, somewhere someone was watching. As they entered Face apartment they quickly made it to the front room throwing everything on the floor. Face then went to his front window pulling the curtain to the side just enough to peep out and not be seen. Once he felt everything was all good he turned around to address Mello.

"Mello, this is what we're going to do, but you have to trust me and know I will never do anything to hurt you. "Without responding, Mello just rocked his head up and down letting Face know at least he was listening.

"Mello you got half of everything, but there is too much money and drugs to be sitting around in my apartment or yours. So this is what we're going to do, you take 100 g's and I'll do the same, then first thing in the morning we're going to the bank and get a safety deposit box and not only put our names on the paper work, but your lil-sister name as well, so in the event anything ever happens to us she'll be good.

That alone put a smile on Mello face knowing dat his lil-sister would not only have access to his money, but Face's too.

"As far as the drugs keep a brick or two for yourself and the rest we're going to put into a storage bin , and as we need something, we just go get it, you feel me?" "No doubt Face !and I just want to thank you and say much love for giving me the opportunity to get this money". "No need to thank me young soldier, we family".

///

Over the course of the summer Mello began to realize his lil-sister was no longer just lil-sis, but a beautiful young lady in the making. It's been 3 years since that day their mother walked out their lives without saying good-bye. Mello was now 17 and Cheri was 14, he did everything a big brother could do to substitute the absence of their parents. He spoiled her rotten from day one and never let up; she was the flyest shorty in the P.J's that brought her a lot of unwanted attention.

"Cheri! Bring your fast as here", Mello yelled from across the street. Cheri couldn't believe her big brother was blowing her spot up, so she responded without thinking. "Damn Mello, you didn't have to sky page a bitch, to get my attention". Bringing laughter into the air from the many men and women that were close enough to hear, but far away to continue their B.I.

As Mello began to march across the street with fire in his eyes, he had every intention to snatch Cheri by the collar, but then Face words came to mind, (The streets are watching) that allowed him to think clearly and make the right move. As he stood over his lil-sister, he quietly whispered in her ear, "Take your young ass up stairs before I embarrass you", turning around on his heels not once looking back to see if she fell in line behind him. Cheri never saw her brother like this before and didn't want to take the chance of second guessing him or his threats , so she fell her ass right in line behind him, because the last thing she wanted to happen was to get embarrassed from the one person who loved her the most.

"Mello, what's wrong? Why are you acting like this?" "Look Cheri," Mello paused trying to find the right words to say. "You are growing up and I didn't realize how much until I saw oh boy all in your face, I almost lost control and did something I would've regretted later. Sit down Cheri, I need to know something. Are you having sex?" "Hell no"! "Are you thinking about having sex"? "Yes and no, I mean I haven't found the right person that makes me feel or made me feel like giving myself to them. It's not that serious with me, but whenever I do, I'll put you with dat."

Mello couldn't believe the way his baby sister have grown and matured over the years.

"Cheri, I guess it's time for me to put you down on game about boys and men alike, and the way most of us think. I know you might not want to be having this conversation with your big brother, but I want you to know there's nothing you can't come to me about because at the end of the day, all we got is each other." "You better believe it, big-bra"

"So peep game lil-sis, all boys and men want to do is fuck something." Get in between your legs just to say they fucked, we love a challenge to where we got to work to get the pussy, the thrill of the chase and the satisfaction of the catch is rewarding with-in itself then we finally get it. Then we're on to the next bitch! Know your worth and understand dat what you got between your legs is a treasure and only should be shared with those you choose to share it with because many will come, but only a few should be chosen but most of all, respect yourself and protect yourself and make these niggas strap up"!!!!!!!!!!

"Damn big-bra' you didn't have to give it to me so raw and un-cut." "Yes I did, because shit been raw and uncut every since moms left. I had to grow up fast in these mean streets and these niggas out here didn't spare my feelings about our moms or the situation she left us in, so all I know is keeping it raw and uncut, you feel me?"

Mello felt good talking to his lil-sister about sex and what to expect dealing with the male species hoping it would bring them closer, but for right now he'll have to trust her and her decision making, that she'll make the right decision when the time comes.

///

During that same summer Mello was coming into his own. Face taught'em the whip game to where he could turn a bird (kilo) into a bird and a half. So instead of having 25 birds, he came closer to 38 of those thangs or 1368 oz.'s, which he sold nothing but 3 grams for a 100, to hustlers and dope fiends alike.

"Fuck this shit Mello! How the fuck my money gonna spend the same as these motherfucking dope fiends?" J-Rock yelled looking at Mello for some type of justification.

"Because your money got printed at the same place theirs did, now fuck the small talk, what you gonna do, get this money or sit here and tongue wrestle a nigga all day."

Mello was getting all type of heat from the way he was handling his business, the dope fiends praised him as if he was the second coming of Jesus, but the hustlers were plotting to repeat history and nail his ass to cross. Mello's name was hotter than fish grease in the hoodz. Niggas wives, girlfriends, and baby momma's from all over the city was shooting through to see dat nigga everybody was hatin' on.

One by one Mello laid pipe like a true dicksmen, taking naked pictures and videotaping some the freakiest shit you ever seen a bitch do. Don't let your so call man have words with Mello because he was quick to expose a bitch hand and let her man know his main bitch was just dat, a bitch! And to add fire to an already burning situation, Mello would walk around all day wearing a naked picture of the niggas bitch with the words stank hoe on his T-shirt. That shit alone hurt niggas feeling

"OH, that clown ass nigga think he can carry me like dat" T-love said. "Calm down Tee. You know dat fake ass gangsta only carrying it like dat because of Face."

"Moe, I don't give a fuck! I'm going to pull dat niggas cap back."   "Over dat trick ass hoe bull-moose.""Fuck naw! It's about respect, he waited until we had words to put dat bull-shit T-shirt on like he's trying to send me a subliminal message, and believe me, I got dat", T-love said as they crossed the streets to the Earl Regents.

Out of all the females Mello ran through there was one he kept around because somewhere in the mist of one of their sex escapade Mello caught feelings. She had more than just a mean head game, Annette (Netta) was everything Mello envision in a female he would call his own. From the first time he laid eyes on shorty, it was love at first sight. Her style alone and the way she carried herself was different from any other female he had ever encountered. She was a little over 5 feet, weighting no more than 130lb, with a caramel complexion that complemented her round face and short haircut only she could rock.

"Boy, take dat bull-shit T-shirt off before T-love start catching feelings."

"Naw Netta, get you some business, before I put your ass on a T-shirt."

"And when you do, make sure it's the one that got your ass deep sea diving."

"Bitch please, I ain't got no shit like dat."

"True dat, but I do, Netta said smiling going up the street before turning around looking at Mello as if to say, act funny if you want to.

It was little things like dat that separated her from the rest. Mello was in love for the first time in his life and carried it as such; he spoiled Netta rotten buying her any and everything. The more he began to love her the bigger the gifts got. First it started off with just keeping her hair, nails and feet done weekly, to shopping sprees to May weathers, to ice out jewelry, to the 3-series 325-1 BMW he got her (which Face disapproved). He was so in love he got to pillow talking about I got this, that, and the other, but I just keep a low profile to keep the haters off balance.

At first Netta thought he was all talk until she started receiving all those expensive gifts, then she realized it wasn't all talk and her man was all he said he was. Netta being Netta, knew she had something special in Mello because she could see through the bull-shit and see true love staring her in the face, so in return she loved him the only way she knew how.

"Take this pussy boy, oh Mello, I feel it in my stomach, don't stop please don't stop, oh I~I'm about to cum."

Mello was loving the sound of dat as he turned her over taking her from behind catching his rhythm glaring at that forbidden hole,

"Yea bitch, take this dick", Mello was saying in between strokes trying to put a hurting on dat glove tight pussy.

"OH Mello, I'm-I'm c-u-m-i-n-g".

Just then Mello took his dick from the warm confinement of her wound, taking Netta by surprise only to surprise her even more by forcing himself into her forbidden hole making her jump and take off running hoping to be set-free, only to realize Mello was still knee deep in her ass. After trapping her bent, over the kitchen table, Mello paused to allow her a chance to catch her breath, but instead she took dat time to cry out to Mello.

"Please Mello, you hurting me, you hurting me, baby."

That shit turned Mello on even more and made his dick just as hard. "Just relax, the worst is over, allow me to please you in ways you never imagined being pleased" Mello whispered in her ear allowing her the chance to stop fighting and enjoy what he was trying to give her.

Netta couldn't believe she was actually entertaining his suggestion by relaxing and allowing him to take her places she never been sexually. Before she realized it the pain turned into pleasure and she began to back dat thang up, meeting his thrusts head on and out of nowhere she began too scream, "OH my god, I'm-I'm-c-u-m-i-n-g, Mello -I'm Cuming".

Mello instantly started smacking dat ass taking her over the edge of no return. (Remember Mello was taught the pimp game to, so he knew how to turn a bitch out). Netta couldn't believe what was going on just the thought of what transpired made her weak in the knees as she and Mello came together, that she almost passed out. Mello feeling her knees give way caught her right before she hit the floor asking her, "You alright" .

The only words she could stutter out her mouth was. "W-h-y m-e". Turning looking over her shoulder. Mello picked his boo up and carried her to their bathroom where he washed her from head to toe, telling her how beautiful she was and how lucky he was to have her in his world. "You know I got it bad"? "What are you trying to tell me"? "I just got it bad." "What are you trying to tell me, Mello?" "I love you"

Netta knew Mello loved her, but to hear him say it was something totally different, he just upped the ante. "I love you more" Netta replied allowing Mello to look deep into her eyes and not only hear the love, but see the love. After that Mello dried his love off and carried her to their bedroom, where they laid in each other arms with a new outlook on life, but more importantly a new outlook on their relationship.

CHAPTER 5

I Saw IT COMING

Cheri couldn't wait for school to start, even doe she was enjoying her summer, the thought of attending Withrow High School over ruled everything because she was stepping with the big dogs. She had befriended a young girl from around the way name Peaches.

Peaches was a little too fast for her age, even doe she was 15, she looked and acted more like she was 25. She too would be attending the Row, the two of them became fast friends when some girls tried to jump Peaches for fucking their man, only for Cheri to rain on their parade and come to Peaches aide.

From that day on they was like sisters from another mother, they had a lot in common, from the way they dressed to the way they looked at life being raised in the hoodz. While "Peaches was sexually active and Cheri not, Cheri lived through her girls wild experiences.

Cheri was in no rush to give up the goodies, but that didn't stop the boys and men alike from trying their hand. Cheri had a love jones for one person in particular and they didn't even know it because she played her cards close to her chest never revealing her hand, not until she felt the time was right.

"Trick, you want to go chill with me and my peeps after practice, you know oh boy trying to holler at you." "Naw I'm good, I'm not trying to put myself into a situation to make your peeps think he got something coming when he don't.

"Trick please, my man's people ain't no rapist, if you ain't trying to give him none, so be it. I'm just trying to put your slow ass down on game that nobody put me down with."

"Okay Ms., put me down with game, what are you actually trying to put me down with." "I knew you wasn't game shy, but for real doe, you got that mystic about yourself. With the fact you're still a virgin, it's the thrill of the chase dat got these niggas taking bets to see who's the first to bust dat cherry, Cheri." "Yea right." "For real trick, and you got to use dat shit to your advantage and make these niggas, not only pay for your conversation, but for being in your presence while selling these clown ass niggas champagne wishes and caviar dreams." "Bitch you are off the chain." "Naw trick, that's what's Up!" After they finished practice and cleaned up they met Peaches peeps in the parking lot.

"Hey love," Peaches said walking up to her man, they embraced for a brief moment allowing him to roam her body and smack dat ass before she pulled away to introduce her girl to her man and them.

"Cheri, this is my man Tyson and his right hand man B-more, and ya'll this is my home girl Cheri." They all greeted each other with head nods and brief handshakes, until one by one they began to climb into Tyson SUV. Once Cheri got situated in the back she counted 5-TV's, not counting the ones behind her and B-more. The music was so loud it vibrated the seats. The next thing she knew as they were pulling off B-more began to rub the inside of her leg ~~ whispering some bull-shit.

"Damn Cheri, 1'm loving dat name of yours and everything about you 1'm trying to make you mine, but you got to play fair first." Taking his hand a little father up her leg trying to reach the goodies.

Cheri stopped his hand before he struck gold letting him know. " Don't play yourself B-more, trying to play me so close like you know me like dat", looking B-more dead in his face.

"Come on shorty, that's the hole point of me trying to get to know .you like dat", putting his hand right where it left off. "Well B-more, let me put you with this, never could you know me like dat and I just met you", smacking his hand off her leg this time.

"OH, you one of those, let's wait a while type bitches?"

"See B-more, I can tell you're the type of nigga that don't get his way, start having temper-traumas and get to calling a sister all out-side her name when you already know my name, and it damn sure ain't bitch and for the record, that shit ain't sexy at all".

B-more was taken back by shorty's word play realizing she wasn't your typical young girl in the hood you could run game on. With dat B-more fell back and told Cheri, "I really like you doe." "That's all good, but get to know me first". Dats just what B-more did as they rode alone 1-71. Peaches reached to adjust the volume of the music to holler at her girl, she could tell something was going on the way they were back their talking and laughing. "Ya'll good back there, Peaches asked while turning around in her seat to look at her girl.

They both responded as if they was singing a song together. "Yea we good", picking up where they left off at before Peaches interrupted them. Peaches was pleased that her girl was enjoying herself now she could focus on her thang and make it do what it do. She wanted to show her girl firsthand how she got down for hers. Peaches began to play with Tyson dick through his pants, awaking his sleeping giant.

"Girl what you doing?" "A better question is what you want me to do?" "Don't start nothing you can't finish Peaches." "Never will I do dat daddy," licking her wet lips making Tyson dick stand-up.

Peaches seeing the reaction couldn't do nothing but smile to herself, so she began to unzip his pants and before Tyson could blink she had his dick in her hand stroking his shit nice and slow. All Tyson could do was try to prepare himself for what he knew was about to come and stay focused on the road.

"You like dat daddy," rubbing the tip of his head with her thumb. "You already know." "Then you really gonna love this," putting her thang down in front of everybody, only coming up to say. "Daddy take me to the mall", before placing him back into her awaiting mouth not waiting on a response because she knew her head game was tight and the way she been freakin' his ass. You better believe he was willing to take her to, North Gate Mall, Tri-County Mall, Kenwood Mall, Forest-Park Mall, or any other Mall in the city.

Cheri couldn't believe her girl was giving -a nigga some head right in front of her, UNFUKIN BELIEVABLE!!!!!!!

//

"HELLO".

"Young soldier, I need to see you a sap" "I'm in the middle of something right now." "I don't give a fuck what you in middle of, meet me at the house." Click! Mello looked at his phone saying to himself, Dam, playboy needs a hug. As he made his way to go see Face. Mello made it to Face place in less than 10 minutes flat, removing his keys Face gave him awhile back. Once he entered he could see Face sitting in living room turning up a bottle of Gray Goose.

"What's good old man", Mello said as he took a seat on the couch. Without responding Face went into his spill, "Dig Mello, this broad you fuckin' wit, she's out of your league", and before Face could continue Mello had got up saying, "Look here Face, I look up to you like a brother I never had, better yet, a father I never got to meet because you taught me so much, but I refuse to allow you to pick who I fuck wit or who I chose to love, it's not going to happen."

Face jumped up and threw his bottle of Gray Goose against the wall screaming, "Sit your 5 dollar ass down before I make change out your ass!" Mello knew shit was real and sat his ass down, but he wasn't giving Netta up for no body. Fuck the bull-shit, the boy was in love.

Taking a deep breath before shit got out of control, Face looked at his young soldier and paced the floor choosing his words carefully. "Mello, I've never told you who to fuck with and I'm not going to start now (Mello felt relived) all I've ever tried to do since day one was try to help you and give you this game I've learned over the years hoping you don't make the same mistakes I did, but I guess that's too much like right. I don't care about who you claim to love, let alone who you fuck! I'm just telling you oh-girl will bring more harm than good."

"So what you telling me Netta don't love me? That she's playing me like one of these corn ball ass niggas out here. you taught me better than dat. Don't tell me you second guessing your teachings like I can't see what it is out here." "Naw Mello, I'm not saying shorty don't love you and I'm not saying she does, only you and her know the true answer to dat. All I'm saying is baby girl got a past, not only dat, the streets are watching and talking about all those expensive-ass gifts you lacing shorty with. The people she knows and the people she be around is the ones that's going to bring you harm, not her, YOU FEEL ME!"

"Face stop talking in riddles, I don't have time to read in between the lines to see where you coming from." "That's your problem young Mello, you don't have time to think and that will be the cause of your down fall, not me talking in riddles."

"Can I leave?" "You welcome to leave whenever you get ready, but remember I'm always here when you ready to listen and understand where I'm coming from."

Mello left Faces apartment unsure of what to make out of the conversation they just shared. On the other side of town the things Face was speaking on was about to bear fruit. Netta was riding down Race St. in her 3 series 325-1 BMW, blazin. Nas, you can hate me now, as she pulled up on the corner of Race and Green. She stepped out her shit like she owned the block with her low rider jeans on and bikini top exposing her pierced bellybutton sporting her lady's Rolex with 2 ct. ear rings in her ears, matching the 3 ct. white gold ring on her finger that will sure nuff have all her girls in her business.

"What up trick," her so called girl friends called out to her. "That's what your man was calling me when I gave him a break from eating this pussy." "Ha-Ha-Ha, so you got jokes to go alone with your new car, clothes, and jewelry." "Naw trick, I'm just doing me and found someone to love me for me and not for how good my head game is." "Yea right, and we all heard it's like dat." "Just keep on hatin' and watch a bitch come up while ya'll still waiting on these no good ass niggas to do right by ya'll."

Before she finished her sentence the one person she wanted to floss on, the most; just turned the corner locking eyes with her. Dat same nigga she once loved that told her not to long ago, you ain't; shit don't have shit, and you never will amount to shit! But look at me now!!!!

"Damn Netta, I see you done hit the lottery" Maniac said looking his ex, up and down. "Naw playboy, pussy just been selling like crack lately, so what you trying to do, window shop or buy a little something", turning around to make sure he caught an eye full.

"OH you got jokes" "Naw, I'm still dat same bitch you told not long ago, how I aint shit, aint got shit, and damn sure wont amount to shit". You would have thought her head was going to come off her shoulder the way she kept moving it from side to side, trying to get her point across.

"You still trippin' about dat old shit", Maniac said closing the gap between them putting his hands around her hips, looking deep into her light brown eyes. "I only told you dat because I knew you would go all out to prove me wrong"; turning her around to get another view of dat back side that was crying out to him," Damn Netta, you looking good," before smacking that ass.

Netta jumped out of his reach. "Oh, no you didn't! You lost that right the day you left a bitch high and dry to fend for her god damn self", pointing her finger all in Maniac face."Bitch stop playin' and get your mother fuckin' finger out my face, you'll always be my bitch until I tell you otherwise." "Nigga please! Tell dat shit to my new man," turning around to get in her car.

"Oh I see your new man let you/take a spin in his little girly BMW," Maniac said smiling to himself trying to read his ex-situation.

"For your information you know what they say about assuming, so I'm going to leave dat at that, but since you all up in my__ business I'm going to put you with dat.!", moving closer to him in order to whisper in his ear before saying, "He didn't have to let me take a spin in something, he bought me to take a spin in" smacking Maniac on the ass before turning back to get in her car.

Maniac was like hot damn! This bitch didn't hit the lottery, this bitch hit the mother fuckin' power ball. "Hold up baby girl," as he grabbed her door before she could close it. "You know all I ever wanted was the best for you, even if I couldn't provide it for you myself. I see he makes you happy and I know you're doing what you got to do, to make him happy as well."

"You better believe it," Netta interrupted "I'm not hatin' on you, but don't forget where you came from or the people who was there when you didn't have nothing", closing her door putting his head threw the window to give her a kiss she wasn't expecting only to whisper in her ear, "Don't be a stranger". "I won't", she replied as she pulled away from the curve playing the same song, you can hate me now. Maniac turned to her girls ."Get the 411 on her and her new man and report back to me A- SAP", turning on his heels not waiting on a response because he knew they knew better than not to.

//

Tyson pulled up in front of North Gate Mall looking at his little freak in the passenger seat next to him wishing they were at his place instead of some fuckin' Mall, but he had to keep her happy, plus school was starting, soon outside the fact she kept him happy in more ways than one.   Without even asking Tyson went into his pocket and broke bread giving Peaches a fist full of money, Peaches took the money and told him.

"I'll be through there later on tonight, so make sure all your other bitches ain't around." "Come on Peaches you know you're the only one." "Yea right, tell dat shit to a bitch dat don't know better," looking at Tyson as if to say, don't play yourself. Tyson couldn't say nothing because Peaches was on point and her word play was bananas. Peaches was happy Tyson had no more to say, so turning to, B-more, "Break bread playboy, my girl company or her conversation aint free, so if you looking for something free, I suggest you take your ass down town and sign up for dat free cheese at the free store."

B-more and Cheri burst out laughing, B-more more so because he couldn't believe shorty cracked on him like dat and not to seem cheap he broke bread. Cheri on the other hand was laughing because her girl was off the chain, dat 80's way! But was surprised when B-more hit her off..

Existing the SUV Cheri pulled her girl close to her as they waved at the departing SUV. "Girl you are too much giving a nigga head while he's doing 70 mph down the high way. I just knew his ass was about to crash into something, I can see us now all in the hospital fucked up with you still with a dick in your mouth".

"Ha-Ha-Ha, Trick you miss your calling". "What's that dick breath?" "With all these jokes your ass should've been on B.E.T comic view." "Picture dat" Cheri said grabbing her girl as they entered the Mall with one thing on their minds, shopping. "Oh before I forget, I got to go see my girl Coco at Christ Hospital," Peaches said leading the way to the Gucci shop.

///

Mello pulled up in his new white on white 745 BMW he just copped from Jack's car lot in Ky. He was in his own world throwing caution in the wind thinking it was time to come from under Face's wings and do him, he wasn't on that robbery shit like Face. He wanted to be a rock star and slang those thangs like how dat go.

He pushed in the security code to the storage bin he and Face kept the kilos of cocaine in. As he made his way through the complex to where their storage bin actually was, he pulled right beside it glancing in his rearview mirror just out of habit before killing the engine. As he exited the car he once again looked around to check his surroundings before pushing the next security code. Once he felt everything was good, he pushed the code in and waited for the green light to appear before pulling the door. He quickly went inside and took inventory of what was left of his part, it's been almost 2 years since the robbery/murder and in that time Mello only sold 15 of those thangs all in pieces. Which he was tired of doing, he was ready to take his game to the next level with or without Face's blessing.

So he packed the remaining 10 bricks he had left only to get curious about how many Face had left." Damn, this nigga still got all 25 of those thangs left, I need to get at those, but not until I see what he got planed."

Mello grabbed his bag and exited the premise thinking about how he was going to became one of Cincinnati livin' legends. As he made his way back to the home front he allowed his mind to wander and before he knew it he was turning into his projects in his white on white BMW with Ky temporary tags playin dat R.Kelly, Ja-Rule, and Ashanti, if it wasn't for the money, cars, and jewels blazin from his speakers.

All eyes were on him because it was a new car flossing down their block in the night of darkness concealing the persons identity. That shit alone was a no-no, especially if you wasn't from E-town or St-Ledgers.   Mello was feeling himself and lovin' all the attention from his peeps not knowing it was him. He went down the street which was cool with the on lookers being the street was a dead end, Mello had to come back up and when he did he better have his ghetto pass in hand or shit was about to get hectic.

As Mello made his way back up the street he knew he had to reveal his hand and reveal it fast because the niggas in this projects didn't play dat flossing shit on their block and especially at night. That shit alone was a sign of disrespect and to disrespect them boy's from E-town was sure way to find yourself taking a dirt nap. So when Mello passed the first couple of people on the strip he called out to them,

"What's good Pee-wee and Snake," taking them by surprise before they could kick the bull-shit off. "Mello, is dat you?" Peewee said hoping he wasn't hearing correctly because shit was about to pop off like the 4th of July. "You better believe it", Mello replied smiling to himself knowing niggas was mad they couldn't touch him and the fact it was him Shinning like new money.

"Damn Mello, you out done yourself with this one." Peewee said putting his twin 9mm back in his waist band letting Mello know he came close to seeing his maker. Once Mello parked he stayed inside his whip just long enough to hit them off with another verse from Ja-rule, you couldn't walk a mile in my shoes, you don't posse the heart that I do, adding insult to injury~ Mello felt like fuck'em. This was the new Mello in the making, somewhat of his coming out party that no one knew they were invited to.

He existed his car with bag in hand concealing its contents, that shit alone made his dick hard knowing he was carrying 10 bricks and nobody knew. Mello made it to his place without any problems, only to enter his domain to find his girl in her birthday suit.

"Hey Daddy, Netta said before bending over the love seat the way Mello liked it. (Ass up face down). "Damn baby girl", Mello said closing the gap between them dropping his bag at his feet ~. ripping his clothes off like they were illegal to wear. Once naked Mello dropped to his knees bringing himself eye level to dat one hole, he placed his hands on her ass cheeks smacking both of them to hear the sound he so badly wanted and needed to hear, "Give it to me Daddy." Mello parted her ass cheeks like the red sea and feasted on dat forbid-den hole for about 5 minutes. The room was filled with nothing, but Netta voice.

"God damn nigga! Eat dat ass, oh Mello I'm about •to c-u-m". Right then Mello stopped to apply 8 1/2 inches of raw dick to her wet awaiting pussy. "Yes Daddy, punish your pussy", bracing herself bent over the love seat.

Mello beat the pussy up for the next 10 minutes, pulling her hair smacking her on the •ass in between of talking shit letting her know how he get down until he felt himself about to erupt, then Mello pulled his dick from her dripping wet pussy turning her around and damn near poked her eyes out trying to find the warm confinement of her mouth telling her, "Taste yourself and you bet not spill a drop", pumping in and out her mouth until he let loose.

Netta couldn't believe she actually swallowed for the first time in her life that the thought of it made her cum again. Mello took her places sexually that no other man ever have, his dick was like dat and his head game was like no other. Netta stared off into space thinking those exact things until Mello broke her train of thoughts, "You al-right?" "Yea love, I'm good I just had to catch my breath because the shit you do to a bitch is breath taking".

Mello just looked at her smiling to himself knowing he wasn't playing fair, the magic stick is a mother- fucker especially when you knew how to use it.

Netta took Mello by surprise looking in his bag at the same time, asking him what's in it. The contents caught her by surprise even more making her jump with dat one look on her face!

"Mello who you done robbed? because that a lot of shit in that bag and I know from being in these streets The person or people you robbed aint going to take that shit lightly. It's going to be like Afghani- stan around here and I'm not trying to lose you like dat, this shit aint worth it," looking at Mello with pleading eye's hoping he would explain or say something.

she was delirious and because for the first time in Netta's life she was actually in love and not with the idea of love itself.

Mello watched his girl go from the sexy little shorty she was, to a frightened and scared little girl that needed answers. He went to her and smacked the shit out of her before she went into a state of shock bringing her back to reality.

"Baby girl, stop all this nonsense! I told you I was dat nigga and dat I kept these niggas off balance by staying low key and out my business, but now I DONT GIVE A FUCK, I'm about to take my game to an whole different level," looking Netta directly into her eye's before continuing. "Either you with me or against me, aint no room for no in between."

Netta was so excited dat Mello didn't rob nobody, even more so, that he was asking her to be dat down ass bitch a nigga needed to have when doing dirt in these streets.

"Yes Mello, I'm down with you until the end, I will follow your lead and never second guess or question your decision. If by some chance you slip and fall and not able to lead us, I will pick you up and together we will make do," Netta stated coming straight from the heart.

Mello looked at his boo before saying, "Now that's what's up," taking her into his arms about to put down round two when Cheri un- expectedly came through the door with bags every- where.

"Oh excuse me, ya'll need to take all dat to the bed room. What ya'll trying to do corrupt a sister or what? It's bad enough I got peep pressure in the streets, but to come home to a live porno is a little too much," Cheri said watching her brother and Netta get ghost down the hall way.

CHAPTER 6

Criminal Minded

While the world and everything in it was moving 100 MPH, Face was on cruise control paying close attention and listening to everything around him by keeping his eyes and ears to the streets. This shit wasn't a horse race where Face wore blinders only seeing and paying attention to the things in front of him.

This was his life, his lively hood and everything he did had to be calculated to the last step because if not, his next move could be his last! Looking at Face and his outer appearance no one would have guessed he was 5 mill strong and the owner of ST. Ledges projects, he didn't have to rob people, sell drugs, or do anything else illegal, but the shit was addictive and he was an addict within himself in need of a fix dat one way!

While Mello was doing him, Face was plotting their next robbery. Face didn't bother fuckin with small fish he'd wait until they got their weight up because if he couldn't clear a mill or more he didn't waste his time. Face was a true student to the game, he studied hard and learned everything there was to know about his Vic? What type of females they liked, to the places they ate at, all the way down to their daily routine, and when it was time to take the final exam, you better believe he passed leaving his Vic's lifeless, bankrupt, and their loved ones making funeral arrangements!

///

Maniac, Smiley, and Corey was sitting at the round table discussing the information they received from Netta so called girlfriends.

"Oh, dat bitch fuckin with them E-town niggas", Corey said looking at Maniac to make sure he heard correctly. "Yea, dats what her girl Quanda claiming anyway." "You know those niggas out dat way be on dat blood shit," Smiley said adding his 2 cents to the conversation.

"I don't give a fuck what type shit them clown ass niggas be on its Hell-Town up in this bitch," Maniac yelled making his point clear.

"Clam down Maniac," Corey said "You know I got a little cousin out dat way." "What the fuck you still talking to me for, get at dat nigga and make this shit happen."

While Corey took to the phone talkin to his lil-cousin, Maniac indulged in a conversation of his own talkin to himself, but loud enough for anyone to hear.

"This nigga thinks he can take my bitch, marry da bitch, and didn't have to marry my ass-too. Hell naw! I'm filing for divorce citing irreconcilable differences. Fuck dat, 1'm takin' everything, my bitch, his money, and his bitch ass life making a gun gesture with his hand whispering, "R.I.P bitch ass nigga!"

Corey lil-cousin on the other end of the phone caught an ear full and began thinking about how Mello played himself puttin his bitch on dat t-shirt and now it was time to pay the piper. "Dig big-cuz, I got you on this end just make sure ya'll make it right and break bread with a nigga afterwards". "No doubt"! CLICK!!!

///

Ring-Ring, "Hello." "What up love?" "Nothing much just tired of lying in this fuckin hospital". "Don't worry as soon as the doctors release you the family sending the G-4.""I'm not flyin' out there; I got business to attend to". "We all do, but LA got the best cosmetic sur- geons in the world and once they finish." "I already know", Coco said cutting her unk off "I love you," Click! "Trick, you didn't have to rush off the phone on my account".

"Bitch please! About time you got back up here to see a bitch." "You-know it's hard trying to juggle all these clown ass niggas, at the same time makin dem pay a bitch worth." "So what's a bitch worth these days?" "All the tea in china ."""Girl, you got to be hangin with Cheri crazy ass real strong because you got jokes." "Yea dats my girl, but she can never take the place of you. Anyway when you going to blow this spot?" "Whenever these crazy ass doctors release me" Coco said gettin frustrated.

"How do you feel?" "What do you mean?" "I mean surviving dat car crash when your moms and pops didn't?" "I can't lie, my world is fucked up; when all this shit transpired not knowing if they made it was my driving force to survive. And once I found out they didn't, it was my will to live and my will power to keep on living, but at the same time I wanted to died, but by the grace of God a bitch still livin", Coco said shedding tears not of sorrow, but tears of pain!

//

Everyday I'm husltin- husltin- husltin was blazin throughout Mello apartment while he sat in the living room trying to decide how he wanted to put his thing down. He wanted to be recognized as a major player in the game, dat nigga everybody came to see, but he knew he couldn't take over the city with 10 bricks, let alone the 25 Face had put away. What he needed as the song continue to play in the back ground (I know Pablo, Noriega, the real Noriega) was his own Pablo or Noriega. His pockets was right, but without a strong connect his dream was just dat, a dream! Just when his mind started to wander, Netta sexy ass entered the room demanding all the attention in her boy shorts bendin over in front of him as if she was trying to clean up the spot, takin Mello mind into a frenzy.

"Girl, you want your daily fix", Mello asked pullin at his belt buckle. "Boy, what you trying to do, make a bitch over dose off da dick?" walkin over to her man smackin his hands away from his belt buckle

"Let me help you with dat."

Right before they could really get started Face appeared like a thief in the night.

"Don't mind me, make it do what it do."

"You'll love dat", Mello said pullin his pants up, at the same time tellin Netta to get ghost.

Once she got dressed and headed out the door, Face and Mello was able to share with one another what they wanted and needed from the other. Mello wanting those 25 bricks and A strong connect, while Face was ready to body bag a nigga and relieve him of his earthly riches. They were so much into their conversation they never heard or realized Cheri came through the door and was now within ear shot of their conversation.

"I understand you're not built for this type of shit and I apologize for exposin you to dat side of the game, but then again I'm not because now you know firsthand what it is when a nigga get caught slippin", Face said lookin at Mello as if he was trying to tell him something without actually coming out sayin it." Another thing, be careful what you wish for because what you wish for today might not be what you want for tomorrow".

"What you mean by dat," Mello asked just to be asking. "Let's just say everything that glitter ain't gold and every closed eye ain't sleep."

Face knew he was talkin over Mello head, but he also knew Mello wouldn't press forward for an explanation because all he really wanted was what he wanted.

"As far as those 25 bricks take them as an early B-day gift and I'll make a call or two to my people in the A.T.L and see about gettin you plugged in." "Stop playin! 'For real Face?" Mello asked not believing his ears, but counting the money he could make if shit was real To think he could get plugged in with some major players in the ATL was unthinkable.

"There's still one thing." "I knew it was a catch 22". "Naw young soldier, I just need you to find some pretty young thang I can throw at that nigga Fat Jeff. "

"That's all; I got plenty of young Shorty's dats down for the cause."   "You got it twisted, I got plenty of bitches like dat .I don't need no season vet that's already been turned out to this game, what I need is a bitch dats green to this shit because I need my Vic to think he came up on something special and treat it as such, not someone when he put his back ground check on her- ass and the shit come back she been fuckin dem niggas from brick city, zone 15,down the way, north side, and those A-1 niggas and treat her as such". "Oh I see where you coming from."

Just then Cheri made her way into the room as if she was trying to audition for the part. "Take a picture, it'll last longer."

Her spill was an understatement because Face and Mello was lookin at her like a deer caught in head lights, wandering how long she been there and how much she might have heard.

"The way ya'll lookin. ya'll going to make a sister buy some bells and tie the shit to my shoe laces." "Ha-Ha-Ha, Miss comic view, you just took us by surprise," Mello said trying to play the situation off.

"Whatever;" turning around to leave just as fast as she appeared, leaving Face and Mello to ponder about what she could have heard verse what she actually heard.

CHAPTER 7

Happy B-Day

Mello B-day was the talk of the city, not because of him or the fact it was his B-day, but more or less because of the open bar, the free food and free admission to one of Cinti's hottest night clubs. The RITZ was the place everybody had to be, it was a place where the who's who went to show off their earthly riches, from the newest whips, to the latest fashion, to the bluest ice. That alone brought the many females from all over lookin to be down, from the girl next door to the hoe up the street, to da bitch around the corner.

The atmosphere was electrifying and so addictive it kept the party seekers coming night in and night out. The fact Mello locked down this spot to throw his B-day spoke volumes, it had niggas and females alike especially the ones dat knew him lookin at him differently. Not believing he had the money or the resources to pull off such an event, and the ones who didn't know him was left wondering who the - fuck he was, and where the fuck he came from.

Curiosity alone caused a serious buzz around Mello B-day that people from all over started showing up at the club before 6:00PM,even doe the party didn't start until 8:00 and by the time 6:30 rolled around the whole parking lot was jammed packed.

The owner and the head security of the RITZ couldn't believe their eyes that someone unknown to most could draw such a crowd.

"Drew, we might need to call for more security." "I know it's damn near 2000 motherfuckers out there." "You think he told somebody about the surprise guest that's going to perform"."Naw because he don't even know, but regardless we need to get more security." "True dat!"

As 8:00 neared security started to let people in and before long the party was on and poppin and the B-day boy hadn't even arrived. Around 11:00 pm Mello and his E-town family made their grand entrance, at least 30 deep not including the females. As if on cue, The Game One Blood sparked the speakers with the DJ shouting out Mello and his E-town family causing everyone in the club to pause and take notice to Mello and company dressed down in flaming red lettin it be known they were blood affiliated.

"Damn playboy, this mother fucka jammed packed and you still got 700 to 800 motherfuckers outside trying to get in," Tight-White said as they made their way to the V.I.P area.

"If they don't, somebody let'em know how we made it do what it do", Mello said watchin two females tongue kissing, "Now that's what's up" turning Tight-White in the direction of the two females.

Netta hearing the comment knew she had her hands full trying to keep Mello away from these thirsty ass hoe's especially the way they were half dressed leaving nothing to the imagination. You would have thought this was the Playboy mansion and Mello was the black Huff. At 12:01 50 cent, it's your B-day rang through the club speakers alerting everybody it was actually Mello B-day and the party was officially on.

Mello made his way to the stage thankin everyone for coming out. "Sin-city, much love for shownin a nigga love", and before Mello could continue someone hollered out. "We love you Mello,"Mello responded "I love you to", bringing laughter throughout the crowd.

Then out of nowhere the sound of Dipset, Dipset, Dipset came roaring through the speakers takin everybody by surprise even Mello. Just like David Copperfield, Jim Jones of Dipset appeared out of nowhere causing even more of a surprise, tellin Mello happy B-day before settin the stage on fire.

The club went crazy with niggas throwing money in the air screaming ballin, the women not wanting to be out done start takin their clothes off screaming good pussy aint cheap and cheap pussy aint good turning the night club into a strip club.

///

Back at the home front Face and Cheri found, themselves in an intriguing conversation after watching an episode of America Gangsters on B.E.T about Free-way Ricky Ross.

"Damn, I didn't know Free-way came through Cinti". "Yea, playboy made a lot of these niggas hood rich . On the low ,a lot of these niggas got rags to riches stories to tell behind dat nigga."

"So what's your story.""Damn shorty, where dat come from?" "I'm just curious, plus oh-boy reminds me so much of you." "Why you say dat?" "The way you go about handling your business, to the way you dress, despite the fact you got money stacked to the ceiling somewhere," Cheri said pausing just long enough for her last statement to sink in. "You're not flashy or flamboyant with your riches. Shit! you don't even own a car, you'd rather catch a bootleg or rent something, but I've seen you give away more money than most of these niggas spend on their pack and they driving big boy shit."

"Damn shorty, I didn't know you was clockin a nigga so close." "Nigga please, I've been clockin you ever since you came into me and my brother's world."

///

The club was still going strong with security finally gettin things under control having the females put their clothes back on.

"Tight-White, who oh-girl with the platinum hairdo? Her and baby girl been giving a nigga these come fuck me looks all night." "Man, that's Cheri-B and Donna a.k.a Freddie Kruger.""Freddie Kruger," Mello said lookin at Tight-White as if to say, get the fuck out of here. "Yea Mello, and between me and you, I hear they play, dat one way!" "Yea!" "Yea, and if wifey wasn't around." "If wifey wasn't around what!" Netta said catching Mello and Tight-White by surprise.

Mello being caught off guard by his baby suddenly rebounded saying. "You know what it is", grabbing her by the hips and began freakin the shit out her ass just enough to get her hot and wet. "Nigga, what the fuck you stop for"? "I need you to make somethin happen." "Shit! Got a bitch all hot and bothered, you wrong for dat," Netta said trying to fix her clothes.

Mello looked at his baby knowing he had the right one because shorty was a wild one."Baby girl, I need you-", Mello said and started whispering in her ear only to end the conversations tellin her, "Make it happen". "Boy, you lucky I love you", turning around to make whatever happen, happen. "Tell me it aint so?" "You'll love dat," Mello said pointing in the direction Netta was headed.

Netta made her way through the crowd gettin stopped and hit on by every baller, to wanna be shot callers before stopping in front of two lovely young ladies.

"Ya'll see somethin ya"11 like?" Netta said lookin back and forth between the two. "Yea bitch, but it aint you", Donna replied lookin pass Netta toward the V.I.P.

"Bitch please," Netta said turning around giving both ladies a full view of what the total package looked like adding, "You got to be blind, cripple, or crazy not to want a part of all this using her hands to rub herself just to drive her point across.

Cheri-B being who she was couldn't allow shorty to get away without at least exchanging numbers. "Dig, I like your style, but to-night me and my girl trying to fuck some bodies baby daddy. So let's exchange numbers and we can definitely do somethin in the near future." "True dat, but I got one better. Dat nigga ya'll been eye fuckin all night, dat be me."

Cheri-B and Donna looked at each other like they got caught with their hands in the cookie jar and before they could explain Netta stopped them in their tracks, "Don't trip, here's two VIP passes, do ya'll."

Cheri-B and Donna took the passes like dope fiends on a mission and before Cheri-B could rush off, Netta grabbed her by the hand. "Not so fast Miss thang, tonight is your lucky night because I'm taking you home with me", lookin Cheri-B up and down before letting go leaving her standing there with dat one look on her face.

///

Maniac and Corey got to the club kind of early mostly staying to themselves observing their surroundings and dat nigga that had his ex lookin like new money.

"Maniac, this party is off the chain. Playboy playin with some major figures." "I know C, this whole set up including Jim Jones had to hit his pockets pretty deep, plus the way these hoe's taking to the bar like fish to water, I know they fucking tonight." "No doubt, because I'm trying to nail me something," Corey said lookin around trying to find dat something. "I don't know about you, but I see what I'm nailing tonight", Maniac replied leaving Corey standing there wondering who the fuck he was talking about.

///

Cheri-B and Donna made their way to the V.I.P area where they were greeted by Mello and before he could go through the formalities Donna was already into character.

"What took you so long to send for a bitch?" "You know what they say?" "What's dat?" "Patience is a virtue", smiling while leading both

ladies to his private booth. "Damn shorty, I Love the' color you dye your hair." "I'm sorry to disappoint you, but I got it honestly." "Quit playing!" "You'll see if you're lucky enough to see the color of my pussy hairs."   "Is dat before or after I turn your sexy ass out?" Mello said turning his attention to Donna. "So why they call you Freddie Kruger?"

"Because my eyes glow in the dark with the fact I got dat over the top head game", grabbing Mellos dick to see if the catch was worth the chase.   Cheri-B knowing her girl knew she was checkin the package. "What he workin wit?"

"Girl, he's workin with a lil-somethin -somethin, but the million dollar question is," Donna said turning in her seat looking at Mello threw her cat like eyes "Can he work it?" Taking it upon herself to unzip his pants.   "Bitch, stop playing and let 'em know how we get down", Cheri-B said giving her girl the cue to do her.

Mello was lost in his thoughts hearing both ladies go back and forth about him as if ,he wasn't there, only to be brought back to reality when he felt shorty slip between his legs under the table and began giving him some of dat famous amos she was legendary for, within seconds Mello knew why they called her Freddie Kruger.

"Damn bitch, get your money"! Mello said lookin at shorty doing her thang. Cheri-B not wanting to be left out or forgotten grabbed 3 of Mello fingers and stuck them inside of her wet dripping pussy, tellin him don't forget about me while suckin on her 2 middle fingers..

Even doe the V.I.P area was full of people doing them it wasn't nothing to see niggas gettin domed up. The alcohol flowing like water, the purple haze being smoked like true smokers, and stacks on deck like 5th Third was enough to make any bitch play fair, but the demonstration that was being put down at Mello table had Tight-White, J-rock, Noodles, and Dirt bert locked in, like dat shit was a world premiere in the makin.

Being dat Noodles was a true go getter he was never the one to sit back and just watch, "Fuck this shit, put me in the game coach", getting ready to replace shorty's fingers with his dick when out of nowhere someone screamed fight-fight-fight!!!

Netta had just made her way from being harassed by some lame ass nigga who thought she really gave a fuck about what he claim he had or what he claim he could do for her, only to run dead into her ex. She tried to   side step him as if she didn't recognize him, but Maniac wasn't going for dat.

"Bitch, where the fuck you going", Maniac said grabbing Netta by the waist? "Nigga, get your hands off me," Netta responded trying to free herself. SMACK! "Bitch, watch your fuckin tone of voice", Maniac said after smacking the taste buds out her mouth. "I told you, you'll always be mine." And the last words Maniac heard was," Imagine dat."

Those E-town niggas set it off dat 80's way! Turning the club upside down seeing Netta being pimp slapped, Maniac never stood a chance.

//

She swallowed it as Mello grabbed the back of her head. "Damn shorty you nice, but a nigga gotta go and Cheri you taste lovely,"licking her juicy off his fingers. Take this for your troubles ".throwing 10 one hundred dollars bills on the table before trying to exit the V.I.P area stopping right at the entrance. "If ya'll come lookin for a nigga ya'll can find me in the E."

Once in the hallway Mello was met by the owner of the club and his head security. "Sorry about the situation, but everything is under control. Your wife is secure and waiting at the back entrance and for what it's worth Mello, Happy-B-Day." "Drew, it's all love.Just make sure my family make it out okay." "No doubt!"

Mello left the club with his wife unaware of what caused a beautiful night to turn into an all-out war zone, but he was glad that him and his girl made it out safely.

"I'm sorry, daddy." "What for?" "They fucked up your B-day." "Naw baby girl, never dat. I enjoyed myself dat one way, plus I got the baddest bitch in the game wearin my chain."

///

For a person who took a hell'va beat down Maniac wasn't dat bad off other than a black eye here and a couple bruise's there, but for the most part everything was all good.

"You alright", Corey asked trying to cut the tension in the air? Maniac not responding only looked at Corey as if to say, What the fuck you think, before tellin him, "Call Smiley and Chelle, let'em know it's on."

"What's on"?

"Nigga! don't question me like you my bitch, just do what the fuck I told yo slow ass to do", Maniac yelled turning to look at the window instead of continuing to look at Corey stupid ass

///

As the morning air found its way through Face's bedroom window awaking Cheri from her sleep, she turned over to her side trying to focus on her surroundings only to realize her surroundings wasn't those she was custom to seein in the morning.

Then as the night began to play back through her mind she realized she was not only in Face apartment but in his king size bed. She looked under the covers to see what she slept in.

"Damn, he saw me in my bra and panties and I didn't get to see the look on his face. Fuck dat! Where his ass at", snatchin the covers back in search of Face. She found him laid out across his leather couch lookin sexy as hell. "I should just go over there and wake his ass up. Naw, that shit would make a bitch look desperate or something. I got to be seductive with my shit, think girl-think! I got it."

Cheri went to the kitchen with nothing on, but what she woke up in and began makin breakfast. The smell of food in the air brought Face from his deep slumber and before he could completely awake and touch his feet to the floor, Cheri was standing over him with a plate in her hand smiling a smile a nigga would died for in the morning.

She gave Face his plate and sashayed her young ass back to the kitchen lookin slightly over her shoulder to see if Face was lookin which he was, only made her say to herself, "Yea girl, make it do what it do;" putting her thing down dat one way.

Cheri wasn't dumb not even a little bit, she knew she was to young for Face being only 16 ,but she wanted Face to see her for who she was becoming and not the little girl she used to be. Face couldn't believe his eyes,"Damn, shorty letting it be known she aint lil-Cheri, but a young lady in da makin",and before Face could go deeper into thought about what he was seeing, Cheri was standing in front of him again with a glass of OJ in her hand with the other one planted on her hip putting weight on her back leg.

"Cheri, go put some cloths on." "Yea right," Cheri said lookin Face directly in his eyes while he looked her up and down. "You act like you aint enjoying the show I'm displaying", turning around to give him a better view. " That's the problem I'm enjoying the show a little to much".

"Dats what I'm talkin bout," turning around leaving Face to ponder her last statement while she went to retrieve her cloths and be out; because B-day or not her brother was going to have a fit when he realized she didn't make it home last night..

CHAPTER 8

Early bird catches the worm

KNOCK! KNOCK!

Mello turned over looking at his alarm clock trying to focus on what time it was. "6:15! Who the fuck at a niggas door this fuckin early!"

"You want me to get dat, baby?" "Naw love, I got to get up and relieve this snake anyway", playfully smackin Netta on the ass before rollin out the bed. "You know, you done started something", pullin back the cover and throwing her legs in the air spreading her pussy lips. "Shit, you done started something."

KNOCK! KNOCK! Hold the fuck on! I'll be right back."

As Mello made his way from his bedroom to the front door he glanced inside Cheri's room, surprised not to see her there and her bed still made.

"Dat got to be her knockin like she's 14 carat crazy this early in the morning. Yo ass better have a good excuse why you didn't make it home last night", opening the door without looking through the peephole.

As he began to open the door Maniac, Corey, and Smiley rushed in with guns in hand making the door crash into Mello causing him to lose his balance and fall to the floor. Before he could blink twice two bodies passed him like star running backs from the NFL, but the third body stood over him pointing his gun-at his chest.

"Where my bitch ?"his intruder demanded. Mello looked at him confused not knowing what the fuck he was talking about. Then he heard Netta screaming. "Get your fucking hands off of me."

Once she saw Mello in the middle of the hallway with a gun pointed at him, she broke away from her would be robbers and ran to her man.

"There's my bitch," Maniac said watching her run toward him.

Netta damn near stopped in her tracks knowing the man behind the mask wasn't to be fucked witt. "No Maniac! Please don't do this."

"Damn bitch, you spoiled my surprise," taking his ski mask off. " One thing I hate about this love triangle," pointing at Mello, Netta, and himself. "There's one too many dicks and only one pussy to go around, when dat shit happens somebody bound to come up short and find themselves sitting on the side line, but today I'm going to change all dat". Smiling as he looked up at his man coming down the hallway.

"I found ten of those thangs and about 50 or 60 g's", Corey said with two bags in his hand. "That's what's up", turning his attention back to Mello. "I see you been doing good for yourself, but my bitch forgot to tell you something. When you wife her you married me too and when you failed to buy me a car like you did my bitch, I found dat to be totally disrespectful."

Mello sat their listing to Maniac wondering what space ship he just got off of.

"Now I've come to reclaim what's rightfully mine", raising his gun.   All Mello could think of was what ~Face tried to tell'em, but was to preoccupied to listen.

"Please Maniac, just take everything and let us be," Netta cried out. Maniac was hurt more than any thang, the bitch he raised had out grown him and found love.

"You know what bitch," trying to disguise his pain and his lose, knowing things could never go back to being what they were. "I want a divorce." Taking the gun off Mello and putting two in his forever love.BOOM, BOOM! Then turned and hit Mello, BOOM, BOOM " Maniac! What the fuck you still standing there for, let's be out! Smiley yelled. They existed from the back door going down two flights of stairs into the parking lot, jumping a fence by the dumpster running through some back yards until they hit Dixmont where a female waited to take them back down the way.

//

Cheri was half way home when she heard the first shot, then the second, the third, and the forth. Her heart started to beat faster and faster the closer she got until she just couldn't take it no more and broke out into a dead run.

She took two and three steps at a time until she made it to her front door, she tried the door knob and when it opened her female intuition told her that wasn't a good sign. Before she could enter Face called out to her with gun in hand.

"Let me go in first", entering the apartment like a trained pro. Once he spotted Mello and Netta laying in puddles of blood he knew from experiences that whoever committed these shootings was long gone by now trying to put as much distance between them and these two bodies.

So instead of checking the apartment he rushed to Mello and Netta hoping to find a pulse, only to find Netta long gone, but his young soldier barely holding on fighting for his life. "Cheri! "Face yelled snapping her out her trans from seein the only family she had left laid out on the floor covered in his own blood. "Call 911 and get an ambulance out here."

While she called for help Face got down on all fours puttin pressure on Mello gun wounds hoping to stop the bleeding. "Just hold on young soldier," Face whispered with tears in his eyes praying a silent pray to the (GAME GOD). "Just hold on," he continued to whisper knowing the two half a dollar size holes in his midsection didn't look too good. "Damn young soldier, fight lil-nigga fight."

Like GOD heard his cries and felt his pain, Mello opened his eyes to see Face looking down on him. "Face, you were right", spittin up blood after every word." "Don't talk Mello, just hold on young soldier, help is on the way". Mello not listening continued to talk. "It's wasn't her."

"Who was it." "It was the people c-l-o-s-e t-o -h-e-r." "Who Mello who?" "M-a-n."

Before Mello could finish he started choking on his own blood cutting off his oxygen ending the pain and coldness from within.

With all the lives Face had taken over the years he saw dat same look plenty of times before and turned to Cheri. "Tell'em skip the ambulance and send the meat wagon."

"NO! NO! NO' Face!", Cheri screamed pushing Face out the way to see about her brother taking him in her arms and began rockin him back and forth telling him. "Don't leave me, please Mello don't leave me, I can't go on without you. I love you, do you hear me, I love you."

Face feeling a sadness from within witnessing his young soldier take his last breath and now watching his lil-sister talking to a dead body. he couldn't take it no more.

"Cheri! Cheri!" Face yelled trying to bring her back to reality only to be ignored. With the sound of sirens in the air Face grabbed Cheri and smacked the shit out her ass bring her back to life.

"Look, I can't stop child service from taking you. So if you're trying to stay with me, I need you to get your things and take dat shit next door ,You can either stay there or go back to my place, but I need you to take dis while I handle this."

Cheri realizing what was at stake went about her business feeling numb with all types of emotions going through her head ,she wanted to break down and scream, but that wouldn't bring her dead brother back or right the wrong. She had to stay strong for the moment in order to take care of what needed to be taken care of because the last thing she wanted was for child service to take her away to live in some foster home. Never dat!!!

The meat wagon came and left, but the police and homicide detective stayed to question Face and anyone else they could harass before calling it a day.

"Mr. Anderson will you accompany us to the station?" "Am I under arrest?" Face asked lookin back and forth between the detectives. "No Mr. Anderson ,but theirs a few more things we would like to ask you downtown." "Well I'll make an appointment threw my lawyer, at our earliest convenience. Will that be alright detective Trigges?"

Trigges hated when people knew their rights especially blacks' even doe he was black himself he wanted to take this nigga back to the station and beat the living shit out his ass until he begged him to lock his ass up for these homicides, that way he could close this case, but with Mr. Anderson knowing his fuckin rights he had to do his job.

"That would be alright Mr. Anderson", handing him his card and leaving. Face looked at the racist detective as if he could read his mind. "Yea right, get me to the stations and beat my ass half to deaf only to charge me for a murder I didn't commit claiming I confessed.

Good try-wrong nigga." Walking right behind him on his way to his place.

Cinti -Ohio is a Jew city with old money, but the law enforcement is a whole different story within its self with corruption from the chief of police all the way down to your everyday cop's you see bending corners in your neighborhood. They're the true thug's and Americana gangta carrying big guns with a badge to back their actions.

In the last decade there has been assassinations and executions of the black man in low income and poverty stricken areas around the city by Cinti finest.

Shit got so bad people took shit to the streets causing a riot for three days, sending a message to their suppressor dat enough is enough, letting it be known, ya'll can get it to!!!!!

Face returned to his apartment to see Cheri sipping on a bottle of Grey Goose and by the smell of things she found his stash of dat purple. Face took a seat next to Cheri on the couch, extending his hand implying puff-puff-pass. She gently took the blunt from her lips and passed it.

"How long you been getting down"? As he puff-puff-pass passed "   "Just started today, you should've seen me when I first lit this bitch up, I thought my lungs was about to burst."

"I see you handling yours, but you can't baby sit the blunt and hold a conversation." Taking the blunt while she continued to talk.

"Face somebody took my brother away from me, today was supposed to be one of the happiest moments in our lives sharing another B-day between us, only to come home to find him dead." Face just listened knowing she needed to vent, but the last thing he wanted was for her to blame herself and not deal with reality. (puff-puff pass).

"Listen Cheri, I feel your pain and your lost, but the reality of it is Mello gone. and we got to deal with this regardless if we want to or not." We got to bury Mello and find the person/person's responsible for this and handle them accordingly. You feel me"? Looking at Cheri waiting on a response. "Now that's what up", taking the blunt before yelling out" C.D 1, track-7,max volume." That Nas feat: ScarFace, you wet/who I want wetted/ I wet who you want wetted/anybody can get it.

//

Maniac ,Smiley, and Corey made it safely back down the way to Chelle's apartment. "Pull around back and cut through the ally," Maniac instructed. They existed the car with bags in hand. "Park the car out front and bring your ass up stairs."

Once everybody got up stairs and found themselves safely within Chelle's apartment they began partying, even doe it was still early maybe an hour or so after the robbery/murder, they got drunk and high all day heading into the night celebrating their come up.

"I told ya'll this lick was going to be big", Maniac said smiling like a kid who just found out about sex. "Yea playboy, you did, but it's getting late. So lets break bread and let a nigga be out," Corey said.

"No doubt C" I'm going to give you and Smiley all the money and two of those thangs. That should come out to be 100g's, 50 apiece."

Corey couldn't believe his ears and by the expression on his face, Maniac knew that Corey didn't like what was being said. "Is there a problem with dat C?" "Hell yea, there's a problem", standing up. "We a team, so how the fuck shit aint adding up, but in your favor." "Calm down playboy, everybody getting 50g's.You,Smiley,and Chelle, but I'm taking the rest because it was my sting".

"Fuck dat Maniac, you know and I know, even Chelle knows, You aint giving her. shit, let alone,50g's." "Okay C, since you all in me and my bitch business tell me what's fair because the last thing I want to do is fall out over something we can work out", trying not to reveal his true feelings.

"True dat Maniac ,true dat! All I'm saying is show a nigga a little more love than this, you know I got to break my cousin off for shooting us the 411." "That's right I forgot all about dat," Maniac said trying to ease the tension in the air. "I got 30g's for fam",bring a smile to Corey's face because for real doe, his cousin wouldn't see it, taking his take from 50 to 80. "Much love Maniac, I know he'll be happy wit dat." "Well get dat shit out the bag and go handle yo business. Me , Chelle, and Smiley going to stay put and do us."

Corey was a little to drunk and to high to be going anywhere, but he had things to do, places to go, and people to see, so he pretended. So as he made his way to grab his ends and his cousin he passed a standing maniac, as he passed him he upped pipe and hit'em once in the head. BOOM! " Dats for being in mines, bitch ass nigga," and began kicking him like the head shot wasn't enough..

The shit happen so fast, Smiley and Chellle jump up speaking for the first time. "Wat da fuck you do dat for"? "Shut up bitch and go get something to clean dis mess up", turning to Smiley. He got greedy, plus he was the only link between us and his cousin that could lead us back to them bodies. Now dats out the way, you already know."

"Don't sweat the small shit, lets just continue to get dis paper and let everything else work it's self out." "Now that's wats up," looking at Smiley glad he didn't have to do him too..

//

Days after the murder was hard on Cheri, but by the grace of god and the thoughts of revenging her brothers death was her reason to live taking one day at a time knowing everyday aint going to be the same and the same aint going to be every day. She already made it up in her mind dat the person or persons who was responsible for her brother's death would die a thousand deaths.

Her girl Peaches rushed to her aide after hearing what had •transpired vowing never to leave her side especially after losing her girl Coco, now that she moved out west.

"Girl we going to make it, I might not know how it feels to lose a close family member and I'm not going to fake it like I do, but you my girl and when you hurt, I hurt". "What would I do without you", hugging her girl. "Hopefully we'll never have to find out."

Face entered the room breaking up there girl moment, "Cheri, lets ride." "Damn Face, you act like you don't see a bitch." "I don't," existing the room. Peaches looked at Cheri with frustration written all over her face, "I'm going to fuck him up." "Bitch please." "I'm serious, I'm going to fuck him." "Give it a rest."

"I'm' going to literally fuck the shit out his sexy ass." "Bitch you a mess, dat's why I'm glad, I got you by my side . You help me ease the pain and make a bitch laugh when she don't want to." High fiving her girl as they exit the room in search of face.

Face took the girls to Jamison and Jamison funeral home on Montgomery Rd, in Walnut hills. Where they brought Mello one of the most expensive caskets in the place, which wasn't a problem until it came down to where Mello would be buried.

"Excuse me sir, where would the family like the burial to be held?" "I was thinking Spring Grove cemetery out on Spring Grove."

"Hell naw, I'm not burying my brother way out there. I want him buried in the same hood he loved and the same hood dat betrayed him." "Okay Miss thang, but let me put you with this. As far as inviting a whole lot of people, I'm not with dat. It's going to be me and you, the only family he got."

"Fuck you Face"! Peaches yelled taking everybody by surprise. "I'm family too and I don't care what you say I'm going and before I don't you'll have to kill a bitch first!"

"Okay Peaches, You good. But we'll see when the times come just how much you're family or just portraying to be", leaving them both standing there with dat one look on their faces. "What's dat suppose to mean?" "Girl, don't pay Face no attention he's going through it just as bad as me".

///

Within the next couple of days they buried Mello, the wake was at Jamison and Jamison funeral home and the burial was at St. Marks in Evanston, everybody got their wishes. and was able to lay Mello to rest.

"I can't believe I just buried my brother", Cheri said with tears running down her face. "I know", both Face and Peaches responded looking at each other as if to let the other continue. But instead Cheri broke the silence, "Shit just ain't the same without him, just the realization I will never see him again or hear his voice is killing me in side. He was my everything when the one person who brought me into this world wasn't. Shit, the bitch didn't even love me enough to stay around, she left that responsibility on a 14 year old boy who needed and wanted the same things he was giving me day in and day out. Not only did she rob me of a mother, the bitch robbed him of the same", she vented between tears." I can't do this no more", breaking down like the weight of the world was on her shoulders falling on top of Mello grave site.

"Come on love," Face said picking Cheri up and carrying her to their waiting limo where he instructed the driver to one of his luxury houses out in Kings Mill.

"Face, who live out in Kings Mill", Peaches asked knowing you had to have gap on deck just to look at a house out dat way, let alone buy one. "We will once we get there", looking out the window as they headed up I-75.

//

"I can't believe these niggas aint got at me, especially cuzzo. They must think shit sweet around here, let a mother fucka keep play-ing games like they don't wanna break bread with a nigga and watch shit start to unfold and the truth come fallin out the sky. Shit, dat 100g's Face offering for any info sounding real good right about now because one way or the other, I'm going to get mines."

CHAPTER 9

It's All Good

"Unk, I'm tired of walking around like a fuckin momma. Plastic surgery on my face, breast implants here, butt implants there, and lipo-suction. I feel like a fuckin experiment." "Don't worry Coco, once everything is completed you'll thank me later." "Fuck dat, I need to get back home, I got shit I need to handle."

"We all do Coco, we all do."

///

RING, RING, RING!

Sweat lady/want you be mine/sweat love song of a life time, was all Face could hear coming through his cell phone , "Baby girl-baby girl."

"Hey daddy," finally realizing who was on the other end. "Max, turn dat shit down!" "Oh, you don't want to be mine?" "I'll always be yours, but right now I need to know what's good at the home front?" "You'd know if you weren't running around with the wonder twins." "Come on Max, don't act like dat." "Act like what? I'm not the one who up and disappeared for the last two months! If I didn't no know better I would have thought you was trying to play me for my shoe size and not my age."

"Never dat baby girl." "So what took you so long to call?" "Dig Max, I should've called, I would've called, and I could've called, but I didn't. Now brush dat shit off your shoulders about a fuckin phone call I'm making now!"

"Fuck you Face! Had me worried not knowing where the fuck your simple ass was, so excuse me for giving a fuck!"

"Baby girl, don't be like dat. I need you more than anything, I need you to be my eyes and ears because shit done took a turn for the worse and I got to make it right one way or the other and everybody on the team got to play their position."

"You know I'll always play my position, I just wanted you to know I didn't like being left in the dark about yo where a bout's, but everything good. Aint nobody running around like they hit the lottery, niggas still trying to get in where they fit in. Oh yea, before I forget, Netta sister came through here lookin for you, she left a number, but I misplaced it somewhere." "Okay, find dat number and I'll get back at you in a couple of days". "So when can I expect you and the wonder twins?" "About another month or two." "Aint dat about something." "Let me find out my baby girl gettin jealous." "Picture dat!"

Face laughed to himself as he hung up the phone thinking about his beloved baby girl. She was the only person he really trusted, not only dat she had access to all of his money and paper work regarding his legitimate establishment within and out the U.S. Let the truth be known, she was the one who turned Face out master minding the robberies/murder of Cinti biggest players puttin him in the position where he is today giving him more game at a young age then most old heads could ever receive in a life time.

///

And I luv it! Maniac was singing as he headed over to Ice-Mike spot on 13th street. He was in his new element ballin in dat 07 black on black Cadillac Escalade Ext sittin on 26's."

Maniac was smart enough not to spend all his ends trying to keep up with the Jones without finding a strong plug because the last thing he wanted was to wake up one morning busted and discussed going back to being dat nigga that aint to be trusted, especially after taking dem thangs to water turning 10 to 15 easily selling nothing, but oz.'s at 650 a pop. You do the math, that close to 400 thousand!!!

As he pulled in front of his destination still playin, I Luv it. He hit them off with other verse, All the real niggas/either dead or in jail, before sliding out his SUV. "What the fuck you want?" "Claim down Self, I'm just trying to see oh boy, matter fact, tell'em I got some ends I'm trying to shoot his way."

"Oh, you got some ends you're trying to shoot at a nigga? Shit, you aint got to go way up there to see oh boy, get down ducking", throwing a pair of dice at'em trying to entice Maniac into a game.

"You know dat aint my thang", hoping Self let it be and allow him to see Ice. After a brief moment he was escorted inside where he was patted down for any weapons, only then was he allowed access to the main floor. "Hot damn, I done died and went to heaven ",Maniac said lookin at all the half-naked Shorty's running around.

"The boss this way," one of the half naked females said leading the way down a long hallway and right before they reached the end his escort turned around and looked Maniac up and down with a mischievous look all over her face stopping at dat bulge in his pants.

"Aint you quite the excited one," pushing him seductively against the wall whispering in his ear. "If all goes well I'll be more than happy to take care of dat," grabbing his dick through his pants.

"Fuck if all goes well," reversing the situation pinning her ass against the wall taking the opportunity to get his feel game on. "My shit so hard, it hurts. "Shh! Don't seem so desperate," biting him on his ear lobes.

"Bitch, fuck all dat shit. I'm trying to fuck something!"

"Poor baby," rubbing the side of his face. "Let momma see what she can do", unzipping his pants allowing his dick to see the light of day. "Damn boy, you'll hurt a bitch with this", stroking his ego while rubbing the head of his dick with her thumb turning him against the wall.

"Bitch stop playin and make something happen." "You'll loved dat," lookin Maniac up and down before slowly sliding to her knees. The anticipation alone was driving Maniac crazy as he waited for her lips to touch pay dirt.

"Oh shit! God damn, yea bitch, make it do what it do", just like dat she had'em climbing the walls. "Don't stop, pleaseeeee, ooooh shitttt", grabbing the back of her head. She took him to the edge of the cliff of cumin only to stop. "Bitch why you stop", not really waiting on a response before taking matters into his own hands bring himself to satisfaction.

"Who's the bitch now"? "Bitch, you lucky I don't beat dat ass." "Whatever, the boss is waiting", leaving him standing there with nut all over his hands.

"Damn,! can't believe I let this bitch play me", using his t-shirt to clean his hands.

"Get your tender dick ass in here before I make dat ass use the emergency exit out this bitch," Ice Mike said surprising Maniac. "My bad Ice", following him into his office. "I know time is money and money is time and the lil-ends I'm trying to shoot your way ain't nothing to how you get it." "Nigga please, a mouth will say anything just like a hoe will do anything, so don't bull-shit me with small talk come from the hip and shoot me some numbers".

"Ice, I got 200g's I'm trying to shop wit", feeling good about himself knowing he wasn't dat nigga known for having those type of ends.

"Now, that's what's up. But let me put you with something, this is not a democracy, this is a dictatorship! If I tell your clown ass to jump, don't waste my fucking time asking me how high, your ass need to be jumping and if I feel yo ass aint jumping high enough, then I'll tell you how high, you know what I'm talking about?"

"Ice, I knew what it was when I stepped to you, I'm just trying to be family and get this money." "I feel dat, but before you can become family you got to clean house." "What you getting at?" "You aint got to be no rocket scientist or no college professor to figure it out, dat you and yo men done made somethin' happen, but for what it's worth, loose lips sink ships, so tighten up any loose ends and let's get this money."

//

"Bitch, get up! Peaches yelled pulling the covers off Cheri exposing her in her b-day suit. "You need to cut dat forest, dat shit aint sexy at all."   "Trick, like I give a fuck about what you think is sexy or not and if you don't put my covers back where you found them I'm gonna.""You gonna what? I'm not the one who want your everglades pussy. hair ass to get up, anyway we outta here." "Where we going"? "Bitch, do I look like Face?"

Within the next couple of hours Face and the wonder twins where dressed and headed down 1-75. Before the wonder twins realized it they where pulling into the Greater Northern Cincinnati airport in Ky.

"Who we picking up" ,Cheri asked watching one of the planes take to the sky. "Who said we picking anybody up"? "Stop playing Face, we didn't even pack anything." "Don't worry, I got us. I think it's time for us to get away, I mean really get away."

They entered the airport where Face picked up 3 reserve tickets he ordered 2 days ago and instructed the wonder twins to gate 24F to await their boarding call while he excused himself to make some necessary phone calls. " "Trick, where you think Face taking us." "Do I look like Cleo from the physic network or am I just as surprised as you to be sitting here", Peaches responded laughing at the expression on her girls face." You know I'm just fucking with you ,but I really have no clue."

Without warning Face appeared telling the wonder twins, "Let's ride, their calling our flight". Last call for 24F to Miami, last call. Cheri and peaches looked at each other like bitch, did I hear last call to Miami and once everything register they began to jump up and down yelling, "We're going to M-i-a-m-i, we're going to M-i-a-m-I."

"Okay wonder twins ,if ya'll don't get to moving, ya'll aint going nowhere," Face said leaving them still jumping up and down.

The wonder twins tried to control themselves knowing when their plane lands they'll be in the M.I.A. Five hours later Face and the wonder twins finally landed in Miami, they exited the plane and took a cab to the Hilton where Face reserved the Presidential Suite.

"Damn Face, I didn't know you where ballin like dat", Peaches said looking around the suite. "Some things are better left unknown than known" Face replied making his way to mini bar.

"Face, what we going to do about clothes? I want to take a shower, but I'm not trying to put on the some panties, that shit is nasty." "I bet you've done nastier things than puttin on the same panties twice", Cheri said laughing so hard tears began to form in her eyes. "I see you feeling better, Trick", laughing along with her girl.

Face sat back sipping on a bottle of Grey Goose glad he allowed Peaches to tag alone because it's been a long time since he saw Cheri really enjoying herself..

"Look wonder twins, take this money and go grab ya'll something to wear or what have you because at 10:00am we outta here." "I thought you said we needed to get away and we leaving tomorrow! Nigga please", Cheri said with much attitude! "Who said Miami was our final destination, just do what the fuck I ask ya'll and stop asking and questioning a nigga so damn much." "Yea Trick, stop asking and questioning a nigga so damn much and do what daddy ask."

Cheri looked at her girl like bitch please, taking the money from Face. "Who side you on anyway," looking Peaches up and down as they left the suite.

While the wonder twins where gone doing them, Face followed up his phone calls from earlier trying to get the wonder twins some fake social security cards and birth certificates alone with driver licenses to make their trip. The girls where gone for more than three hours when Face started to worry," What's taking them so long to pick up a few items ",only for the wonder twins to come marching through the I door.

"What's going on in here, and who's all these people, and why you got this place looking like the DMV," Cheri asked as she made her way through the suite stopping right in front of Face.

"Look at you, you haven't been back for 21 seconds and here you are asking 21 questions. Sit your ass down and observe your surroundings you'll learn more," bringing laugher throughout the suite.

"You don't have to carry me like some little girl you got to chest ties." "Well start acting your age and not your bra sizes" ,bringing even more laugher. "I don't have to take this shit," turning to leave.

Face got up to chase after her knowing he may have went a little too far. "Cheri, Cheri, bring your spoiled ass here." She stopped right out side the door knowing she didn't have enough money to get far.

"Look at you, with your lips all poked out like a nigga really done something to you . "Why you got to clown me in front of strangers?" "The same reason you asking me a thousand questions in front of strangers. In my line of work that's not a good look, all you need to know is that I need you and peaches to take these pictures so I can get ya'll some fake ID's to take where I'm trying to take ya'll."

"So where you taking us, dat we need all this?" "There you go again asking so many damn questions, I told you before there's two kinds of people in this world ,those who listen to listen", and before Face could continue Cheri finished his sentence. "And those who listen to respond."

"Actually! So which one have you been lately;" Face said smiling. "Now fix your face and go handle your business and let me do me" ,taking her by the arm leading her back into the suite and right before she completely passed him ,Face smacked dat ass.

"What you do dat for," loving every minute of it looking back over her shoulder. "A nigga gonna have to find something else besides talking", smackin dat ass again making Cheri jump. "I'ma fuck you Up." "Tell me something I don't know."

//

"Max, when your boy coming back?" "I didn't know he left." "Stop playing, Face hasn't been around since Mello death."

"Nigga, go get you some business and stop asking so many damn questions."

"Well, when you hear from him, tell'em to get at me." "You done fell and bumped your head, tell'em to get at you, like you somebody important, yea right." "Bitch, if it wasn't for my respect and loyalty to Face, I would have hit you in your dick sucker."

"Let dat be the reason you don't feel froggy because if you ever put your bitch ass hands on me, Face is the last nigga you got to worry about", putting her hair into a ponytail and taking out her ear rings. "I'm not even going to waste a bullet on your worthless ass, I'm going to shoot you a fair one," and without warning Max hauled off and hit'em straight in the eye.   "   "Bitch"! Grabbing his eye. "I'm going to beat your old ass."

"Don't talk me to death," and before T-love could get a good run at Max, Tight-White, Dirt Bret, and Noodles intervened.

"T-love, you done lost your god damn mind if you think we gonna let you jump on Max."

"Noodles man, dat bitch stole on me."

"She what", bringing laugher between the five of them.

"Yo ass lucky, I didn't follow up and hit you with this over hand right." "Picture dat Max," T-love responded with a slight smile on his face. "I didn't know you had it in you, but I didn't come to cause no harm, I came to let ya'll know I might have some info that Face might need."

"Spit it out nigga", Tight-White responded.

"Naw playboy, I got 100g's worth of info", turning to leave letting it be known he had to be compensated for his information.

"Bitch ass nigga," Tight-White said trying to get at T-love.

"Hold fast Tight-White", Noodles said holding him back. "We need to get at Face first before we do anything.

//

"Bitch, what's wrong with you"? "I'm not feeling the name they put on my ID". "Cheri, you too much. What name they give you"? "Yvonne Blout, but a bitch 21 now."

"You act like they put Bull-Mouse and your real age on da damn thang," bringing laugher between the both of them.

"I guess you're right, but what you workin witt?"

"I'm Tracey Bell", turning around like she had a new look to go alone with her new name. "And a bitch 23 ,watch out! I'm goanna set somebody club on fire, you better believe it", high fiving her girl as they boarded a flight to Cancun Mexico.

Once landing they couldn't believe their eyes and the beauty of such a foreign land and why so many immigrants left their country to come to America. "Shit girl, I need to sneak my ass over here." "Aint dat the truth," Cheri responded.

"Ya'll need to quit it, regardless of how beautiful this place is, anit no place like home."

With dat they hailed a taxi cab. Where to signor?" "The glass house," Face responded.

After damn near 2 hours of driving through the mountains they pulled up to a house made of mostly glass where they were greeted by the in house maid and grounds keeper.

"Signor Face, we're glad you finally made your way back home, we were beginning to worry." "No worry Maria, I've just been tied up handling things back in the states and I haven't had the chance." "No excuse, you should have called, now come, me fix you meal."

The wonder twins looked at each other like, what the fuck! While watching Face being carried off.

"This place is banana's, slap me and let me know I aint dreaming." SLAP! "Trick what the hell you do dat for," looking at Cheri as if she lost her damn mind. "You said, slap your dumb ass and that's what I did ,so be careful what you ask for," laughing at her girl.

"For-real doe, do you think this place is Face's or is he trying to play mind games like he got it like dat?"

"Peaches ,what reason would he have to do dat, let alone, what would he gain? When we both got it bad, dat one way!" "You aint never lied, but shit aint adding up", Peaches said as they follow behind Face.

The glass house sat on the edge of a cliff with a bird side view of the ocean, it featured over 5400 sq. ft. of living space,4 bedrooms, 1 master suite, all with adjoining bathrooms. It has state of the art security and surveillance cameras, surround sound in and out the house with everything voice activated. A sunken living room, a chief type kitchen with marble floors and granite counter tops, theater room and a dinning room you dare not eat in, leading to a balcony/deck that lead to a water fall that spilled into a heated pool Jacuzzi ,to top it off it had a retractable roof.

"Fuck this, where's my baby daddy"? "Bitch please, you better get in line and step your game up and I'm not talkin' about your head game either," Cheri said lettin it be known what time it was. The next three weeks were something out of a fairytale, Face expose them to a life only a few experience, but many dreamed about.

"I can't believe how much fun I'm having, this shit is so unreal it's like we're celebrities." "You better believe it," Peaches responded.

"But girl, let me put you witt this, I've been kickin' it with the ground keeper Ortis and bitch you'll never have guessed what he put me on to about your boy. This nigga is paid, I'm not talking hood rich paid, I'm talking gettin out the game paid, not only do he own this bitch ,he own a sea food restaurant, a car dealership, and part owner of one of the biggest hotels over here, no tellin' what he's workin' witt back home.

This nigga living in an 3bd room apartment in' the projects like he aint got shit like the rest of us, I can't believe, "was the last words you heard before Cheri cut in. "Damn trick, catch yo breath. You haven't came up for air yet. Fuck around and pass out if you want to, yo ass be laying on your back lookin' for a bitch to mouth to mouth your ass", walking away laughing so hard she fell to the floor holding her stomach. "Oh, I see Ms. Comic view is back", laughing just as hard.

Face sat in his office watching and listening to the wonder twins do what they do ,feelin' good dat he was able to allow them the opportunity to escape their present state of being if only for the time being because sure as there was a heaven and a hell, the people responsible' for young Mello death would go through hell in search of a heaven.

For the last three weeks Face was planning how and when he would bring the wonder twins back to reality and set forth his plan of revenge and stage the necessary steps that needed to be taken in order to make everything come full-circle, the longer he continued to listen and watch the more he wanted to say, fuck this shit! It's now or never he reason and before he realized it, he was standing over them

"Peaches," taking her by surprise. "I want you to read this book, the art of seduction", and before he could address Cheri she jumped in.

"What you got for me?" Instead of Face getting' mad, he responded. "I want you to read the art of war." "What's all this about?" "You would be the first to ask, instead of holding tight and allowing me the chance to put you up on game."

Cheri knowing she fucked up, made a mental note to start doing the little things Face been trying to teach her.

"Once ya'll finish reading these books, I need ya'll to look at these porno tapes and before you ask why Ms. Thang let me continue, I want ya'll to know everything about pleasing a man and a woman, then I want ya'll to read the first chapter of Genesis in the bible about how Eve tricked Adam to partake in eating the forbidden fruit."

Without a second thought, Face left as quick as he appeared. When Cheri felt Face was out of earshot she asked? "What you think this all about?" "I don't know ,but I already know the art of seduction and when I put my thang down, no is not options."

"So why he give you dat and me this?" "If I knew the answer to dat, I'll be able to tell you why you ask so many dumb ass questions.""Okay bitch," Cheri responded knowing Face would be shaking his head right now.

CHAPTER 10

You Shoulda New

"Fuck Smiley, he gotta go!" Maniac told himself as he dialed his partner in crime.

With everything going the way it was, it was time to clean house, Maniac was never the one to get attached to anything or anyone especially when money was involved. Loose lips sink ships was the only words going threw his mind as he drove down Main Street waiting on Smiley to pick up.

"What's good?", Smiley said picking up his phone.

"You already know. "Nigga, I was just thinking about you." "Yeah right, that's why I haven't seen your ass, but in traffic." "You know I've been at them ends just like you." "That's what's up, but dig I need to get at you." "Wats up?", knowing what time it was when Manica come calling.

"I got somethin' beautiful in the making just meet me at Chelle's around 8." "No doubt", CLICK!

Shit was about to go down, but he had to call Chelle and give her a heads up. "Dig, I'm sending Smiley yo way around 8, hold'em down until I get there." Chelle being dat down ass Chick never questioned Maniac, she was down for whatever. "I got you boo." "I already know," hanging up thinking about making a U-turn to go get a shorty he had passed at the bus stop.

Just like clock work Smiley showed up at Chelle's around 8 looking for Maniac to be there. "Where's yo boy?" "He'll be here in a minute to entertain yo tired ass", moving to the side allowing him to enter.

"That aint what yo freaky ass was saying a couple of days ago," brushing pass her. "Nigga please, I wanted some dick and you so happen to be the one I called. So don't play yo-self thinking it was more than it actually was 'cause believe me, if it was," pausing as if she was trying to find the right words to say. "I woulda been call you back over, not Maniac! Anyway, what you want to drink?" "Bitch , you know what. I drink ", mad that he couldn't have his way like Maniac.

Chelle just smiled thinking we'll see who the bitch is when my man gets here as she went to get their drinks. Several drinks later Maniac finally decide to show his face.

"Damn nigga, you tell me to be here at 8 and here you are showing up damn near a hour or so later. "Nigga you sound like one of my bitches, roll something up," throwing a bag of haze on the table.

"I'm going to grab me something to drink and by the sound of thangs, you need a refill."

Maniac made a b-line to the kitchen where he put two drops of eye drops in Smiley drink and made his way back to the living room.

"Here you go playboy." "Where's mine," Chelle asked looking for her drink. "Bitch, fall back and let two bosses boss", not paying her the least bit of attention. "So how life been treating a nigga?" "I can't complain, shit been real lovely for yo boy", sipping on his drink. "But you know I'm always down to put some work in." "That's what's up, but let's chill and get liquored up and put some haze in the air."

About 30 minutes later Smiley was sensing something wasn't right, even doe he had nothing ,but love for his boy they were never on no social type time, so for this nigga to be sitting here talking about shit that didn't amount to nothing caused him to wonder.

"So what's the occasion", bring the bull-shit to a head. "It got to be an occasion for a nigga to parlay? What you to good to kick it with me and my bitch? I guess what they say is true." "What's that, Manica?" wondering where he was going witt this." "Money change niggas!""Naw playboy I'm dat same nigga, dat ride and die nigga," taking the rest of his drink to the head. "I'm just saying, we aint never been on no social type time, so why now," trying his hardest to stay focused.

"You right," realizing he almost slipped by not staying on course to his reason for calling. "Chill nigga, I was just trying to get yo mind right before giving you the spill on this new caper",looking at Smiley rubbing his eyes as if his vision was getting blurry and he couldn't see. "Playboy, playboy, you alright? you don't look too good," standing directly in front of him trying to play dumb like he didn't know what the deal was.

Once he realized Smiley was totally knocked out he got down to business. "Bitch, wash these glasses and pull the car through the alley", he order looking around for any more physical evidence.

Chelle being use to the verbal abuse never took his words personal, she just went 'about her business being all she could be playing her role in Maniac twisted world .

As Chelle went to get the car, Maniac carried his boy down three flights of steps to the back entrance leading to the alley where Chelle was waiting.   "Bitch, get out and help a nigga." Chelle jumped out the car to assist her man only to be caught off guard with a straight jab followed by a left hook.

She took the jab like a camp, but the hook took dat ass to another place leaving her laid out on the ground next to Smiley.

Maniac quickly looked around to check his surrounding before pullin' his 9mm ,once he felt the coast was clear he let loose dat canon fillin' Chelle and Smiley full of holes before taking off under the cloak of darkness telling himself, don't get it twisted!!!!"

//

"Tight-White, what's up witt you?" "Nigga, I'm about to put this work in", loading his twin glocks" and if you aint trying to ride, you already know." "Naw playboy, I don't already know," Dirt Bert responded" but I do know you better check yo self before getting caught up in some bull-shit." "Call it what you want, but I'm not gonna lay back while this nigga got info about my nigga, acting like he can't reveal it unless we grease his palms with a 100g's.Picture dat", strappin' his twins in place!

"Slow down Tight-White, you know if you fuck this up, who you gotta answer to," blocking him from leaving.

"If Face got a problem witt me gettin' at this nigga, so be it! I waited and waited to hear somethin' from dat nigga, I'm not waiting no damn more," looking at his boy as if to say, don't be dat one standing between him and T-love.

//

"Baby girl-"

"Oh baby, please come home," cutting Face off. "What's going on Max", sensing something wasn't right. "Me and T-love got into it about a month ago and I had to hit'em in his shit." "You what", not believing what he was hearing. "Yea daddy, and come to find out he got some info." "Info about what?" trying to hurry her story along.

"I don't know, he only wants to holler at you. His punk ass trying to collect dat 100g's." "Did he hurt you," wishing a nigga would. "NO, the boys where on location and stopped things before they got outta hand." "Where the boys around when he claimed to have this info?" "Yea."

"Look Max this is not a joking matter, get at Noodles and Dirt Bert ASAP and tell'em, I don't give a fuck what they gotta do hold Tight-White down until I get there."

"What's wrong", hearing the worry in his voice. "Tight-white is a hot head and I know in my heart he's not gonna lay back while dat nigga claim he got some info, just do what I asked and let'em know I'm on the first thing smokin' dat way!

//

"Ice's, you know yo boy's people came up witt them daisy." "Come on Self, you know I played dat nigga like a violin, he was so eager to be down he woulda killed the bitch that gave him life if I hinted at it," laughing at his last remark.

"So what's next?" really wanting to know the reason for even fuckin' witt a nigga like dat. "We gonna pump'em up and let'em have his way and use'em like the bitch he is." "You know we can't trust'em, especially if he'll kill his own." "Don't worry Self, once we pump dat ass over a mill or two, it's rock- abye baby," letting his right hand man know what time it was."Dat's what I'm talkin' about."

//

"Maria, call me a taxi", Face yelled from his bedroom as he gathered his things.

"What's going on Face and why you'~ packing?" Cheri asked seeing the urgency in what he was doing.

"I got somethin' I need to go handle", never looking up from what he was doing. " Stop Face, you're scaring me!"

"Not right now, Cheri," dropping everything he was doing to look at her before continuing to pack. "Don't you do this Face, don't you dare shut me out, when all I have left is you." grabbing his hands stopping him from packing.

"Cheri, I don't have time to explain just trust me and know I have yo best interest at heart", turning to grab his suit case saying ,""I'll be back within a week."

///

"Look at you", admiring his nieces' beauty. "Man or woman got to be blind, cripple, or insane not to want you,"

"Unk, what's the purpose of all this"? "You'll understand when the time comes, but for right now all I want you to do is get use to the unwanted attention you'll attract with yo new look 'cause truly you are a sight to see." "Unk, none of this matters, I'm just trying to get home." "Patience Coco, patience."

///

"Fuck you, Tight-White!!!" "Naw nigga, fuck yo self, you'll get better pussy", smackin' T-love across the mouth. "You think this shit a joke, I got somethin' for dat ass," walking toward the basement.

"Pump yo brakes," Noodles said grabbing Tight-White by the arm. "Let Face handle this, his plane touchdown tomorrow." "Hell naw," snatching his arm away. "You think I'm gonna baby sit this nigga until Face gets here! Imagine dat," opening the basement door yelling, come here boy.

Within seconds Bolow came charging out the basement into the kitchen looking back and forth between Tight-White, Noodles, and Dirt Bert before settling its eyes on T-love.

"Dat's right boy, watch'em, watch'em Bolow, watch'em."

"Noodles, Dirt Bert, get yo boy, I told ya'll everything, untie me before this shit turns into somethin else," T-love pleaded.

"It turn into something else," Tight-White responded. "When you tried to play us outta pocket for dat 100g's,knowing you was the one."

"I didn't know they where gonna kill'em," cutting Dirt Bert off. "Just like you don't know" "Fuck all dat, get'em boy," Tight-White ordered letting Bolow loose.

Bolow ran at T-love with such force when he jumped into'em it caused Bolow to knock T-love and the chair to the floor where Bolow had his way, biting him from his face, to his chest and arms, all the way down to his legs taking big plugs of meat outta everywhere leaving nothing ,but the bones to be seen.

"Dat's right, get'em boy, get'em," Tight-White yelled in between T-love screams, while Noodles looked on wondering how in the hell they were gonna explain this shit to Face.

//

"Ya'll what," Face yelled not believing the half of it." "The shit happen so fast I couldn't." "You couldn't what Noodles? you and Dirt Bert where supposed to keep dat nigga in check, we don't need no lose canons running around or no walking time bombs, dat shit can backfire in a niggas face and have all our asses sitting in Lucasville doing 23 and 1,and believe me, dat aint a good look." "I know Face, but what's done is done."

"Nigga is you listening to yo self or you just talking to be talking, ya'll let Bolow eat a nigga alive. I'm not mad about what ya'll did, just the way ya'll went about doing it." "I sent the cleanup crew in."

"Come on Noodles, the cleanup crew can't do nothing for dat crime since ,but burn dat bitch down and ya'll need to get rid of Below." "What for," not trying to hear none of dat.

"Bolow got a dead man's DNA in'em and you asking me what for" throwing his hands in the air on his way to the mini bar. Face stood in front of the mini bar trying to pull his thoughts together as he poured himself a drink. "What ya'll get out dat nigga," turning around to look at Noodles.

"After the smoke screen, he finally came clean and told us about his cousin Corey gettin' at him, in the mist of their conversation some nigga in the background was' holding a conversation witt somebody about Mello wifeying his bitch and that he was going to get at dat nigga."

While Noodles kept on talking Face was focused on Noodles last statement, (Wifeying his bitch) then going back to what Mello told'em (It wasn't her, it was somebody close to her, M-a-n) That shit kept playing around and around in his mind until it came to him.

"Dig, do you know Netta's sister?" Face asked out of nowhere taking Noodles by surprise. "Yea, but what's that got to do witt this?"

"She came through here looking for me and I bet she holds the missing pieces to this puzzle", taking the rest of his drink to the head.

///

"Here, take one of these," handing Cheri a pill with a smiley face on it. "You been acting like a little sad puppy every since Face left," Peaches whispered gettin' all up in Cheri's space making funny faces.

"And what you been doing?" looking at the pill before taking it.

"Bitch, stop asking so many questions and roll somethin' up," throwing a bag of purple beside them while she played bar tender.

"Trick, where you come up at", thinking back to the last time she sparked some of dat. Peaches not even paying attention asked her. "Where you put them tapes Face gave us." "What you need them for," splitting a blunt down the middle.

"Look Cheri", turning around to look at her. "Face gave us those tapes for a reason and I'm not trying to hear his mouth about why we haven't did our part, so stop playing and tell me where you put them tapes. "The mere mention of his name had Cheri feeling tingly inside.

"Trick, look beside the entertainment center," puttin' her rolling skills to good use. Peaches gathered the tapes going through them one by one taking the ones with girl on girl action and leaving the rest.

"Trick, what you got me watchin?" sparkin' the blunt. "I aint got you watchin' nothing, you need to ask Face that question," passin' Cheri her drink. " "Damn its gettin' hot in this bitch", taking off everything, but her panties and bra."I don't remember feeling so fuckin' hot the last time."

"Bitch save all dat rap for a motherfucka that's trying to hear it. Just watch these ho's doing what they do, you just might learn something," smiling to herself, hitting Cheri to pass the blunt..

Not 10 minute later she watched Cheri playing with herself. "Damn my pussy is on fire", feeling how wet she was. "Don't pay me no attention, do you" ,encouraging her to do whatever.

Just like dat Cheri pulled her panties to the side and went at herself not giving a fuck who was in the room while watching three females sucking and fucking the shit outta each other. Things had got so bad she imagined herself with the three females on the tube doing her that she took her panties completely off moaning to the pleasures she was conflicting to herself.

"Oooh I-I-I'mmmm-Cummmminggg", she screamed out with her legs spread wide open with three fingers inside her wet pussy.Without warning Peaches slid between her legs and began sucking on her clit causing Cheri to scream out. "Oooh yesss, just like dat, don't stop, pleeaaassse dooont stopppp", grabbing the back of the person head between her legs only to realizing it was her girl.

."Bitch what the hell", jumping off the couch feeling embarrassed looking at her juices around Peaches mouth. Peaches seein' the look in her eyes knew she wanted more. "Lay down and let me finish," looking deep into her girl's eyes.

Cheri wanted so badly to lay her ass back down and feel the magic her girl tongue provided, so instead of responding she just stood-there afraid of what she was feeling inside with her pussy screaming , bitch lay yo ass down.

Peaches being Peaches took that as a sign to do her and gently laid Cheri back on the couch placing her on her stomach and began suckin' dat thang from the back. "Yeessss, oooh, yeeeesss, eat this pussy", pushing it back into Peaches face."I'rmmmmmm cuummmmiinggg", burying her face into the couch.

//

"Face this is Seal, Seal this is Face," Noodles introduced them.

"Excuse me, but what type of Jeans are those 'cause you wearing the shit outta them", Face asked. "Apple bottoms," Seal responded turning around to give him a better view at what she knew he wanted to see.

"Bitch, J-rock gonna knock yo head off," Dirt Bert said outta no-where. "Fuck J-rock, I'm what the people want", smackin' herself on the ass. "True dat shorty, true dat," Face and Dirt Bert said together.

"Anyway," rolling her eyes at Dirt Bert before turning her attention back to Face. "Thank you again for lookin out." "Don't mention it, I did what Mello woulda wanted me to do plus Netta was family and I take care of family," eyeing Seal up and down.

"And I bet you do," staring directly at his dick. "You see sonethin,' you think you can work witt," grabbing himself. "Not only dat, I see something' that will have a bitch doing back flips", shaking her head at the sight of that print." The way you're holding I know you got a bitch," looking around his apartment to make sure she wasn't there. "Don't worry, aint nobody here, but us," seeing the way she was looking around."

"Instead of me calling you Face, I should be calling yo ass James Bond or , Mr. 007.""Why is dat?" "Shit, witt yo missing in action ass", bringing laughter throughout his apartment. "Oh, you got jokes?" laughing just as hard. "Not so much I can make a living, but on the real I've been trying to get at you, to put you witt something' that's really real", looking at everybody in the room!

Face heart began to swell inside his chest anticipating the information that was about to be revealed. "My sister ex-boyfriend came up outta nowhere, around the same time Mello and-."

The pain was still visible to the point she couldn't bring herself to say it. "I know dat nigga, and I know ain't nobody gave him shit .At first I didn't think too much of it' cause him and his little crew would do a stickup or two ,to stay above water but these niggas were ballin, dat one way! That is until lately." "What you mean until lately?" Noodles asked. "His whole crew been gettin knocked off, everybody except-." "Corey," Tight-White hurried to say cutting her off.

"Naw, M-a-n," Face said alone with Seal finishing the rest causing everybody to look his way wondering how he knew oh boys name.

"Mello died tryin' to give me oh boys' name", answerin' their question before they had a chance to ask. "You had a fuckin name all this time and didn't tell no body? Fuck you Face!" Tight-White yelled standing to confront him.

"Nigga, sit yo ass down before somethin' pop off yo ass ain't ready for", giving him that one look. "The only reason I kept dat shit close to my chest 'cause I knew there was a shake living amongst us, and I didn't want what I knew to get back to the enemy, but by the sound of thangs oh boy is taking out anyone who could link him back to these", catching himself as he looked into Seal eyes.

"Don't pay me no attention, I want dat bitch ass nigga to feel my pain and my lost before we lay his ass to rest. "That last statement took everybody by surprise causing Face to look at her differently, but smart enough not to comment only saying, "We'll see."

///

"Revenge is like, the sweetest joy, next to gettin' pussy," Maniac sang. "Pac was dat nigga, I'm tellin' you he woulda love to fuck witt a nigga like me," showing off his new tattoo as they drove pass Findlay Market." Its M.O.B, money over bitches", pointing at it on his arm. "All day every day and all bitches ain't women, You know what I'm talkin' about, Rob?"

"You already know, but I ain't trying to ride around all day listening to you spit like you trying to cut a demo, stop pump fakin' and throw a dog a bone, until I see a better day!"

"I got you, the bull-shit ain't nothing. I know how you get down and when you shoot to the D ,grab me some of them E pills," throwing 10g's in his lap.

"Dat goes without saying, but what up witt dat situation about yo people and who put dat work in," Rob asked puttin' them ends away.

"It's a big mystery right now, don't no body know too much of nothing, but let me get wind of somethin', you better believe it's gonna be the 4th of July around diss bitch"!

Rob just sat back listening trying to read into what Maniac was saying, even doe things where a big mystery about his crews demise there was a lot of speculation going on with Maniac being the number one suspect.

"I feel you, and if I hear anything, you already know.

//

RING, RING! "Hello," Cheri said answering the phone feeling exhausted from the night before. "Get up sleepy head, and where's Peaches? "Umm, she's around here somewhere", looking at her laid across their bed.

"Dig, I need ya'll to stay put for a minute." "For a minute, come on Face, make up yo mind. You said you'll be back and now you want us to stay put, what up witt dat!""Calm down, Cheri! Things are coming together and I need a little time to sort things out before I put this play down."

"I'm not gonna interrogate you over the phone like I would've if you where here, but I hope whatever you put together, you involve me." "I got you, ya'11 just read them books and check them tapes out, and every thang will be every thang. Now let me go before you change yo mind and start interrogating a nigga." "Oh, you got jokes?" "Naw love,I'm just fuckin' witt you", laughing knowing he didn't want to get her started"Be Careful." "You already know," hanging up the phone pondering his next move.

Cheri hang up staring into space wondering what was going on that Face would want them to stay put. She hoped whatever he was up against the game God would bring him back safely, just when her mind began to race it was like déjà vu all over again.

"Good morning to you too," looking at Peaches wiggle between her legs."Ooooh shiiiitt, god damn bitch, get yo money," grabbing the back of Peaches head pushing her pussy into her face.

//

"Don't worry unk, I'll keep a close eye on her and if harm should come her way, I'll take care of that accordingly." "I know you will J, that's why I'm sending you", never looking up from his newspaper.

"My transfer should be good by the end of this week, so I'll be needing to make the necessary arrangements." "No need J, I got everything already in place just be ready when the time comes," turning the page in his newspaper.

CHAPTER 11

I'm watchin'

With Maniac caught up doing him moving 100mph, he never noticed the eyes dat be that covered his every move from sun up to sun down memorizing everything he did, from the places he ate, to the people he encountered and everythang in between even calculating how much money he was clockin'.

The eyes dat be shadowed Maniac every day until it was satisfied and comfortable enough to allow him to move around freely.

"Face, when we gonna touch this nigga?""Patience, Dirt bert patience-" "Patience my ass! It's been damn near a month and you'll still preaching this patience shit! Me, Tight-White, and Noodles can body this nigga before the sun goes down." "True dat, but then what?" "What the fuck you mean, then what? Dat nigga be dead and, Mello can rest in peace."

"See Dirt Bert, that's the difference between me and you", pouring himself a drink. "While you simply want revenge, I want more than dat. I want this nigga to pay for his actions, at the same time feel my pain and understand my loss when he took my young soldier away from here."

"So what you gettin' at?" "I'm not only gonna touch this nigga, I'm gonna touch the very thing he love the most first, then I'm gonna touch his pockets turning his whole world upside down before I lay his 'sorry ass to rest!" "Damn Face", Dirt Bert said trying to envision everythang Face just put out there. "Make no mistake about it, I knew you where game tight, but damn you're one shrewd and conning motherfucka!" "I know," turning toward his window sipping his drink.

Face stayed up late into the night planning his first move all the way down to his last, like playing a game of chess. He wasn't content with a simple check, he wanted to checkmate his man leaving him no room to escape, let alone get away!!!!

//

"Dat's 500g's right there", Maniac said pointing at the duffle bag on the floor. "I've been puttin' dat work in." "Yea Maniac, you being makin' it happen, but understand shit ain't the same and niggas are lookin' at you differently, the same way you where lookin at niggas when you didn't have. So be careful 'cause. Lot of dem would love to take yo place", Ice Mike responded.

"I don't give a fuck what they love or what they don't, I'm doing me and if they got a problem witt dat! Get at me!" "Oh, you Mr. Bad Ass," Self-asked wanting so badly to pull this niggas cap back?"

"Come on Self", Ice interrupt looking at his partner in crime lettin him know to keep his cool. "Maniac family", turning back to Maniac assuring him all was good. "Yea nigga, lighten up! We family now, let's get this money while the getting' is good." Maniac said makin his exit." Oh, what time ya'll gonna drop dat off," turning around at the door. "Same time, same place" Ice responded.

After Maniac left Self let it be known what's on his heart. "I'm tellin' you Ice, I don't like dat nigga and I don't trust'em. I've been watchin' dat nigga and I know he's closer to dat ticket than you think" "So what 'you saying?" "Men lie, women lie ,numbers don't! Do the math and let's get rid of this nigga!"

//

Out West, Unk was watchin' Coco closely, he could see the look in her eyes. That look dat was thirsty for sornethin' she already had in her. So he tried his best not to force feed her, but fed her with a long handle spoon allowing her to consume it slowly little by little makin it easier to swallow and digest 'cause the last thing he wanted was for her to get choked up and become game shy and have an allergic reaction to diss game, that was already in her blood line.

" Unk, it's all coming together .I see the big picture." "I knew you would Coco, you had a different upbringing, a different grooming, a different schooling, it was just a matter of time before the game you where breast fed since birth would bear fruit.

"Thank you Unk, thank you for everything," Coco said trying to catch her tears while giving him a hug. "Most of all, thank you for respecting my wishes and my decision to go back on my own."

"Shh Coco, before I change my mind," He whispered in her ear before breaking their embrace. "You remind me so much of yo mother, it's killing me inside to let you go like this, but I can't shelter you from life's experiences, let alone, its trials and tribulations." "I have to give you the room and the opportunity to make yo own decisions, as well as yo own mistakes. Learn from them and use them as a guide when faced with somethin' similar, but most of all use them as a stepping stone and not a stumbling block!"

///

Due to Face presence back in the hood, the streets where more than just watchin, they were paying attention especially after one of their own mysteriously disappeared when all he knew was the hood, never traveling to far from it.

"I'm tellin you Joann, they killed my baby". "Girl, you better keep yo thoughts to yo self and yo big mouth shut." "I'm not scared of them." "Bitch, you don't have to be, but will it matter when you're dead", lookin' at her girl sideways making sure she understood where she was coming from."I'm just saying."

Joann threw her hands in the air as if she was trying to stop traffic "I'm just saying will have yo ass 6ft. under somethin' and yo kids Motherless. Now take my advice and leave dat shit alone and do what you do best." "And what would that be," Bull-moose asked knowing her girl.

"Put yo fuck'em dress on and make it do what it do, to provide for you and yours and whenever you find the time, say a prayer for dat nigga 'cause T-love was good to you and them kids, despite his hoein' ways and yours." "That he was," Bull-moose responded thinking how much she really miss dat nigga.

///

"Det. Triggs this is Det. Jones" Capt. McCoy introduced. "He just transferred in from um-." "California, and you can call me J," Det. Jones said extending his hand to Det. Triggs. "That's right, anyway I'll let ya'll get better acquainted later," motioning both Detective to take a seat passing them folders. "Gentlemen we have a serious situation on our hands. As you look through these files I assembled, you can clearly see the similarity between these double homicides in question. All of them consist of a male and female killed witt multi gunshot wounds. Now turn to page 8, you'll see the ballistic test shows that our last two double homicides where done by the same person, better yet, the same gun."

"So how do these two connect with the first one?" Det. Jones inquired looking over his report. "I just have a gut feeling." "No disrespect Cpt. from what I'm reading the first one was done more professional than the other two." "How is dat," Triggs jumped in saying. "See Det.Triggs, the first one there's nothing to go on. There's no DNA, no shell casing, no finger prints, nothing! They even burned the place to the ground, while these other two were done sloppy. We have DNA, partial prints, shell casing and almost anything else we need to break this case", as he flip threw his report he come across something he knew the CPT wanted him to see.

He flip back and forth to make sure he was reading everything correctly before speaking on it. "So our last double homicides have more in common than just a gun," Det. Jones spoke out loud.

"What the hell you talking about now", Det. Triggs flipping through his report trying to find what Det. Jones was speaking on.

"So Mr. Smiley was at the sense and took part in a double homicide, that much we know for sure, due to his DNA found under Ms. Netta's finger nails. Then months later he's found dead alone witt another female by the same gun that killed the first two! So my question again, how does these two connect witt the first one? Better yet, what part do I play in all this? I'm not a homicide detective, nor do I wish to become one I work vice," Det. Jones said looking back and forth between the Cpt. and Det. Triggs. " "True dat, and you will continue to work vice", the Cpt. insured him, but around here we do what's asked and needed of one another, not necessary what we're assigned to," making his way to the door. "Now find our man," leaving both Detectives with dat one look on their faces.

//

After months of being ate up by that platinum head her girlfriends Peaches was giving her she was wide open and turned the fuck out. She never consider herself to be gay or into women like dat, but the way Peaches been puttin' dat work in, she couldn't think let alone figure out how she allow herself to be hoodwink.

"Trick we need to talk." "About what," Peaches responded going back and forth from the bathroom to the bedroom brushing her teeth. "Don't play dumb, like you don't know. Got a bitch going crazy off dat magic shit you been lacing me witt for the last couple of months." "Good," she said taking Cheri by surprise gaining her full attention. "What the fuck you mean good," gettin' all up in Peaches face preventing her from leaving the bathroom.

"Bitch! Fall back and let me put you witt something," side stepping her to go take a seat on their bed. "Just like Face been trying to put you witt game, I got a little somethin' somethin' I'm trying to put you witt to." "What's dat, beside pressing yo tongue on my shit every night," walking right up on her as she was sitting on the edge of the bed.

Peaches looked up from lotioning her legs knowing this day would come where she would have to snatch the veil from her eyes, the veil that protected her from the naked truth and the reality of the situation.

"What I did, I did for a reason," standing to look Cheri eye to eye. "I would rather turn you out myself and keep it real, than allow the next motherfucka to do the same and not, having you think and feeling one way when it's actually another."

Cheri stood their stunned with her feelings caught up in the matrix, not knowing how to respond or how to react. She just stood there with tears free fallin' unable to fully understand what was going on. "I-I-I can't believe you did this to me."

"Cheri, I know what I did was wrong, but try to understand where I'm ,coming from first before passing judgment," pausing long enough for both of them to take a seat."I don't know what Face got in store for us ,so a bitch got to stay witt a backup plan. You know how I get down, I use what I got, to get what I want. So if we both got to be about this, I don't need you fallin in love cause a nigga got a mean head game and slanging dick like how dat go, never dat!"

"Trick ,you too crazy," Cheri responded smiling for the first time. "Naw bitch, dats real talk!In diss game you got to detach your heart from yo pussy and be able to distinguish sex from love 'cause in the end niggas play games just like bitches do!!!"

CHAPTER 12

Home sweet Home

"Ooh Mami, you sure nuff can get rich easy", one of Coco admires yelled out reading the words across her shirt as she strutted pass.

"I bet she get down dat one way" ,his partner jumped in saying as they watched Coco break necks on men and women trying to catch a better view.

Even doe she was extremely exhausted and fatigued from her 6 hour plane ride, Coco was still stunning to say the least drawing all eyes her way as she stepped through the Greater Northern Cinti airport.

She knew her presence would be the talk of many conversations long after she left, that when she bent the corner to take the escalator down to baggage claim, she ran right into a pedestrian almost losing her balance if it wasn't for his quick hands.

"Damn shorty, you alright?" "What it look like," she responded with much attitude removing his hands from around her waist.

"My bad shorty," throwing his hands in the air. "You damn near ran me over and got the nerve to have an attitude! You need a hug." "Is dat yo best pick up line besides calling me shorty?""Naw, but for what it's worth, lose the attitude you'll have a better day", holding eye contact before slowly walking away thinking to himself, Damn shorty can get it.

For the first time Coco came across someone who wasn't captivated by her presence or mesmerize by her beauty, someone who seemed to care less about either and to top it off, he didn't even asked her name, with his sexy ass.

"Excuse me," gaining the attention of her mystery man. "Where's my manners, I just had a long flight and I-." "No need to explain just show love to the next nigga you run into", leaving Coco standing there with dat one look

///

."There he is", Cheri said pointing Noodles out as he wove through the crowd.

"What took you so long?" greeting him with a hug. "Probably somewherer, hoein, " Peaches added. "Imagine dat," he responded turning around to give her a hug too." "Yea, imagine dat," she whispered in his ear.

"Damn ya'll lookin' good, I hope the little get away served its purpose." "And you know it," the wonder twins responded high fiving each other. "Boy, its somethin' you had to be there to witness. Who knows, we probably woulda let you get down providing you woulda been a good little boy," Peaches said seductively.

Noodles stood there trying to read between 'the lines, but with Peaches freaky ass one could only imagine what she was hinting at, so instead of driving himself crazy about it, he grabbed their luggage saying, "Let's get outta here before I book us all a flight, especially the way ya'll talking."

The wonder twins laughed grabbing the rest of their luggage knowing he woulda love to be a part of what they were talking about. As they navigated their way through the airport, they never paid attention to all the stares and the many eyes that seem to be following them.

Peaches was always a show stopper and carried it as such, she was a young Stacie Dash with her bow-leg ass with a walk that made males and females take notice. As for Cheri, she favored Rocis, oh girl on 106 an park literally with a lot more back yard to go in them jeans.

Even doe, she wasn't fully aware of her star potential as her girl, she was still a star in the making.

"Oh baby thank you, I knew this day would come," Maniac mother said with tears in her eyes. "I just wish Netta was here to share this moment. She always believed in you, that girl would cry herself to sleep worried about some you." "I know Ma," he whispered felling guilty. "Do you like it?" trying to change the subject.

"Oh baby, I love it," stopping to give her son a hug." "Dats what I'm talking about," returning the hug as they stood in the kitchen.

Maniac was feeling dat one way, seeing the joy in his mother eyes now that he moved her out the hood into a 4bd room house of her own.

"You aint mad I moved you way out here?" "Boy, don't be silly, Madison Ville aint that far that I can't make it back down the way to see my girls. Shit, I might not be able to keep them from out here, speaking of, which," reaching the back door. "That beat up thang I got for a car is another story within its self, so do the right thang," making eye contact with her son as she made her way to the backyard whispering, "Home sweet home."

///

"Face, now that the wonder twins are home it's time to stop playing captain save a hoe and let them ho's be. This whole ordeal with Maniac shoulda been over," Max strongly stated. "Don't worry baby girl, I got diss." "You're not hearing me! You spending too much time on this worthless ass nigga when we got bigger fish to fry."

"Max, clam down. I got diss, You know me better than dat," taking a seat right across from her. "Right before this shit transpired with Mello, I was searching for somethin' young to use as bait."

"Shit, by the looks of thangs you still searching." "Naw baby girl, that's where you're wrong. I got some young thoroughbreds in the making." "The wonder twins? Nigga please! They aint built for this shit," laughing at the thought. "Probably not, but I'm gonna use this whole situation with Maniac to my advantage and turn'em out to game they never knew existed and if they take to it, you already know."

Max sat there listening and analyzing the conversation along with the situation realizing Face might be on to somethin' especially with both girls blinded by revenge leaving them vulnerable to be mislead and misguided.

"If you play yo cards right, you might be able to pull this off. Speaking of which, what you gonna do with them ends Mello put away for Cheri," changing the subject knowing he was on top of his game.

"What I look like giving a 17 year old damn near a mill ticket to do as she please? The little bitch will be broke within a year wondering how it all got away, naw baby girl, she aint ready for dat, but when she is, she got dat coming."

///

"Damn! Coco screamed grabbing her foot after running into the corner of her entertainment center. "You alright"? "Yea unk, I'm fine. I just seem to be running into things lately", she explained thinking about her mystery man she ran into earlier."But every thangs good, I just need some type of income."

"Don't worry, I've set up a bank account witt fifth third in Norwood to hold you over, plus I took the initiative to grab you some wheels." "Ooh unk, thank you .You always seem to know what I need before I get the chance to ask. So now that's taken care of I can get about my business." "That you can Coco, that you can."

Coco hang up happy about her new living arrangements, back account, car,and anything else she needed. all she had to do now was find her man.

///

"Trick, what's on the agenda for tonight"? "Shiiit, I'm thinking let's put these I.D's to good use", Peaches replied going through her things trying to find somethin' to wear. "Matter of fact, I know this little spot called Vito's I want to turn you on to-." "Is dat right," Face jumped in saying taking the wonder twins by surprise. "Face, I don't know what type time you on, but keep sneaking up on a bitch and watch me get jet-le in this piece," breaking into a karate stance.

Face and Peaches glanced at each other wondering who was gonna be the first to burst out laughing only for Cheri to laugh first. "Oh, ya'll think this shit a game," playfully kicking and chopping at Face. "Ya'll go ahead, fake defending Cheri's attack. "And enjoy ya'll self 'cause come tomorrow we gonna really put those I.D's to good use," grabbing their attention! "What that's supposed to mean," the wonder twins asked? "Don't worry, ya'll see soon enough," looking them straight in the eyes. "It's time to put our play in motion and stop playin!" bringing them back to reality of the situation at hand!

CHAPTER 13

Tighten up

The next morning the wonder twins woke up with slight hang over's, but more importantly they woke up thinking about the things Face put out there knowing in the back of their minds things where about to take a turn for the worst.

"Cheri, you ready to make it do what it do," trying to see where her girls head was at as they got dress? "Bitch please I've been ready since day one and the thought of finally gettin' the chance to get at these niggas, got my pussy wet." "Is dat right," looking at her girl with a half-smile. "But seriously, what part you think we gonna play in all this?"

"What's witt the 21 questions?" stopping what she was doing. "I'm just wondering," seeing the way Cheri was looking at her. "Wondering my ass, You better get yo shit together and man the fuck up," Cheri said with authority sensing Peaches was having second thoughts. "Whatever part Face need us to play we gonna make it happen," staring Peaches down lettin' her know the bull shit aint nothing.

Peaches stood there feeling the effect of her girls words and before she could defend herself, she noticed Face standing in the door way shaking his head. "Now that's out the way, let's be out," Face commanded taking Cheri by surprise.

"Boy," grabbing her heart as she turned around. "I'm gonna fuck you up one of these days." "Picture dat!!!"

The wonder twins followed Face out to his truck not knowing what to expect or how they were going to go about gettin' at these niggas that their stomachs where doing back flips.

"So what's the plan?" Cheri asked climbing into his truck. "Calm down baby gangta," puttin' the key into the ignition."Before I put ya'll witt diss, I got to make sure ya'll ready and not just seem to be." "What the fuck that's supposed to mean," Peaches asked feeling his statement was directed at her.

"Peaches, I know everybody aint built for this shit, let" alone able to take a nigga away from here and be able to sleep at night .So I'm not gonna put you or anybody else in a situation to fail or expose ya'll to anything you can't stomach." "How you know what' I can stomach and what I can't?" "I know everthang, I know yo strengths and yo weakness and before everythang is said and done, yo shit gonna be air tight and not just game tight," Face explained pullin' out the drive way.

As they headed down 1-75 Face began to paint a brighter picture giving the wonder twins a better view and understanding into what he was trying to put together explaining why he chose the books he did and why Peaches read the art of seduction and Cheri the art of war stressing the importance of team and how everybody had a role to play.

"I'm tellin' ya'll it's much more at stake than just revenge", bringing the picture to life. "This nigga not only robbed Mello of his life, he robbed him of his life saving." "What you talking about?" Cheri asked.

"Don't to many people know this, but Mello was a millionaire." "Get the fuck outta here," looking back and forth between Face and Peaches not believing the half of it.

"Yea Cheri, and we gotta get dat back", pullin' into Target world where he instructed them to sign up for the target range expressing how important it was to learn how to handle and shoot a gun 'cause you never know when one might need to use one.

//

"Tight-white, what's good playboy?" greeting his partner in crime. "Nothing much just trying to stay focused making sure shit running smoothly around here." "That's what's up. speaking of which, where's Noodles," Dirt Bert asked looking up and down front street before settling against the fence in front of the projects.

"That nigga took off to the mall, he's talking about shooting through Annie's. What you trying to get into", looking away to make sure the dope fiends where gettin' taken care of. "You know me, all work and no play 'cause the day you layoff is the day they pay off", grabbing his boys attention. "Give it to me straight up, no chaser", turning to look Dirt Bert head on.

"You know Face been having a nigga keep tabs on oh boy from time to time just to make sure he's keeping his same routine and aint changed nothing up. Well, I decided to hit'em on the grave yard shift just to see what time he be gettin' out and about, so I'm laying in the cut talking to this little freak on the phone when our boy makes this late night run. I'm tellin' you Dirt, I think our boy led me to his stash house." "Get the fuck outta here," wasting no time asking, "Where dat shit at?"

"Fall back," seeing the look in his man's eyes! "Like I was saying, oh boy took me on a spin through Madisonville to this little spot ducked off on one of those side streets across from that park out dat way, but the crazy part about it all, the spot ADT and camera up," shooting Tight-White the disappointing news.

"Can we infiltrate it," dismissing the disparity in his man's voice?" "Anything possible, but I know once I put Face witt this he'll come up with somethin.

///

"Maniac, when we gonna hook up again?",Raytonya asked as they pulled in front of her spot?

"Don't worry, I got you," hittin' her off for a job well done. "But don't call me, I'll call you," making her feel like shit.

This was the life of a niqqa having his way and playing a bitch for what she's worth.

"Oh, it's like dat," snatching her ends out his hand jumping out his SUV. "You aint shit," slamming the door. "Little dick mutherfucka" she screamed to the back of his tail light as he sped off. "I'm gonna get yo punk ass, you just watch!!"

Life was good for a robbery boy turned dope boy, but his life was empty inside missing the one thing everyman deserved one time or another regardless if they want to admit it or not. Every since his true love Netta, Maniac have yet to find love, let alone someone to love him for him, but had plenty of females to love him for the things he could provide. As he headed down the way, he allowed Kanya West to set his mood. I'm not saying she's a gold digger, but she aint fuckin' witt no broke nigga.

///

With Det. Jones coming into the picture Det. Triggs felt the need to step his game up, especially after fallin' outta grace with the Captain. He was feeling more pressure than ever to come up with somehing that he began working 16 hour shifts hittin' the strip with a vengeance puttin' pressure on anybody witt two legs and those unfortunate only to have one, be it man or woman he didn't care.

Little by little Det. Triggs began gaining more and more information only the streets would know placing a couple of niggas in intensive care and sending a few females to the emergency room, letting it be known the house nigga done came off the porch.

///

"Face, I'm not feeling this bull shit, me and guns don't get alone", Peaches said giving her gun back to Face. "I already know," ejecting one out the chamber after taking the clip out.

"So why you got me all up in here with Ms. Sharpe shooter?" pointing at Cheri doing her thang. "Don't worry about dat," motioning for her to follow him outside so they could have some privacy.

After climbing into his truck Face turn the ignition to allow the AC to blow. "I never envisioned you killing a nigga witt a gun, but dat pussy is another story within its self," laughing at his own statement while grabbing the blunt out the ash tray.

"Oh, that's what you want me to do? Kill a nigga witt this pussy," knowing Face never said anything he didn't mean.

"All I want you to do, is do what you do best, but understand your role is very important and shouldn't be taken lightly," passing her the blunt. "This nigga in question aint nothing, but a big ole trick and being what he is ,bitches cater to'em."

"So you want me to follow suit and get in where I fit in?" "Naw Peaches, dat shit only going to get you in the batter box with a wet ass and a couple dollars in yo pocket. The game plan I'm gonna put into play only require for you to get on base and if the opportunity present its self to steal second, make it happen 'cause once I come up to bat, you already know," watching her take the last of the blunt to the head.

"So how do me and oh boy cross paths for all of this to come into play?" "I'm going to give you a couple of locations I know he'll be. I'm not saying he's gonna bite right off, but when he do just be independent and present a challenge and watch this thang take a life of its own."

"I'm buzzin' like a mutherfucka and the shit you spillin' is A1, matter of fact, the shit sound so good I know you can sell sand to a beach and water to the 'ocean, but how in the hell am I'm gonna play this independent bitch, when a bitch can barely make ends meet", looking at Face for the million dollar answer.

Being the nigga he was, Face paused looking at his young thoroughbred as if he was lost for words inching closer until their lips where touching before seductively kissing her, whispering," That's where Daddy comes into play." bringing a smile to both of their faces.

//

Annie's was jumping with females lined up around the corner while Noodles and Tight-white where off in the club doing what they do.

"Let me get two double shots of Remy and two coronas," Noodles ordered as they checked out the dance floor. "Man, you see oh girl with the fish net body suit," Tight-white asked pointing toward a 'group of females.

"Damn, I see some bitches tonight that should be having my baby", Noodles yelled before getting bumped into. He turned around ready to let a nigga have it, when he was hit with some déjà vu shit. They stared into each eyes until she broke the silence. "If I'm not mistaken, aint you the one who told me to show love to the next person I ran into? And I bet it never crossed yo mind you'd be the one, Mr. Mystery man?"

"Damn nigga ,who the fuck is dat?" "Hi, my name is Coco and you are?" extending her hand. "I'm whoever you want me to be and then some," taking her hand into his.

"Pump yo breaks, playboy," looking at his boy like he done lost his mind."So Ms. Coco, let me buy you a drink," turning to flag down the bartender who seemed to have got lost. "Naw, I'm the one who bumped into you .Let me buy you a drink," taking Noodles by surprise as she went into her Channel purse.

"Pimp nigga pimp," Tight-white whispered in his ear.

"If you gonna buy me a drink, you gotta hit my nigga off too," causing Coco to look up from her purse. "If the situation was reversed, you already know." "Boy, you too much." "Two double Remy and co-ronas," the bartender interrupted looking at Noodles. "Don't look at me the lady buying," pointing at Coco. "Let me get the same," paying for all their drinks.

"Nice meeting you Coco and hopefully we'll get the chance to meet again," Tight-white said shooting her a slight wink before going to find shorty witt the fish net.

While Coco and Noodles sip on their drinks every nigga and female in the club was staring in their direction, if not directly, indi-rectly wondering who she was.

"If I didn't know no better, I would think all these eyes were on me, but seeing you standing in front of me, I know better." "Nigga please," looking up into his eyes. "I'm the same person you left standin at the airport not caring one way or the other who I was or what my name might be," puttin' her hands around his waist. "OH, you got it like dat?" breaking into a smile. "You 'tell me," she softly whispered in his ear.

///

The following day Face was about his business, eager to get things under way, He wasted no time puttin' Peaches witt the necessary information along with keys to a nice condo in Hyde Park and a BMW truck sittin' on something real lovely, not to mention the 20,000 dollar shoppin' spree and a job working, as a real estate agent.

"Fuck, if I knew shit was gonna be this sweet, I woulda signed up to fuck the nigga," Cheri said with attitude looking at all the stuff Peaches had gotten. "Cheri, I ain't got time for yo shit. Now fall back and let this shit unfold." "Yea trick, fall back," Peaches jumped in say-ing shooting her girl a half smile and a wink. "Bitch! I'm gonna give you something to wink about," charging across the room.

"Hold tight baby gangta," Face yelled grabbing Cheri around the waist before she could get at Peaches. "Let her go, Face," taking her ear rings out. "I'll be the last bitch she runs up on."

"Look at you", turning Cheri around to look at him." I got too much time and energy invested in this and I be damn if I let you or anybody else fuck this up, so if you got a problem with the way I'm puttin this shit together, I suggest." "Suggest what, Face!" Stopping him from finishing his sentence. "If you think I'm going somewhere, you are sadly mistaken," snatching his hands from around her waist.

///

"Nigga, where everybody at?" Tight-white asked looking down at his watch.

"Everybody up stairs, we just waiting on Face and the wonder twins. " "Man you missed somethin beautiful last night, I mean beautiful", hittin' the last of his Newport." Noodles came up dat one way! I'm tellin' you Dirt Bert, shorty was so bad they had to break out before baby girl 'caused a riot."

"Yea right, you act like Hallie Berry was on his arm."

"Man, fuck Hallie Berry with her white boy baby daddy. I'm tellin' you baby girl 5ft 4 coca cola bottle red bone with a tattoo on her ankle, and the only different,her licence plates say Coco instead of Angle."

"Tight-white, you had me. You had me good," laughing and pointing at his boy." you been listening to too much R. Kelly, and had one too many," holding his stomach from laughing so hard.

"Believe what you want, but if I tell you there's cheese on the moon, take some crackers," leaving Dirt Bert standing there with dat one look as he went up stairs.

///

By the time Face and the wonder twins arrived everybody in attendance where in deep conversation. Face wasted no time settling things and gettin' things under way.

He introduced the wonder twins to Seal aka (Apples) before taking the floor. Face captivated his crew like a true leader demanding their attention while he reveal the art of revenge, he was precise and to the point leaving nothing to their imagination.

"If there's anyone here", stopping to look back and forth between Max, Dirt bert, Tight-white, Noodles, Apples, and the wonder twins."Let them speak now or forever hold yo peace 'cause once this thing take flight ain't no turning back".

Everybody looked around at one another hoping all was good 'cause the last thing anybody wanted was a mutherfucka down witt cold feet."

//

Nigga, be easy", Ice Mike said running money through his money machine. "He's a dead man walking."

"Fuck all dat, dead men don't walk, I'm trying to lay his ass under something," passin' Ice a stack of money.

"Is dat before or after we take his shit," making sure it was about the money and nothing else.

"What type of question is dat," looking at Ice wondering why he was trying to shoot some bullshit under him."You think I was on that one bus?" "I don't know, you tell me," rubber banding 10,000 dollars stacks together. "A dead man can't lead me to dat pot of gold, let alone separate mine from his, not knowing his was mines to began wit," bringing a smile between the both of them. "That's what I'm talking about," Self said thinking about how bad he was going to do Manica.

CHAPTER 14

Oh I think they like me

"Big Poppa, how long it's gonna be," Maniac yelled looking down at his ice out Presidential Rolex.

"Boy, don't you rush me or my crew with that bull shit, when you done brought dat big ass truck in here," pointing at Maniac SUV heading toward his office.

"Damn, I came in here every week and these slow ass mutherfuckas can't get a nigga outta here within an hour," Maniac bitched to himself rushing out side to go hollar at a couple of Big Poppas workers. "Ray- Ray, you and Greedy go help them slow ass niggas, for I can get outta here."

"If you ain't paying, I'm good. Me and Greedy got the next one," stopping in mid-sentence as a dark blue BMW truck pulled up. It wasn't the truck its self that stopped him in mid-sentence, but the female who got out of it.

"Hot damn! How can I help you?" 'Ray-Ray jumped to asked eyeing her from head to toe. "You can start by puttin yo tongue back in yo mouth." "Calm down Miss Lady," Maniac intervened. "My man didn't mean no disrespect, he just got beside himself seeing someone as stunning as yo self," puttin his arm around Ray-Ray shoulders.

"I don't have time for small talk, if it don't make dollars, it don't make good conversation," handing her keys to Ray-Ray with the instructions to detail her truck and steam clean the engine looking Maniac up and down before turning to walk toward Main St. leaving them standing there with dat one look.

"I got to have lil-shorty," Maniac whispered watching her strut down 13Th Street.

//

"Man, did you peep those hips and dat ass on Cheri?" Dirt Bert asked Tight-white. "I always knew shorty would grow up to be somethin' real nice, but damn," grabbing the front of his pants. "Yea Cheri like dat, but don't you sleep on Peaches sexy ass, shorty been stuntin' on niggas since she was 12, witt her bow-legged ass."

"Ya'll niggas need to quit it, eye fuckin' dat jail bait," Noodles jumped in surprising his boys. "Jail bait my ass," Dirt Bert corrected him still grabbing his dick through his pants. "Both of them tricks turn 18 this year. Matter of fact, I got somethin' real lovely for'em," smiling the whole time.

"I hate to ask, but what's dat?" Noodles asked out of curiosity. "I'm gonna wrap diss dick up witt a red bow and tell'em happy B-day", bringing laughter amongst the three of them. "I expect somethin' like dat from Tight-white, but you my nigga, I ain't feelin' dat." "Feel what you want, all I'm saying is both of them ho's got it going on, if they go, I gotta get'em," lettin it be known he'll nail their ass to the bed post.

Noodles just stood there shaking his head knowing if given the opportunity he'll 1et'em have it to. "Only if my nigga could see his sister now", he whispered looking to the sky hoping Mello was looking down on them." "Nigga, what you mumbling about now," Dirt Bert asked not really caring one way or the other.

"Nothing, I was just talking to myself", watching his girl turn the corner. "There she is", leaving his boys without a second thought rushing to her car.

"Dirt Bert, that's shorty I was tellin' you about," elbowing him in the side. "Wait until she get out."

"Nigga shut the fuck up! Let me see what she's workin' witt," lookin' on as Noodles leaned inside his girl window.

"What took you so long?" grabbing her cell phone from her ear pushing the end button. "Girrrl, you gonna make me climb through this window." "No Noodles," pushing him from trying to climb in. "You promised me you were going to take me, to see America Gangster, you know I love me some Denzel, and if I let you get started, we'll never make it, not tonight anyway."

Noodles just laughed knowing the truth when he heard it. "I got you," looking into her hazel eyes. "But first I need you to meet my boys," opening her door as if she didn't have a choice in the matter.

Dirt Bert and Tight-white sat back watching as Coco stepped out her car. "Nigga, I told you what it was," Tight-white said smiling from ear to ear, as Dirt Bert just stood there not believing his eyes.

"Coco, this is my boy Dirt Bert and you already met my nigga Tight-White." "Hi, Dirt Bert," she said extending her hand." I've .heard so much about you." "I wish I could say the same, but believe me the pleasure was all mine," pausing to admire her beauty feeling his lil-man growing inside his pants.

"So we meet again" Tight-White intervened breaking up Dirt bert moment. "And I must say, you look more beautiful than the last time we meet. I didn't know if it was the drinks or if it was actually you, but by the way you done stopped the flow of traffic around here, I shoulda known better."

Coco smiled taking his comment in stride, she turned around to observe her surrounding and wasn't the least surprised to see all the eyes looking her way.

As she continued to look over the projects and the people standing out and about, to the people in their windows, she caught a glimpse of someone that caused her heart to jump.

"Baby, you alright?" Noodles asked seeing the expression on her face "Yea boo," taking another look at dat window only to find no one there. "It's just too much testosterone in the air," pointing at his visible hard on, then his boys. "My bad, my nigga," trying to cover up the obvious.

Face appeared in his window to catch Noodles and his female companion leaving wandering how he allowed himself to get enticed by someone he didn't know, let alone formally get introduced to.

He allowed his imagination to take on a life of its own imagining what it would be like to have shorty in his stable, not taking into account the pro's and con's of such a task and believe me that was unlike the Notorious Face!!!

///

Peaches returned to Big Poppa's detail/car wash to find her BMW shinning like new money. "How much do I owe ya'll?" digging inside her Prada purse."Don't worry Miss lady, that's been taken care of ," Ray-Ray replied trying to sound all professional causing Peaches to look up from her purse."Excuse me!" "Yea, the gentlemen that was out here with me took care of dat and he gave me this card to give to you." Peaches took the card as if she was going to keep it only to tear it up.

"Tell yo homie, yo nigga, or whatever you call'em. Tell'em if he gonna pay for something,' he got to come better than dat," handing Ray-Ray a 100 dollar tip before jumping into her truck. "Oh yea, since you in the business of relaying messages, tell'em he ain't never came across a bitch like me," laughing to herself as she sped off.

//

"Baby, what's wrong," grabbing Coco around her waist. "It's like you're not even here. The whole time you been playing me off as if nothing's wrong,when you know I can sense somethin' ain't right. You didn't even watch the movie, the mutherfucka end up watching you," trying to look deep into her hazel eyes.

"I'm not in the mood for talking," kissing him forcefully on the lips. "So what you in the mood 'for," kissing and sucking on her neck. "You want me to make love to you," gripping her ass with both hands as he put tongue down her throat trying his hardest to bring her back to the here and now.

"When you're in a relationship, you gotta become one with yo significant other," biting his nipple threw his shirt. "Ahh! You hungry or something?" "Only for you," unbuttoning the first button on his shirt. "You got to know when yo girl needs to be held and when she doesn't, when its time to make love, versus when it's time to fuck," ripping his shirt from his chest. "Oh, you on dat?"

"Shh," putting her finger to his lips whispering" What's under-stood don't need to be talked about."

Without another word being said, Noodles reached under her skirt tearing the g-string from her person pushing her hard against the wall before turning her ass around so fast, she almost lost her balance.

"That's right, take what you want," bracing herself as he forced himself between her folds."Yess, ha shittt," she screamed out loud as Noodles assaulted the pussy from behind. "Handle yo pussy," biting down on her bottom lip.

Within minutes her juices ran freely down her legs and on to

Noodles dick causing him to speak out in between his pistol like stokes.

"Girrrrl, you're so fuckin' wet," concentrating on keeping his rhythm. " "Know when to call me yo girl," forcing herself to look over her shoulder. "And when to handle me as yo bitch," meeting his thrust head on burying her head under somethin' to muffle her screams.

///

"Bull-Moose, you always knew how to handle yo business," Det. Triggs said zipping his pants up. "Only if yo lil-boy friend knew how many times he done kissed yo ass with my dick on yo breathe," laughing at his statement. "Matter of fact, I haven't seen that wanna be thug in a while anyway," turning to see Bull-Moose eyes full of tears.

"And you won't," wiping the tears away that seem to be flowing like a river. "Bitch, what you talking about," wondering why she had to fuck up the mood with this crying shit? "He's dead Triggs, he's dead! They killed my baby and think I don't know," grabbing her things knowing she done said to much to the wrong mutherfucka.

"Bitch, where the fuck you think you're going," grabbing her by her weave throwing dat ass across the bed before she could make it out the door. "Now start from the beginning and you bet not leave nothing out, or I'm gonna, You already know!"

As if Bull-Moose just signed a recording deal, she sang her heart out adding to information Det. Triggs already knew and puttin' him witt things he didn't. All this new information was making his dick hard and the thought of leaving was not an option.

"Was that hard," standing to show her dat print in his pants, "Now do something to make me feel better," smiling to himself knowing he was on the verge of breaking a major case wide the fuck open.

///

"Don't worry Unk, I'll be about dat business soon enough. Just give me a minute to get settled in and familiar with my surroundings."

"J, you're one of my best soldiers, I believe in you and yo ability to handle whatever needs to be handled, or I wouldn't have sent you. My niece means the world to me ,so protect her at all cost, even if you have to "That goes without saying," knowing he'll have to sacrifice himself before allowing any harm to come her way. "These streets will bleed red before I let harm come her way!!!" "I know you will ",J , I know you will", Unk said hanging the phone up.

CHAPTER 15

Closing In

"Face, Face! Man, I'm sorry to interrupt you, but dig, you need to hear this." "What's dat Dirt Bert"? Looking up from his computer.

"Det. Triggs been trippin', got the whole block hotter than a muther-fcka asking questions he ain't got no business asking." "Questions like what?" "I don't know how to say this, but oh boy knows about T-love and got us in the middle of it,"

Instantly the hairs on Face neck stood up. "Hold tight Dirt Bert." Standing lookin' at'em half crazy then at the pager on his hip making sure it was on as he walked toward him stopping within inches giving the spy pager a chance to do it's thang before continuing cause had it went off, he woulda knew Dirt Bert was wired for sound and more than likely their conversation was being monitored.

"First of all, don't be coming in here talking about some nigga this and we nothing, you feel me?" Looking Dirt Bert dead in his face before returning to his laptop. "My bad Face, I just got off my square hearing what I heard."

"Dig Dirt Bert don't let some punk ass Detective get you off yo square," motioning for him to take a seat. "He's shooting in the dark hoping to find dat needle in the hay stack. Without a body, a murder weapon, and a motive ,he can ask all the questions he want and then some cause he damn sure ain't gettin' no confession ,you know what I'm talkin' about?" "Yea Face, I feel dat. I'm just curious to know who planted that seed."

"It's not that hard baby boy, once you put everything into perspective and deal with the basic elements of the situation." "I don't know Face, it's too hard to tell especially witt so many haters in the mist." "True dat, but think," Face said pausing long enough for Dirt Bert to do just that."Envision T-love here and Det. Triggs over there and who could be the go between cause dead men don't talk, let alone relay messages."

Dirt Bert listened closely putting everything together in his head realizing there was only one person T-love woulda felt comfortable around to share his deepest thoughts witt.

"I'ma kill dat bitch," Dirt Bert vowed jumping outta his seat rushing for the door.

"No you ain't," stopping him dead -in his tracks. "That's what he want us to do," standing to look out his window for a moment before turning around."He hopes we put one and one together and go handle shorty while he's laid in the cut waiting to hummer a nigga head in the dirt. Naw Dirt Bert we smarter than that, we gotta represent thinkers and be able to see around the corner before actually turning it, and if Det. Triggs become too much of a problem," lookin' Dirt Bert straight in his eyes. "He can get it to!" "Better believe it," Dirt Bert responded shaking his head up and down.

After Dirt Bert left Face went back to his laptop looking over the blue prints of Maniac mother's house, he studied the layout from top to bottom memorizing everything from the biggest detail down to the smallest.

Normally the cameras or ADT wasn't a problem, but with the electric box moved inside the house it was damn near impossible to disconnect unless killing the entire blocks electricity, but the more he played with different scenarios he finally came to the conclusion, why force my way in when I can send a familiar face and be invited in.

///

"Trick, don't look! But there go dat nigga." "Who?" Cheri asked looking over her shoulder catching eye contact with Maniac. "Bitch I told you not to look, now he know I saw his ass," pulling Cheri toward the escalator inside Kenwood Mall.

Maniac had noticed Peaches from a far recognizing that walk from anywhere, he was waiting on the right opportunity to make his play, but now that his cover was blown he had to man up and go get at shorty following them up the escalator.

"Bitch, who the fuck is dat," Cheri asked looking to see if he was following them as they ducked inside Exclusive.

"That's Maniac," Peaches responded knowing she fucked up once his name left her lips and seeing the look in her girls eyes. "Don't you dare do anything crazy," grabbing her arm as Maniac entered the store.

"Damn Ms. Lady, I made the mistake once by lettin' you get away with out catching a name and I'll be damn if I make the same mistake twice, witt yo sexy ass."

Peaches and Cheri looked at each other and started laughing. "Where you find this clown," Cheri asked pulling her girl hand trying to get as far away before she let this nigga have it.

"Damn Ms. Lady, I come in peace, but the look in yo eyes tells me you haven't been fucked good in months", Maniac said not about to let oh girl get out on'em like dat. "Oh, no he didn't" Cheri screamed turning to cuss his ass out.

"Hold tight," Peaches said through clenched teeth. "Don't fuck this up, just walk away and let me play this nigga for what he's worth."

Cheri stood their staring at Maniac for a moment then back to her girl with pleading eyes knowing without her gun she would be no match, deciding a good run is better than a bad stand.

"Maybe we can get together some time and I'll let you take care of dat for me," Cheri said blowing Maniac a kiss easing the tension between them. before turning to her girl "When you're finished, I'll be in the food court," allowing her girl to do her thang.

Peaches looked on as Cheri walked away with her back to Maniac gettin' herself together before going into character. "I'm not the one to apologize for someone else's actions, let alone to someone I don't even know" turning to look at Maniac. "Don't even trip sexy, yo girlfriend is the last thing on my mind," admiring Peaches natural beauty.

"I'm trying to catch a name and get to know you better and if anything else transpired outside dat we'll deal witt that when it comes". Smiling showing off his platinum grill.

"That's cute, and I guess I'm supposed to be impressed by yo word play and blinded by all yo ice. Like I told you before," stepping within inches of kissing him. "If it don't make dollars, it don't make good conversation," turning on her heels. "Hold up, Ms. Lady," grabbing her wrist before she could slip away." just wanna know yo name."

"No, no ,no, Mr .Man," smackin' 'his, hand until he let go. "You grab what's yours not what you want to be and I promise you, if we ever run into each other again, I'll give you more than just my name," leaving Maniac standing there with that one look on his face.

///

"Fuck this shit, I'm gonna split dat bitch in two." "Naw Tight-White, preventing him from leaving. "That ain't how dat go, we don't need no added drama on our hands especially witt this Maniac situation about to bear fruit", Dirt Bert expressed.

"More importantly Tight-White, keep yo eyes on the prize and stay focused," Noodles added."Cause one never knows when this fool might pull a nigga about this bull-shit, turning nothing into something,' you know what I'm talkin' about?"

"Listen to you nigga," Tight-White replied not believing how they where coming at him." If dat bitch ass Detective pulls me and I'm dirty, he better be ready to hold court right then and there cause I'd rather be carried by six than judged by 12 and if ya'll so happen to be riding shot gun, know what time it is," mean mugging his boys on his way out the door leaving them wondering where do they go from here.

"I love dat nigga, but he needs to get his shit together," Dirt Bert said pacing back and forth. "There's to much at stake and before I let'em fuck this up, I'm gonna." "You gonna what," Noodles snapped."I don't know where your mind at or what you thinking, but I ain't trying to hear none of dat."

"Nigga if you wasn't so quick to respond and just listen, I'm gonna tell Face to send his ass down south until this thang blows over cause the last thing we need is a nigga that ain't trying to listen and get his self fucked up as well as ourselves." "True dat, but before you do all that let me hollar at'em first." "No doubt and when you do let'em know, love is love."

///

While the family was occupied with executing their plans against Maniac, Max had her sights set on somethin' much bigger. She had her mind on taking down another notorious king pin in the city as she cruise through Mt. Auburn. She could smell his presence and the money circulating through this area.

"I'm gonna fry yo fat ass," she whispered to herself turning down Glencoe. She couldn't believe Face would put something like this on hold to chase some five and dime robbery boy turned dope boy, but then again she knew a lot was at stake fuckin' witt a nigga like fat Jeff.

This nigga had the whole Mt. Auburn on locks making Glencoe his million dollar spot. Fat Jeff was making dat weight money, the type of money you had to weigh or spend a life time counting it.

"What you need old girl," one of the hustlers yelled breaking her train of thoughts. "That be me," another hustlers instructed the other one telling Max "pull into the lot."

This was Max daily routine eyeing fat Jeff lay out trying to formulate a plan to get at'em.

"What it be Max? got dat blueberry, I'm tellin' you it's better than dat purple." "C'mon Tommy, you know what I like", hoping he wasn't trying to slid her no bull shit.

"I know, but I'm trying-to -put you witt this", pullin' a ounce from his pants. "Smell it, yea dat what I'm talkin' about. If you don't like it or ain't' satisfied bring it back and I'll give you a ounce of dat purple free of charge," causing Max to look up from the bag in her hand.

"Don't play witt me Tommy." "C'mon Max, never dat. You spend too much money for me to fuck up a good thang, plus dat bad for business something fat Jeff ain't having," bringing a smile to her lips.

Max paid Tommy and made her way back up the hill watching fat Jeff surrounded, by a couple of females thinking to herself, "The power of pussy is phenomenal and if presented right, the cause of any mans down fall."

///

"Joann, I fucked up. I'm tellin' you, I done fucked up", Bull-Moose yelled pullin' her hair running from room to room.

"Girl, what the fuck you talkin' about?" Seeing the look in her girls eyes as she began to pack. "Stop all this running and tell me what the fuck is going on" ,grabbing Bull moose by the arm.

"I got to get outta here before they kill me." "Before who kill you," lookin' at her girl like bitch stop playin'. "I was fuckin' witt Triggs and I told'em something I shouldn't have and now it's gonna come back on me."

"You what!" Joann yelled." " You better not told'em what I told yo stupid ass to shut the fuck up about," lookin' at her girl hoping she didn't.

"It just slipped and once it did he was all over it," she explained making Joann began to pace back and forth pullin' her hair trying to think of a somethin' she could say or make right the wrong. "You gotta go tell'em, you got to tell Face everything and hope he let yo stupid ass live." "Bitch, is you crazy!" "Naw bitch, but you is, if you think you can run and he won't find yo simple ass. This way he'll have a better understanding of what happened versus coming to his own conclusion thinking you set'em out there." "I don't know girl, I like my chances better cause the catchin' comes before the hangin'."

///

"Det. Triggs, can you come in here for a second," Det. Jones yelled as Triggs walked passed.

"I'm on my way to the computer lab to run some names through the data base but how can I help you?" "WE"RE SUPPOSE to be working together, but it seem you been trying to avoid me at all cost. I didn't ask for this, I was more or less pushed into this, I've been goin' through these reports over and over again and it seems we have a better chance at crackin' these two more so than the other one."

Det. Triggs stood there laughing to himself listening to the detective go on and on about nothing realizing while this young punk was in the office going over reports he was out there hittin' the pavement making shit happen.

"Is there something amusing detective," snapping Triggs outta his thoughts. "Now that you mentioned it", ceasing the opportunity to put this young Detective in his place. "I don't take kindly to strangers especially the ones trying to show me UP in front of my captain," stepping further into Det. Jones cubicle.

"So yo best bet is to stay outta my way, I didn't ask for yo help and I damn sure don't need it," knockin' his report on the floor takin'

Det. Jones by surprise. "I'm warning you, stay outta my way young punk."

Det. Jones sat there motionless trying to control himself as he watched Det. Triggs exit his cubicle knowing if it had been another place under different circumstances Det. Triggs woulda gotten more than he bargained for, finding himself caught up in a maze screaming for a nigga to come and save his ass, but for right now." I'll be just dat", he whispered lookin' at the mess on his floor. "

///

Trick, let me get you outta here before we end up catchin' a case," playfully hittin' Cheri on the arm.

"I'm good, I just got rattled seeing oh boy face to face, but before its all said and done I'm gonna fucked dat nigga", standing to trash her fish sandwich before turning to say. "I'm gonna literarily fuck'em", causing the people in ear shot to turn around hearing Cheri outburst.

"True dat!" Peaches responded wanting so badly to change the subject seeing so many eyes and ears upon them.

"That's what's up, but for right now we need to be finding somethin' to wear cause I be damn if I'm going to the Picnic/pool party looking like one of them broke down ho's and you know its gonna be a lot of'em." "Bitch, you are off the' chain and you ain't never lied," high fiving her girl as they laughed ready to do some major shopping.

///

"Boy, slow yo ass down and pull yo pants up coming through here witt dat loud ass music waking up the whole neighborhood," Ms. Joyce screamed at her son. "Mom please, fuck these mutherfuckas around here, matter of fact, go put this money away handing her a duffle bag full of money."

"Boy, don't you get grown", pointing her finger in his face. "I love everything you done did for me, but before I let you play me like one these two bit ho's you got kissing yo ass, I'll give you all this shit back and move my ass back to the projects."

"That's what I'm talkin' about," Maniac yelled picking his mother up in the air turning her around in circles loving how gangta she was.

"Boy, put me down before I get light headed and forget to put this money away", causing Maniac to stop immediately ."I thought so", laughing straighten herself up. "Seriously baby, when you gonna settle down and make me some grandbabies, you know I ain't gettin' no younger?"

"Funny that you asked-dat, I met this girl who reminds me so much of Netta it's driving me crazy." "Oh baby, you got to let that girl go I know its hard, but she's gone and you can't replace her with some Look a Like!" "Naw mom, it ain't nothing like dat, she just got a sharp tongue like Netta and the way she carry herself, I can't explain it. She's doing good by herself, but she could be doing a lot better fuckin' witt a nigga like me, You feel me?"

"Naw I don't feel ya," Ms. Joyce said laughing at her son. "So when I'm gonna meet this soon to be baby momma?" "Soon enough mom, soon enough," kissing her on his way out the door.

Maniac was feelin' dat one way inside as he climbed into his SUV, he had accomplished so much and exceeded his own expectations, all he needed and wanted was someone he could call his own and the more he thought about it, the more oh girl came to mind. "Damn shorty, why you gotta play so hard to get," He whispered pushin' his truck down Madison Rd. wishing she was right there beside him.

CHAPTER 16

The Picnic/Pool party

"Dirt Bert, did the catering service have enough grills, did you call to see what time they where coming to set the stage up ,did you find a company to do the fireworks, did you?"

"Clam down Max, I took care of everything I needed to and then some. I know how special this day is", pulling a chair for her to relax while he massaged her shoulders ."I got a couple of runs to make before we shoot to Hyde park, so roll somethin' up and get yo lungs right and I'll be back before you know it," making his way out the door. "Did you book anyone for the entertainment?"

"C'mon Max," getting aggravated that she kept on asking so many damn questions. "Face gonna handle dat," Closing the door behind him before she could throw something else at'em.

The 4th of July was like no other holiday on the calendar and for the few who knew it, this was the day Face came into the world and being that he wasn't big on celebrations, Max was excited when he mentioned what he wanted to do.

His plans was to throw a picnic/pool party in their neighborhood park offering free BBQ, drinks, and live entertainment ending the night with a message in the sky only a few would understand.

///

"Noodles who you taking to the picnic?" "It ain't who I'm taking, it's who ain't coming. You know my ho stroll like dat." "True dat!" But since Coke came into play, I don't know playboy." "Who the fuck is Coke?" pausing to think who he could possibly be referring to. "You talking about Coco?" "Naw nigga, Coke!" Shorty who got'em fienin, Tight-White joked poppin' tags on the outfit he planned on wearing. "Fumble the ball if you want to, shorty be standing on my side line."

"I don't love dem ho's, I love money and if don't make dollars, it don't make sense," refusing to admit his true feelings for her. "Pimp nigga pimp", turning to face his boy. "You can say what you wanna say, but I know within yo heart there's another story to be told" Tight-White said seeing the look in his mans eyes."

"Now that you into reading niggas, we need to talk", Changing the subject to somethin' more meaningful. "Talk about what?" feelin' the mood swing.

"That little stunt you pulled the other day ,ain't what time it is especially when a nigga trying to put you witt somethin'." "We ain't little boys no more running through these projects screaming fuck the world, we young bosses making more money than a lot these muther-fuckas gonna see in their life time." "We didn't get this far by not thinking, let alone going against one another, ain't no big I's or little U's never have, never will be."

"It's always been about us. DB and 'I Love you more than love it's self, but don't alienate yo self from dat and move without thinking cause yo actions not only effects you, but us as well, you know what I'm talkin' about?"

"Damn homie that's real talk, I can stand here and give you all types of excuses, but dat shit won't hold no weight or right the wrong. I'll admit I've been on some other type of shit lately thinking only one way, I take Mellos death personal and the last thing I'ma let happen is for one of my niggas to get caught up in some bull shit, even if I got-ta."

"Naw playboy," stopping Tight-White in mid sentence." Ain't no I

nothing! We all gonna do our part," lettin' his boy know he's not alone.

By 2:00 in the afternoon everything was in place the catering ser-vice had about 30 grills smokin' with hamburgers, hotdogs, ribs, and steaks. For the people who didn't eat red meat they offered grilled salmon, turkey burgers and chicken. SelfMade entertainment set up the stage on the baseball field along with the VIP tents for Face and company while the people doing the fireworks took over the tennis court. It being fenced in allowing them the security they needed at the same time keeping everybody out of harm's way. The Pepsi Company provided portable stands throughout the park making it easier for eve-ryone to get something to drink.

The front entrance to the park was blocked off causing everybody to enter at the far end of the park by the drive thru. This caused problems being everybody used the drive thru as a parking lot.

"Move yo cars, this no parking lot, this business," one of the foreigners came out yelling pointing at everybody.

"You better take yo rice eating ass back inside and lock dat door before a nigga beat dat ass out here." "Me not scared, me call police," the foreigner responded fleeing inside. "Call yo momma to, punk bitch," another person yelled throwing a brick at the door the foreigner rushed his ass into bringing laugher through out the crowd as they headed into the park.

Even doe, it was a picnic/pool party the females represented the pool party to fullest in their revealing outfits. These girls was sporting some of the coldest one and two pieces you ever want to see on a female. Then you had the ones ,coming through in body suits and daisy dukes leaving somethin' to the imagination, but still had a nigga feelin' dat one way.

"Tight-White, who you invite?" "Nigga, who I invite? I don't invite sand to a beach or water to an ocean, don't you see all these fine honeys running around here," pointing at all the many different females walking through the park. "Before it's all over witt, you know how I get down, I'm nailing a bitch to the bed post", causing Noodles and Dirt Bert to laugh.

"Dirt Bert who you got coming through?" "Nigga, I'm witt Tight-White, what I look like inviting a bitch to diss shit?" "I don't know, but here comes sugar and her girlfriends," Noodles responded pointing in their direction. "So you tell me what you look like," laughing seeing the look on his man's face as the ladies approached.

"Hi baby," Sugar said standing in front of her so called man. "I need to hollar at you for a minute," pullin' him to the side while her girls Ebony and Christina entertained the boys.

"Noodles, why I haven't heard from you lately," Ebony asked pushin' her body against his. "You know what it is, love me when I'm there and when I ain't continue."

"Pimp nigga pimp", Tight-White said lookin' at Christina camel toe. "Damn shorty, you on display dat one way, what you trying to get into",puttin' his bid in before the next man did. "We'll see cause the last thing I want to do is waste yo time and mine," lookin' directly at the dick."Shiit, don't even trip about dat, good things comes in small packages," grabbing his joint. "I hope so cause I hate to embarrass you," looking at'em side ways. "How is dat", wondering what type of games shorty on.

"It would be a shame if I allowed you to get my juices flowing and got you home and pulled out a magnum and you just a lifestyle type of guy", placing her hands on the prize as she whispered in his ear.

"Ya'll ho's ain't shit," Sugar yelled shaking her head. "I can't leave ya'll alone for a minute, come on these niggas ain't nothing, but some male prostitutes anyway," guiding them through the crowd as the boys looked on. "Man, I'm trying to fuck the shit outta Christina tonight."

"Yo if baby don't come through here I'm gonna knock Ebony ass upside the head my mutherfuckin' self." "Fuck Sugar and them bitches", Dirt Bert commanded taking everybody by surprise knowing his ass was love sick over shorty for real.

"Don't get tight cause Sugar trying to get at them ends or is it you ain't trying to see yo bitch on stage settin' dat thang out for all these niggas to see," Noodles joked knowing a lot of these niggas bitches was gonna make it do what it do for that little money Face was giving away to the winner of the wet t-shirt contest, best bikini, rounding it off on some shake what yo mamma gave ya type shit.

"I don't give a fuck what dat bitch do," Dirt Bert said with a attitude wondering how the fuck he knew what him and his bitch was talkin' about.   In the mean time you could see females jockeying for position pushin' and shoving one another trying to get their names on a list whether it be one or the other cause there was only room for 30 of'em, ten to each contest.

All to spilt 7500. First place in each contest gets 1000,second gets 500, third gets 300, and everybody else take home 100. So you might win a lot, you might win a little, but one thing for sure, a bitch was gonna win somethin.

///

"Face, look at what you done started, them girls need their ass whipped the way they carrying on," Max strongly stated not believing her eyes. "Don't get bent outta shape", Face responded pattin' Max on her knee. "You witnessing the change of times, a different era, a different generation and I love it", smiling a smile only Max recognized.

"The only time you smile that hard when there's money to be made and you're the only one on top of it." "Pause game baby girl, you ain't got to be on top of everything, let somethin' miss you some time."

"Nigga please, what you got cookin'," turning to give Face her undivided attention. "The illusion of something for free is really an investment to be filmed, package ,and resold at later date and time", Face said knowing she didn't have a clue.

"What the fuck you talkin' about," she inquired not fully understanding what he was insinuating.

"C'mon baby girl, when have you known me to give away anything, let alone a lot of money to a bunch of strangers that ain't puttin' nothing on a niggas plate," lookin' at Max like she shoulda known better.

"Yea right," she said. "I didn't know what to think when you came at me about this, I was more surprised than anything, so instead of saying somethin' I just played my position taking into account it was yo B-day and all ,but I still don't see how you gonna recoup yo investment at the same time make a profit when you ain't charge nobody nothing."

"That's the difference between me and you, I can envision and see the unseen versus you only seeing what's in front of you", kissing Max on the cheek to ease the blow he just delivered. "I got more than 100K invested in this thing mostly toward the entertainment." "Entertainment! Nigga please, these local acts and DJ ain't put no dent in dat 100K," laughing that Face would try to insult t her intelligence witt dat bull shit.

"If you wasn't so quick to respond and just listen, I got somethin' beautiful in the makin' that's gonna shut this mutherfucka down when they hit dat stage, I'm gonna package this whole event like girls gone wild, but this gonna be called, The 4th of July the nasty nati way.

All I gotta do is sell 10,000 copies at 19.99,you do the math", smiling at his baby girl and mentor as Cheri and Peaches approached their tents.

"Hey Max", both girls said giving hugs and kisses before turning to do the same to Face. "I feel like I'm over dressed," Peaches said lookin' at all the half naked females walking around in different directions. "Me and you both," Cheri added taking a seat next to Face while adjusting her Gucci shades.

"What them ho's about to get into", Peaches asked taking a seat next to Cheri as 10 females took to the stage.

"Sin city, what's really good", Larry Kelly yelled out to the crowd passing out wife beaters to the ten contestant on stage. "Maybe ya'll didn't hear me or I didn't say it right. E-town, what's really good", he yelled again receiving a response only those from E-town could give.

"Nigga, shut the fuck up and get this shit poppin,"someone yelled bringing laugher throughout the crowd and from Larry Kelly himself. "So without any farther delays," he turned to the females seeing if they were ready while 10 guys stood at the bottom of the stage with super soakers in hand and buckets of water at their feet ready to make it do what it do.

As if on cue the music dropped and niggas got to spraying and the females got to jumpin' up and down. What started as a wet t-shirt contest end up being more than one expected, then again maybe not.

All it took was for one female to feel she wasn't gettin' enough attention and off came the t-shirts causing the crowd to go into a frizzle.

"Yea shorty, get about dat money",a couple of ballers yelled out throwing money onto the stage making the other nine get about theirs and step their game up. "Now that's what I call a chain reaction," Larry Kelly yelled into the mic bringing laughter throughout the crowd.

That was just one of three events with the next one not living up to it expectation, especially after the wet t-shirt demonstration.

"Get these stuck up ho's off the stage," one dude yelled causing the rest of the crowd to start booin'. "Hold up, hold up ya'll, I got' this." Larry Kelly pleaded with the crowd. "I know how ya'll feel and the feelings are mutual and I be damn if I let ya'll down. Security, get these bitches off my stage," bringing cheers throughout the park. "Face my bad, but they wasn't representing the bikini contest like they were suppose to," turning to get Face's approveal only to receive a thumbs up and a head nod."Dat's what I'm talkin' about," smiling at Face before turning back to the crowd. "DJ, drop dat shit and let's get this thang poppin."

This was the contest Sugar had been waiting on, she was nothing short of a show off and now that her ass got fatter, you better believe she wanted to show it -off and what better place than in front of an audience that wanted her to do just that. All nine girls including Sugar stood on stage bobbin' to the sound of E40)feat' T-pain.

"Hold it, hold it," Larry Kelly told the DJ. "Cut dat shit off," Turning to the contestants "If ya'll ain't trying to make it do what it do, ya'll can get off my stage right now," walking back and forth in front each contestant fannin' himself with the prize money. "Since I didn't give them other hookers nothing I'm doubling down on this one," bringing a smile to everybody on stage knowing first place just went from a stack to two.

" DJ," Larry Kelly said puttin' the spot light on' em." I need you to dig deep and come up with somethin' that's not only gonna make'em shake it, but represent what they mamma gave'em," throwing his mic in the air basically saying jump this mutherfucka off.

Mystical came blazing threw the speakers, shake yo ass/show me what you workin' witt, bringing the crowd to life and sending the females into action. You had a couple of them pop, lock, and drop it while a few broke into splits and some doing the hypnotize, then you had Sugar running through a ray of moves before turning dat thang to the crowd and hit'em witt the thunder clap drawing all eyes- on her even the females on stage witt her. "Damn shorty, how much," a nigga yelled catchin' her attention that she looked over her shoulder smiling.

Seeing Sugar was stealing the spot light and on the verge of winning first place, a few of the females knew drastic times caused for drastic measures and really set dat thang out taking off everything bring ooH and Haa from the crowd.

Sugar looked on smiling knowing they had to come up witt something if they wanted to compete. "Ya'll ain't said nothing," coming outta her shit as well puttin' it all out there for everybody to see.

The guys who had the super soakers started spraying the naked bodies on stage taking the whole event to another level.

"c'mon Face, this shit done went to far," Max said standing to go do somethin' about it. "Naw baby girl," grabbing her by the arm. "you know what time it is, let me enjoy me on my earth day and see how far these ho's gonna' take it."

Just then one of the females went into a head stand spreading her legs far apart exposing the goodies in such a way the crowd went crazy puttin' pressure on the others to come witt somethin' more creative.

Sugar with her back against the wall seeing she no longer was holding the spot light sprung into action positioning herself behind shorty doing the head stand and began eating her pussy while she was still doing a headstand. "Hot damn, we got us a winner," Larry Kelly yelled into the mic breaking everybody outta there I can't believe this shit look. "That's what you call a head rush," standing next to Sugar as she wiped oh girl juices from her lips, and as the crowd began to chant her name.

Face smiled knowing after all the footage was collected and edited he'll have a timeless piece on his hands.

"What yo nasty ass smiling about", Cheri asked hittin' Face playfully on the arm.

"You wouldn't believe me if I told you," he responded still smiling." "Try us," Peaches jumped in saying.

"Face, Face," Max said pointing toward the stage," as Dirt Bert appeared outta no where grabbing Sugar by her wig. "Bitch, you lucky I don't put my foot in yo ass," he whispered in her ear. "Now take yo winnings and throw dat shit to the wind," giving her dat look lettin' her know he wasn't playin', but dead serious. Without a second thought she threw everything into the wind lettin' it rain onto the crowd.

"Now, introduce me to yo new friend", smackin' her on the ass." "Daddy, this is Keisha," taking hold of her hand. "That's what's up," holding his arms out inviting them to take hold as he exited the stage.

"Pimp nigga, Pimp," the crowd yelled along with Larry Kelly lettin' it be known. Pimpin' ain't dead, it ain't the ho's dat scared, it's the niggas." "You ain't never lied," Face whisper to himself watching Dirt Bert do his thang.

//

"Maniac, I talked to one of my girls in Evanston and they having some type of pool party with free food, drinks, and entertainment and if you ain't doing nothing lets slide through there," Raytanya said headed toward the bathroom.

The mere mention of Evanston had Maniac leery. "Naw Ray, I'm cool, lying back on the bed. "Well if you don't mind, I'm trying to get there and the least you can do is drop a bitch off, I'11 find me a ride home", she yelled from the bathroom. "I bet you will, even if you gotta suck a dick, turn a trick to make it happen", He responded laughing at his own statement".

//

The whole event was winding down, KP and Rob-J two of Cinti up and coming rap artist just finished settin' the stage on fire with local hit, Ciney America most wanted.

The lights on stage where shut off bring even more darkness into the park; the only light being provided was that of the swimming pool which was packed to capacity.

The saying, freaks come out at night was an understatement a crew of strippers from Sneak and peak was workin' the park dat one way, suckin' and fuckin' and doing whatever needed to be done, to get at them ends. The DJ was still spinnin' the ones and twos keepin' the crowd going while Dirt Bert, Sugar and their new friend lounged beside the pool smokin' on somethin' real lovely. The park was still crowded anticipating the fireworks ending the night on a beautiful note, as Cheri, Peaches, Face, Max, Noodles, and Tight-white chilled inside their tent sippin' and gettin' their lungs right.

"Noodles, where that hot lil number I keep hearing so much about?" Face asked. "I really don't know, to tell you the truth, she said she was coming through, but I guess she got caught up," taking the blunt from Max. Outta nowhere the sound of let me reintroduce myself, my name is Hov, then the lights to the stage came back on revealing the man behind the voice.

"OH hell naw," everybody screamed inside the park while Face sat back smiling lookin' at the pool area spill out onto the grass in front of the stage clashing with the people already there.

//

"Damn! What the fuck",Maniac said pullin' into the drive thru lookin' at all the young ladies in bikinis. "I'm cool right here," Raytanya said opening the door to get out. "Hold tight, let a nigga park first," grabbing Raytanya by the arm." Yo ass still gonna have to find you a ride home." "Fuck you Maniac, it's plenty of niggas out here that would love to give a bitch a ride home," gettin' tired of his bull shit.

"They got Hov performing on stage," a couple of females yelled trying to get their friends attention." " Hov performing," Maniac whispered to himself realizing them E-town boys doing it real big out this way.

//

"Where you at?" Noodles asked happy to hear her voice. "I just pulled into the drive thru." "Alright, make yo way toward the stage and I'll come down to get you." "Noo, I'm not gettin' outta my car until you come and get me. Shit, the way these niggas acting and disrespecting these girls, I'm not in the mood to be sittin' down town waiting on yo slow ass to come bail me out for fuckin' one of these clowns up."

"Don't trip love," laughing at how crazy she sounded. "I wish a nigga would, but to be safe. Stay put I'm on my way," pushing the end button as he stood giving Tight-White the signal to ride with him.

Face never being the one to mis much noticed the urgency in Noodles movement and the unspoken words spoken between them knew something was up.

"Playboy you alright." Looking to roll with them. "yea Face, I'm good, I just gotta go get my girl before one of these nigga's get it twisted." "Where she at," Peaches and Cheri asked wanting to see what all the hype surrounding oh girl only to receive a gesture of him pointing toward the drive thru as they exited the stage."

C'mon girl," pulling Cheri's arm. "Lets go see what this trick workin wit cause if she aint right I'm gonna laugh in the bitch face."

The wonder twins left on a mission right behind them when outta nowhere Cheri spotted him.

"Peaches, Peaches," she called until Peaches turned around.

"Theirs go yo boy," pointing in his direction. "Aint dat about some-thin'"" she responded undecided if she should continue on their mission or go put some work in and before she could figure out what to do, Cheri interrupted her thoughts. "The sooner you play this nigga, the sooner we can," "Don't even mention it," leaving Cheri standing there to finish her own sentence.

//

"It took you long enough," Coco said playfully punching Noo-dles on the arm. "Probably had to get rid of yo other hoe's," looking at Tight-White to confirm or deny." "I don't know nothin' about dat Ms. Coke, but my nigga been missing you dat one way," Tight-White said smiling at both of them.

"Yea, Yea, Yea, tell me anything, but what is this coke bit"? "That's just me being me separating myself from the rest while they callin' you Coco, I'm shortin' it up to Coke cause believe it or not you just like a drug." "And how is that," she responded being curious? "Addictive," Tight-White replied lookin' at the way them low rider ca-pris where outlining every curve on her body, not to mention her small waist and tone mid section she had on display wearing a simple bikini top. "True dat",Noodles agreed lookin' around at all the attention she was generating by her presence.

"I hate to break up this moment, but a nigga tryin' to get back before Hov finish doing his thang" Tight-White said making his way back inside the park. "Let's go sexy," Noodles added grabbing hold of her hand leading them into the park.

"Baby, let's go back to my place and I promise to deliver a performance worth seeing, but the catch to it all it's for yo eyes only" pullin' Noodle under a small tree. "C'mon Ms. Coke, I mean Coco. I want you to see Hov up close and meet my people" "I'm not star stuck like a lot of these people, I like his music, but he's not the one," wrapping her around his waist.

"Whats about my people" "I aint going nowhere," kissing him softly on the lips. "There's gonna be plenty of time for me to meet who ever you want me to meet, but right now I just want to enjoy my mans company".

//

Hov was on stage the last 45 minutes doing what he do taking the crowd on a journey through his life struggles and accomplishments with his catalogue of hits starting witt Reasonable doubt, to everything in between ending his performance on some America Gangsta shit

"We the dope boys of the year/drinks on the house/the roc boys in the building," Hov spitted not receiving the response he wanted. "Hold it, hold it," he yelled at the DJ to cut the music. "Ya'll on dat?" turning to the crowd."Ya'll gonna play me?" not even wanting on a response. "Ya'll out there lookin' way to tough," and just like that,30's the new 20's came blastin' threw the speakers giving the people what they wanted, some hood shit.

"Ahh, dat my shit," Peaches yelled throwing her hands in the air positioning herself not to far from Manica as she song alone with Hov."I'm from the era where niggas don't snitch you from the era where snitchin' is the shit."Manica notice her instantly wasting no time making his way over there. "Ya'll respect the one who got shot/I respect the shoota," he spit in her ear causing her to smile knowing the nigga was open and aint even got the pussy yet.

///

Cheri and Tight-White made their way back to the tent just in time to see Face standing with drink in one hand, blunt in the other spittin' alone with Hov."I use to let my pants sag not givin a fuck/bay boy, now I'm all grown up/I used to cruise the used car lot puttin' chrome on the truck." This was unlike Face, a part of him no one ever seen. He was never the one to get intoxicated out in public, let alone let his guards down around a bunch of strangers, but with this being his b-day the people close to him let it go without question.

"We use to ball like that," Tight-White joined in puttin his arm around Face's shoulders. "Now we own the ball team, holla back/ now I got black cards good credit n stuff bay boy now I'm all grown up." After Hov finished his song he got Face attention and let'em know love is love before disappearing into the night just as fast as he appeared.

"Where's Noodles and his girl," Face asked giving the signal to start the fireworks. "They shoulda been right behind me," Tight-white answered."And where's Peaches," he asked turning to Cheri?" "She's witt Maniac," catchin' his facial expression after it registered what she had said. "I wanna touch dat nigga so bad," Face said through clenched teeth. "But I'm gonna let it play out.""Dat's right," Max said seeing the look in his eyes. "We have to much at stake to allow our emotions to run wild and make decisions we normally wouldn't make if we wasn't intoxicated," puttin' Face back on point.

"That's why I love you so much," Face said kissing Max roughly on the lips. "Hit Peaches, Noodles, and Dirt Bert, on their blackberries and let'em know the sky will reveal it all," turning to Cheri and Tight-White tellin' them the same.

For 15 minutes straight fireworks lit up Evanston park ending a beautiful event that would be the talk of the city for years to come. People started pairing up to continue their affairs at a more secluded location. Simultaneously Noodles, Peaches, and Dirt bert received their message on their black berries not fully understanding the contents until the final display of fireworks hit the sky reading, "The world is ours", bringing a smile to everybody within the family.

"If you let me, I'll give you a reason to smile everyday," Maniac said lookin' deep into her eyes. "What make you think I don't already have a reason to smile everyday," Peaches replied puttin' her blackberry away. "Maybe you do, maybe you don't, I'm only speaking on the couple of occasions." "Shh!"Peaches whispered. "You talk too much, let's go before I change my mind."

///

"Let's ride," Noodles said pullin' her hand after reading the message in the sky. "The way you smiling, you act like that message was meant for you." "Some things are better left unsaid like the best sex I ever had started off witt a shot of head", Noodles said laughing at his last remark. "Boy, don't make me beat yo ass out here," remembering their first sexual encounter.

As they wove through the crowd when outta nowhere Ebony jumped in front of them."Noodles, you leaving witt me?" "Not right now Ebony," brushing pass her still holding Coco hand. "Dat ain't what you was saying when that bitch wasn't around." "Who you callin' a bitch," Coco said snatching away from Noodles. "Bitch please, jump out there if you want to, I'll have dat ass lookin' stupid out here." "C'mon love, she's just in her body, but she'll get over it," Noodles said grabbing hold of his girl. "Naw Noodles, let me go. If I let her disrespect me once she'll do it again." "Yea nigga, let the bitch go cause every time I see dat bitch, I'ma let her have it" ,Ebony barked. "Let me go, I don't want to embarrass you," Coco said calmly not attempting to break loose from his hold. "What I look like lettin' my girl cat fight out here with this bitch?"

"I'm sorry you feel this way, so let me apologize," and before Noodles had the chance to respond Coco slammed the heel of her sandals down on the bridge of his toes causing him to loosen his grip and within one swift motion she stepped outta his hold turning around and karate chopped him to his wind pipe breaking him down to one knee. "if you keep yo ho's in check I wouldn't be going through this," she whispered in his ear before turning to get at Ebony ass.

On stage Face, Max, Cheri, and Tight-white watched the whole scene unfold in disbelief. "Man, somebody go get the karate kid - before she kill shorty," Face said laughing that Noodles was still bent down on one knee holding his neck unable to do anything. Tight-White took off to break up the fight while Cheri followed suit to see about Noodles.

"Okay Coke, she had enough," Tight-white said pullin' Coco off her prey. "The next time she call me a bitch, she'll ask me first, I bet dat." "That she will Coke, that she will," shaking his head.

By this time Noodles was finally able to stand with Cheri's help as he gathered his bearings about himself."Girl, you damn near crushed my esophagus", he said rubbin' his neck feelin' embarrassed about the whole situation. "You shoulda let me go instead of trying to protect dat bitch." "Dig, if I woulda known yo ass was gonna get Jet-Le on a nigga, I woulda never grabbed yo ass in the first place," bringing laughter through out the crowd. "Now c'mon and meet my peeps before I steal on yo ass, got my toes hurtin' and so more shit," He mumbled walking toward the stage. As they took to the stairs one by one, Face and Max stood at the top waiting to take jabs at Noodles for what had transpired.

"Playboy, you might need to take some karate lessons," Face joked lookin' pass him to catch a better glimpse of Coco as she made her way up the stairs. Within seconds Coco found herself frozen in time seeing her man, Max, and Face standing together, she began to sweat profusely causing her to become faint and before anyone realized it, she had fallin. "All shit," Tight-White yelled trying his best to catch her from falling off the side of the stairs being that he was right behind her. Face and Max stood there unable to fully understand what had happened while Noodles jumped off the stage to see about his girl." "Coco ,Coco," He screamed. "Talk to me baby, talk to me", Feelin' her pulse. Coco laid there hearing his voice, but for the moment lost in her thoughts trying to piece somethin' together that already fit.

///

"Turn right here," Peaches instructed navigating Maniac to her condo. She knew she couldn't fuck'em tonight and risk him running away after gettin what he wanted, she had to play her hand accordingly and present a challenge somethin' he wasn't use to, making him more intrigued than he already was.

"Pull over there" pointing in front of her condo digging inside her purse looking at him as he put his truck in park and killed the engine. "What you do that for," causing Maniac to look at her crazy and before he could answer she went on to say, "You thought me and you where gonna-. Boy, you a mess," shaking her head from side to side pullin' her keys out. "Don't get it twisted, I'm no angle, but I'm damn sure ain't one of these ho's you accustom to fuckin' witt either," turning to open the door. "Hold on Ms. Lady," Maniac said grabbing her arm." You gonna leave me again without giving me yo name?" Peaches turned around and looked him dead into his eyes."One thing you will learn and get to know about me, I say what I mean and mean what I say and I told you already you grab what's yours not what you want to be," looking down at his hand until he let go. "Thank you," climbing outta his truck. "Hold on Ms. Lady, you also told me if we ever run into each other again, you'll give me more than just yo name. "I already did, you just failed to realize it", blowing him a kiss as she shut his door .

He quickly opened his door and stood on the running broad looking over the top of his SUV. "Ms. Lady, let's not keep playing games, either we gonna do this or we ain't." "Call me and we'll talk about it," walking up to her door. "How I'm gonna do' dat when I don't even have yo phone number?" "Look on yo front seat", puttin the key in the door as he quickly ducked his head inside to retrieve the piece of paper on his seat and true enough it was a phone number. "You didn't put yo name on it doe," Mania yelled before she made it inside. "I'll tell you when you call," Peaches yelled in return closing the door behind her.

With all the excitement no one noticed Det. Trigg's lying in the cut sizing his man up. He wanted so badly to make his presence known by shaking a niggas tree just to see what he could get to fall, but thought better of it, knowing Face wasn't the one he could easily intimidate remembering the last time they bump heads.

Naw, he had to shoot at the body to touch the head, cause once the body get weak the head will fall he reasoned knowing from years of expericncc outta every crew there was a potential snitch that hasn't been tested.

He just needed to find which one had the most to lose, better yet which one was on some love shit cause believe it or not, outside of the fact of wanting to stay free the female played an important role in a lot of these wanna be thugs decision to flip not wanting to unhand cuff the ho and allow the next man his turn.

It wasn't until later that Det. Trigg's saw what he was lookin' for. "God damn, where dat bitch come from, I know damn well he ain't trying to leave that", feelin' his dick gettin' hard. "I'll bet my last dollar on dat," smiling as he quietly exited the park.

"DB why I have to throw away my winnings like dat, I coulda brought you somethin' nice witt that money." "Save that shit for one those bitch made niggas, you can't do nothin' for me, but get diss dick right," holding his shit in his hand. "And that I do, ain't dat right?" Fallin' to her knees motioning for their new friend to join them.

Sugar knew what type of nigga she was dealing witt and did everything within her powers to keep their relationship exciting even if she had to take a couple of ass whipping from time to time for some of the shit she knew she had no business doing, but as long as it kept him chasin,' she didn't give a fuck.

CHAPTER 17

What Happen

"I'm sorry Face ,I really wanted to make it, lord knows I did" Apples said stopping to give him a kiss and a hug. "But I had to handle my business." "That you did rubbing on her butt thinking of all the ways he wanted to put dat dick in her. "I shoulda got a job at UPS cause FedEx got yo girl workin' dat one way." "Don't worry girl," squeezing dat ass. "Once this is over you can tell FedEx to kiss yo ass. Matter of fact, let me see what dat thang look like outside them jeans." "I'ma show you more than what it look like", fumbling with her belt buckle.

Face was in need of some dat 80's way, he had got so wet on his B-day he didn't get the chance to punish nothing, but seeing Apples in them low rider Apple bottoms had'em feelin' dat one way.

"Yea, c'mon outta dat", seeing her standing in front of'em' with nothing, but a red tong. "Turn around," he instructed wanting to see the shape of that thang, as he unbuckled his pants."Dat's it, shake somethin' for daddy. Now let me see what yo neck game workin' wit," Pullin' his joint free. Apple turned around ready to do whatever he wanted her to do. Shit this was Face and a bitch had to be crazy no to want to be a part of this especially seeing what he was workin' witt.

"I knew it", she said happily positioning herself between his legs. "You been trying to keep all this from a bitch," taking hold of his tool teasing the head with her thumb. "You like dat," lookin' at the expression on his face before placing him gently into her mouth. "Yesss, just like dat," he whispered lost within his thoughts thinking about Co-co sexy ass that he or Apples never heard Tight-White and Dirt Bert enter the apartment. They stood there for a second enjoying the show as Apple worked the shit outta the dick, not to mention the back shot was one that belonged in black tails.

"Bitch! ",Tight-White yelled. "J-rock gonna beat dat ass," laughing seeing how fast she jumped off the dick. "Ya'll dead wrong," Face said covering himself while Apples regrouped from the initial shock of being caught in the act. "Ain't no shame in my game," she assured them gathering her things. "Let that shit be," Face said not about to let her get away. "Go catch a shower and I'll be there before you can get lather up," smackin' dat ass before she had the chance to exit the room.

"I see why she got dat nigga J-rock fucked up" Dirt bert said watchin' her throw dat ass."If you need some help with dat, hollar at yo boy." "Believe me I got this. But what happen to you last night?" "Me, Sugar, and our new friend had our own fireworks poppin' off, you know what I'm talkin' about? "That's what's up, but has anybody talked to Noodles?" "He's still babysitting oh girl," Tight-White answered. "She had a an anxiety attack or somethin', but she good, I hollered at'em this morning."   "That's good cause I need everybody on top of their game, its time to make a play on oh boy." "That's what I'm talkin' about," Tight-White said ready to put some work in.

"Tight-White told me, oh boy was at the park," Dirt Bert said. "Yea, that he was and from my understanding he left witt Peaches, so I need to get up with her and see where she at witt'em cause once we shoot this move at'em he's gonna need somebody to run to." "You better believe it," Dirt Bert agreed knowing all hell was about to break loose.

//

"Don't keep coming at me witt dat bull shit," Coco screamed trying to avoid another altercation. "I'm tired of hearing, I played witt shorty when I shouldn't have and I never meant for this shit to happen, keep dat shit to yo self cause I could care less. I'm hurting Noodles, I'm hurting in ways you'll never fully understand." "Help me understand," he pleaded placing her hand on his heart. "I know I probably broke yours, but please don't break mine by pushing me away."

Coco stood there heart broken in pieces vowing not to shed one tear, at the same time trying to sort things out and put everything into perspective. She was at a cross road in her life torn between two worlds, one she could never get back, to the one that will never be the same.

"I will never push you away," feelin' how fast his heart was beating. "But I need you to know something," pausing to collect her thoughts. "There may come a time where you might question what we have." "What are you talkin' about?" he asked. "Shh!" she whispered puttin' her finger to his lips. "'Even my love, but understand I will never do anything to intentionally hurt you." Noodles stood there listening lookin' deep into her eyes seeing the pain hidden behind them, he wanted so badly to question her, but decided against it when he heard her say. "I love you and always will no matter how this turns out."

///

"Nigga, what the fuck you so happy about," Self asked wanting to smack the shit outta his ass just because. "Damn Self, every time I come through here you got dat one look on yo face, take a little bit off dat before I get to thinking you really want it witt me," Maniac said tired of biting his tongue and being played like some lame.

"If I don't, then what," reachin' for his hammer. "Ya'll niggas worser than some broads," Ice Mike intervened turning to look at his man hoping to calm his ass down and put him back on point. "Let's get money and leave that other shit for them ducks out their." "Ice, you know I ain't for dat drama, I'm about gettin' this money, but if a nigga want it ,he can get it," Maniac expressed giving Self a menacing look. Self stared back wanting to let'em have it, but fell back knowing his day would come.

"I was just fuckin' witt his ass making sure he keep dat edge about himself and not allow this money to soften his heart cause in this game it kill or be killed", returning the same menacing look. "Now that's out the way, what you shoppin' witt'", Ice said gettin' back to the money.

"Instead of the usual put 10 more witt it," Maniac replied. "I'll shoot you them ends later on," making his exit. Seconds later Ice turned to Self. "You was about to jack off 700 thousand, please help me understand this cause if ain't about the money, what is it about?" " It's about Corey plain and simple even doe his body hasn't been found."

"You talkin' about yo girl lil brother Corey?! I didn't know he was running around witt Maniac," feeling remorseful cause he was the one who told Maniac to clean house. "I didn't know." "Naw Ice, this was before he came through here, I remember when baby was saying she hasn't seen her brother, then Maniac and Smiley names started ringing. I didn't put it together until I saw how quickly he put Smiley and Chelle to rest, I haven't told nobody, not 'even my girl." "Don't worry Self, after he take care of this load, I'm gonna let you pull the plug on dat nigga."

//

"Hello!",Peaches said flipping through some papers on her desk.   "What it's gonna take for me to see you?" "I wish it was possible, but I'm at work." "What kinda work you do and what time you clockin' out cause I'm trying to see yo sexy ass." "I'm a real estate agent and my last showing ain't until-.Hold on for a second. Hmm, 3:30," she blurted out.

"Dig, if it ain't to much, let yo boy treat you out to Benny Hanna's, say around 6:00." "That would be nice ,but once I make it home 1'm in for the night." "C'mon Ms. Lady, I'm just tryin to kick it, plus I haven't eaten shit all day and I need to put somethin' on my stomach." "I tell you what and I hope I don't regret this." "What's that," Hoping Ms. Lady come out and play witt a nigga, and see what pops off. "Swing by my spot around 6:30 and I'll cook us a little somethin' and you can save yo money."

Maniac took her last comment in stride he wasn't use to a female trying to save him anything especially some money at dat, let alone swap a free meal to cook him one."

That's what's up, Ms. Lady. So what should I bring?" "Just bring yo self and Maniac." "Yea Ms. Lady." "Naw, that would be Peaches," hanging up before he had a chance to respond." "Peaches," he said only to hear the dial tone realizing she had hung up. "Damn, I'm feelin' shorty hittin' the Red Bank exit on his way to his moms to get those ends.

//

"Nigga, I'm coming down the ave right now," Noodles said cruising up Montgomery Rd. "I'm surprised you didn't call in sick," Tight-White joked. "C'mon playboy, how many times I gotta tell you, I don't love dem ho's. I stick'em, lick'em, and drop kick'em." "Pimp nigga pimp ,but let me find out you just blowin' hot air at yo boy," laughing knowing Coco had'em gone dat one way especially the way his ass jumped off that stage.

"Damn!" "What's wrong playboy?" "One time just pulled me."

"You straight?" Remembering the conversation they had the other day. "I'm good other than gettin' my lungs right."

"That ain't nothing, but a ticket and mutherfucka wanting to search yo shit." "You already know, just have somethin' twisted when I get there." "No doubt!" Click.

Noodles pulled over about 30 yards from his destination; he could see the front of the projects and his people standing out and about, as he continued to enjoy his blunt. He wondered what was taking the officer so long to approach his car when outta no where a DT car pulled in front of 'em. "What the fuck!" was his only words when he saw Det. Trigg's exit his car approaching his shit.

"License and proof of insurance" Det. Trigg's demanded. "Ya'll short staffed or have they finally demoted yo ass," Noodles asked laughing as he handed over his license and insurance still puffing on his blunt.

"Yo P.O know you get down like this?" "I don't give a fuck what he know or don't, its non reporting probation anyway you know what I'm talkin' about?" blowing a cloud of smoke his way. "That it might be, but for right now I need you to exit the vehicle", Det.Triggs barked.

By this time the uniform officer was standing next to Det. Trigg's. waiting on instructions."What you pull me over for?," Noodles wanted to know since Trigg's punk ass was on the scene. "Det. Trigg's wanted."

"Don't worry about it officer Lloyd, I got it from here," turning to Noodles. "I need to ask you some questions pertaining to T-love." "Hold tight, I don't socialize or converse with police, if you want to ask me any questions, you need to go through my lawyer," Noodle explained looking at Trigg's like he was crazy. "So go ahead and write my ticket, search my car, do whatever ya'll gotta do, but don't waste yo time or mine witt this bull shit." "Search'em while I search his car," Det. Trigg's ordered Officer Lloyd.

While things seemed to look like a routine traffic stop in the hood with officer Lloyd searching Noodles and Det. Trigg's going through his car, Noodles felt somethin' wasn't right, but couldn't put his finger on it. Det. Triggs was pump fakin' like he was searching ,but instead planted a small hand gun inside his glove compartment.

"Officer Lloyd", Det. Triggs called out. "I'm outta my element will you please finish searching while I have a moment with Mr. Noodles." Officer Lloyd did what he was asked while Det. Triggs stood back waiting on everything to come about.

So much time had transpired Tight-White began to get worried, he had called Noodles cell a couple of time only to keep gettin' his voice mail .He remembered him saying he was coming down the ave. meaning he couldn't be dat far out ,so Tight– White hit the strip in search of his boy and just like he thought, Noodles red CTS Cadillac was down the street within eye shot. As he got closer he could tale someone was busy searchin' his shit while Noodles and what look like Det. Triggs standing in front of a police cruiser. "See ya'll done held a nigga so long my family done came lookin' for me," Noodles said seeing Tight-white coming. Just then Officer Lloyd exited the vehicle with a small caliber 22. in hand." Det. Triggs," he called holding the gun in the air. "Where the fuck you get dat from," Noodles asked in disbelief. "That shit ain't mine," backing up seeing the set up being put into play. "Ya'll got me fucked up," and before he could take off Det. Triggs tazzed'em.

"Yea mutherfucka! You thought I didn't know you had rabbit in you," laughing sending another electric current through his body. Without thinking Tight-White took off running ready to take on the detective and the officer to set his nigga free, he came within a couple of feet before Triggs pulled his 40 cal. seein' him coming all alone.

"Give me a reason not to send your ass away from here," pointing the gun directly between his eyes. Tight-White stood froze in his tracks looking at Det. Triggs then to the sky tellin' Mello to make room for'em. "No Tight-White," Noodles yelled from the pavement. "Tomorrow is always a better day," breakin' him outta his trans. "Yea Tight-White! Tomorrow is always a better day," Officer Lloyd said pushin' him against Noodles car. "But today yo ass going downtown." "

///

"What the fuck happen", Face screamed not believing the half of it. "A 22, c'mon Dirt Bert." "Yea Face, and they got Tight-White on assaulting a police officer, resisting arrest and some bull shit. His bond been posted, but Noodles got to sit for a minute cause his probation officer put a holder on'em." "I can't believe this shit, all because Bull-Moose we got this detective gunnin' at us, I shoulda let Tight-White handle dat," Face said pacing back and forth. "No you shouldn't have" ,Max interrupted. "We stay witt the same game plan. Tight-White will be out in a couple of hours and he'll be able to enlighten us on what the fuck happen, so until then we gonna chill and let this thang play out."

///

"Tell me what I wanna, hear and I can make all this disappear." "My momma didn't raise no rat, it's all man here," Noodles said with pride. "So there's something to tell, but you ain't willing to tell it", Det. Triggs questioned trying to get'em to slip."I saw that hot lil number you was witt at the picnic, I know you ain't trying to leave dat behind. Shit, if I was you I'll be thinking of a way to make it home tonight instead of going up stairs cause somethin like that ain't gonna spend to many nights alone, you know what I'm talkin' about?"

Noodles sat there hand cuffed beginning to get aggravated knowing this pig set'em up and now trying to play him like some bitch. "Dig, I don't give a fuck about no ho or this bull shit ass case, so you can quit wasting my time and get me up stairs." "Suit yo self, but just know I'm only a phone call away," throwing his personal card on the table knockin' on the door lettin' the officers know he was finished.

While Noodles was making his way up stairs he couldn't stop his mind from racing thinking about the last 30 somethin' hours leading up to now. He was so consumed with his thoughts, he never heard the C.O tell'em his new address ,after not seeing Noodles move the officer told'em. "Young man, I'm not speakin' Chinese, grab yo shit and stand in front of the elevator to the left and don't forget yo address S4- C-18,"turning to the other inmates awaiting theirs. Noodles grabbed his bed roll and as he began to walk the elevator opened.

"What's yo address," another officer asked stepping off the elevator allowing Noodles room to get on. "S4-C-18," Noodles replied finding a spot to stand among the other inmates on the elevator. "We going to the same pod," one of the inmates said standing next to Noodles. "What the fuck is S4-C-18?" "South building, fourth floor, c pod, and cell 18. You ain't never been in before," The old head asked trying to continue the conversation hoping to find a friend knowin shit can get rough for a old timer, especially the way these young dudes carry it. "I've been in I just never made it up stairs and the only reason I'm making it now, my punk ass P.O put a holder on me." "That's yo story," another inmate said bringing laugher within the elevator. "Naw nigga ,dat's real!"

//

Knock, knock, knock!

"Who is it, ,Peaches yelled coming to the door. "Damn you early" "You lucky I wasn't camped out waiting on you to come home, how bad I wanted to see yo sexy ass," Maniac said following her inside. "You got Somethin' real nice here." "It ain't much, but its mine," offering him a seat. "Would you like anything to drink?" "What I wanna drink ain't served in no glass," lookin' at dat muffin between her legs. "Be nice, the last thing you want me to do is give you somethin' I know you can't handle. So once again, would you like somethin' to drink?"Lookin' at the expression on his face. "Just give me what you want me to have and if I can handle it, get me, me."

"Boy, you are a mess," turning to check on her meal before grabbing them somethin' to drink. "Dinner will be ready in a minute, I hope you like my lasagna. "If I don't, don't even worry about it, there is to many other things I like about you," smiling as he took a sip of his drink.

Peaches sat the table placing butter rolls and Caesar salads out before bring the main course to the table, they ate until their appetite where satisfied moving to the living room to continue their conversation.

"What's in your portfolio, what type of investments have you made? The one thing I cant stand is for a man not about his business! How long you expect to keep on doing what you're doing?" "What is it, you think I do," Maniac asked wanting to hear what she had to say. "You ain't got to be the sharpest; knife in the drawer, but with that big ass truck sittin on 24's and all the TV's, to all that jewelry you wearing, to dat knot in yo pocket, I can easily say we ain't dealing witt no 9 to 5" "True dat! I'm running a million dollar operation that causes me to work more hours than the average person ,so yea, we ain't dealing witt no 9 to 5."

"That's cute how you played witt my words to answer my question, but the facts still remain the same, You throwing bricks at a glass house and eventually its gonna come crashing in and I can't have dat in my life, been there, done dat."

"Look Peaches, I'm feelin' you. You got a head on yo shoulders and making it happen for yo self, not to mention you can burn", rubbing his stomach. "But I don't have the game to put it down like I would like to and make the investments I need to be making. "It's not that you don't have the game, it's that you ain't seekin' it," getting up to retrieve some books she needed to plant her seed. "They say, if you want to keep somethin' from most black men, put it in a book," giving Maniac a couple of books pertaining to corporations.

"What the fuck are these?" Looking at the books then at her dumb founded. "Even if I decided not to fuck witt you, I'm still gonna give you this game, cause if it don't make dollars it don't make sense," Peaches assured him. "Hold tight, the reason why I'm here is for you to fuck witt a nigga, I'm not on some lets be friend type shit I'm trying to make you mine." "If that's the case, You need to be about yo business and read these books."

///

"What the fuck happen?" Face asked lookin' at Tight-White. "I really don't know, shit ain't adding up ,we don't fuck witt no .22, what the fuck we gonna do with that other than make a mutherfucka made. Plus he said, all was good when one time hit'em witt the disco lights, somewhere between him gettin' pulled and me gettin' there Det. Triggs showed Up."

"Triggs showed up," Max asked looking at Face wondering if they where on the same page.

"I bet you a dollar to a penny that mutherfucka had somethin' to do with that, but what's his reason, what's his angle for going at Noodles," Face wondered.

"We under estimated the enemy and now that he made his move, we need to stay a couple of moves ahead of'em cause if not he'll have all our asses cased up," Max strongly stated giving Face dat one look. "Ya'll shoulda let me have my way and none of this woulda happened," Tight-White spazzed thinking killing' Bull-Moose was the answer to their problems.

"Naw Tight-White, killing' oh girl won't erase what was said only confirm the real of it. Let me play chess witt dis nigga, you just tighten yo game up and beware of what's out there cause this mutherfucka ain't playin' fair, but neither am I." Face and Max stayed up late into the night after Tight-White had left leaving them the opportunity to think clearly and formulate their next set of moves.

"Do we kill'em?" "Naw Face, that shit gonna cause more harm than good, we ain't trying to get the alphabet boys involved, we can handle oh boy it's just gonna take a womans touch to do it," Max explained smiling wondering why she hadn't thought of this before.

//

Cheri laid in her king size slate bed out in Kings Mills unhappy about a lot of things, she wanted some type of stability and security. Even doe, Face provided everything she wanted and needed, she hated having to depend on someone else especially with her girl having her own place, truck, and a job she had grown to love made her want to get the same just as bad, but somewhere along the line Face forgot to make dat happen.

Just when her thoughts where getiin' the best of her, the sound of her ring tone snapped her outta it. "Hello," she answered only to hear J-holidays song I'm gonna put you to bed, to bed, to bed. "Hey bitch," Peaches finally said after turning the music down in her truck. "Trick, it's almost 3 in the morning." "I don't give a fuck if it damn near five in the morning, I'm feelin' dat one way and I need you to put me to bed, to bed, to bed," she sang to J-holidays record. "Just bring dat ass on out here, I'm gonna do just that", Climbing outta bed to gather the many toys she would need to make dat happen.

//

"Mr. BOOZER, you have a visit," the co called over the intercom waking Noodles outta his sleep. "Who the fuck coming to see a nigga this early ",he mumbled making his way to the sink. Even doe it was early the pod was in full swing with people playing various •table top games, to people watchin' TV, to people sweating the phone trying to see if their girls made it home from the club last night.

"Mr. Boozer, you have a visit," the co called again making Noodles hurry about his business. As he stepped outta his cell he noticed Ethy and old school standing outside his cell bent over the railing.

"What's good playboy," Noodles said giving his hood friend a pound. "Me and old school on security until you decided to wake yo lazy ass up." "C'mon Ethy, shit ain't that serious", looking back and forth between the two. "Maybe it is, maybe it ain't, but you never know how one of these niggas might act if given the opportunity to get outta jail. Det. Triggs ain't no joke, if he set you up once ain't no tellin' what he's capable of," Ethy said puttin' Noodles back on point. "You ain't never lied," Noodles responded taking his time gettin' to the sally port replaying the conversation over and over again realizing he had to stay on point cause somethin' wasn't right. "Which way to the visiting room," he asked the officer behind the bubble?" "Door to yo right, up the stairs ,window one", the officer replied. .. ...   Noodles took to the door and up the stairs ,half way up he could see Coco standing on the other side of the glass looking more beautiful than he ever imaged.

"Hey sexy", picking up the phone. "How you find me?" "When you didn't come home last night and yo phone kept going straight to voice mail, I got worried and started calling hospitals, jails, and every-thing else I could think of until I found my baby. I was going to pay yo bond, but the people down stairs said you got some type of holder on you." Noodles sat there listening knowing if he had to do these couple of years, one for the ccw, and the other for his probation violation she'd drive him crazy and the last thing he need was a bitch playin' mind games acting like she's down for a nigga, but really down for a niggas bank roll.

"Hold tight, pause game," he said shaking his head from side to side not really wanting to let go, but knew it was somethin' that had to be done. "I can't do this." "What you mean you can't do this?" "I can't put yo life on hold because of mine, that's for them lames, you're to young and got yo whole life ahead of you and I be damn if I stand in the way of dat, but if the opportunity presents its self for us to get back together once I touch pay dirt, you already know."

Coco stared into his eyes not believing he was actually trying to let her go, not realizing she needed him more than anything and let-tin' go wasn't an option.

"You are my life," she mumbled trying her hardest not to shed one tear as he hung up ending their visit. "No Noodles, don't you dare leave me, don't you dare walk away, don't you," she yelled beating on the glass. Noodles walked down the stairs refusing to turn around knowing he couldn't allow himself to get emotionally caught up into somethin' he had no control over.

Soon as he hit the sally port he ran into Ethy and old school on their way to rec. "Lets ride play boy," Ethy said turning the corner into the hallway where a crowd was stuck lookin' up at a stunting' female one would ever encounter. Upon Noodles entering the hallway she began bangin' on the window again screaming. "I Love you, I love you," causing everybody to turn around wondering who could possibly have shorty acting out in such a way. "I see you still got'em going crazy," Ethy said wishing he could change places to get at this one.

"Mr. Boozer," the officer yelled over the intercom. "You need to go tell the young lady her visit is over and to stop beating on that glass." "Picture dat," he responded easing his way into the gym hoping the pain he felt inside would soon pass.

Before long 3:30 had snuck up on everybody, this was the time of day some enjoyed and others dreaded. "Mail call," the officer yelled coming through the door. He went through a series of names until going on a long stretch callin'. "Mr. Boozer, Boozer, Boozer, matter of fact all this shit belongs to you." dropping everything in his hand on the table ."Oh yea, you got a package too. Once I finish the other pods mail I'll call you out to get it." Noodles stood there lookin' over all his mail seeing every piece had Coco name on it.

"Damn it yo first mail call and you doing it like this," Ethy said helping him gather his mail. "Tight-White, knows how this thing goes. Shit, the nigga sent you every fuckin' mag in the store.""I wish I could say he did," stopping to give old school the Jet, Ebony, and the USA today. "But this oh girls, work," climbing the stairs to his cell. "The one banging on the window?" "Yea man," feeling the affect of his actions.

Within minutes the officer was calling his name again, he stepped outta his cell to see the officer holding up a bag.

"Old school, can you grab that for me" Noodles yelled. "I got you," old school replied seeing how good Noodles people was carrying him wishing it was his people doing the same.

"Like I was saying," entering his cell. "I ain't never did no time before, but I ain't no fool either to think niggas ain't gonna be at dat and she won't go. I don't need that shit on my brain while I'm doing this, you know what I'm talkin' about?" "Naw!" old school intervened giving Noodles his bag. "I've been living on this earth for the last 60 somethin' years and counting. I done had some of the flyest, to the ugliest, from the richest, to the poorest, but never have I had a bitch fly me in the way lil -mamma did you, that means a lot and say's a lot." "So what you gettin' at old school?" Noodles inquired wondering what type of game old school was about to lace him witt.

"Lil mamma got genuine feelings for you. You can either accept it or ignore it, but the facts still remain the same. I don't know the extent of ya'll relationship or how you get down, but you'll be a fool not to allow lil momma the opportunity to earn her stripes when it's obvious she's trying when a lot of these females ain't, I see you got a winner on yo' team, but me seeing it ain't doing you bit of good, if you don't see it for yo self! Now let old school see dat smooth mag over there and I'm gonna get on out ya'll way," leaving Noodles and Ethy to continue their conversation.

//

"Max, I'm sorry! I didn't mean for none of this to happen. Please Max, don't let Face do nothing to me please, I got kids to raise." "Calm down girl, you shoulda came to Face and let'em know what was said versus him trying to figure it out." "That's exactly what I told her ass," Joann jump in saying. "I told yo ass not to run, got me caught up in yo mess." "Look girls, I'm here cause I need ya'll help," Max said looking mostly at Bull-Moose.

"Whatever you need we gonna help",Joann answered for the both of them. "Just tell us what it is and it's done." "Thats all good Joann, but I need Bull-Moose to speak for herself," waiting on her to do just that.

"Max, I'm down for whatever you need me to do, but please don't ask me to kill nobody." "Never dat, all I need you to do is do what you do best, at the same time feed Triggs some info and retrieve some." "That's all",Bull-Moose asked feeling relieved. "I thought you was gonna tell a bitch to fuck and suck the whole hood," causing Max and Joann to burst out laughing.

"That shouldn't be to hard wit yo nasty ass. Probably already done it," Joann added causing them to laugh even harder.

//

"Face we been down there everyday this week. The nigga got somebody breaking da door down like they never seen his ass before. Visiting don't start until 8am,I swear we made it down there at 8:01 and a mutherfucka beat us out. You know I was mad."

"Don't even trip. Cheri, I need ya'll to get there at 7am if dats wat it takes. I need my man to know we on top of everything and Bobo won't be able to see him until the end of next week after he finish some murder trial he's workin' on," turning his attention to Peaches. "How dat thang coming along wit you and oh boy?"

"It's coming, I got'em open and he haven't even tasted the goodies." "That's wat up cause shit 'bout to go down and you need to be prepared when he come running for yo love and affection."

"Don't worry about my end just take care of yours and watch everything else fall into place."

//

"You got a nigga feelin' dat one way, but how long it's gonna last. How long can I depend on you being there?" "As long as you allow me to and even then I ain't going nowhere, I love you Noodles and I don't care if you got to do two years or 22yrs we gonna make it, I'm not saying it gonna be easy, but baby believe in what we have, believe in us, and believe no matter what I'll always be there."

Noodles and Coco relationship took a turn for the better, he realize no matter how many times he refused her visit she always came back the next day lettin' it be known, if she couldn't see him nobody could. "You been knockin the hinges off these doors all week, you ain't allowed my peeps a chance to come through." "I'm not giving my visit up for nobody, if they wanna come they need to come witt me cause other than dat, ain't nothing happening so tell all yo other bitches what time it is!"

"Okay lil momma, I ain't mad at cha, but dig, I need you to relay a message to my peeps." writing something down on the tablet he had wit'em. " "Who, crazy ass Tight-White."

"Naw lil momma, you didn't get the chance to meet him," Noodles answered writing something down on the tablet he had wit'em."Was he the guy standing on stage with you and some older lady?" "Yea, that's him. I didn't know if you seen him before you passed out."

"Yea, I saw him," she responded feelin her heart race and her hands began to sweat. "Here," snapping her outta her trans. "Give him this message," holding the tablet against the window. "Soon as you leave I need you to take care of diss, you got me lil momma?"

"What's up with this lil momma piece?" Coco asked trying to remember what she just read. "Old school blessed you witt dat." "OH, you lettin' niggas name me now," she joked gettin' her mind right to take care of her mans business. "Never dat! But dig, don't you put no more money on my books, I'm good. Thanks for all the letters, cards, pictures, and the mags you been hittin' me witt, that shit really means a lot and helps me get through some rough spots when I find myself thinking about you the most and missing you just the same." "Is dat right," lookin' at'em side ways. "Cause in the beginning you had me crying myself to sleep all because you wouldn't let me love you." "That's was then and this is now, just don't leave me!" "Never dat!!!!"

Coco left the visiting room around 9:30,even doe visiting where only suppose to be 15 minutes long Noodles worked his hand and the guard allow'em to have his way. As she started her car she mentally prepared herself to deal with his people knowing eventually she would have to.

"Hello," Face said answering his cell. "I have a message from someone close to you, I just need to know what time and place we can meet." Face paused not believing his luck, he was finally going to meet Ms. Lady face to face and Noodles wasn't going to be no where around to witness the work of a nigga trying his hand.

"If you're not to busy, you can shoot through here "Where is here," Coco asked knowing he was trying to feel her out." "My bad, you know where yo man get down at," Face asked already knowing she did. "I'll be there in ten," hanging up without gettin' a response.

//

"Hey sexy, when can I see you," Maniac asked pulling up outside Peaches condo seeing her truck parked in the drive way.

"You tell me, Mr. Man, I haven't seen or heard from you in about a week" "It ain't nothing like that, I just wanted to read what I needed to before I got back at you cause believe what you want, I'm about mines," touching the hood of her SUV realizing she'd been out and about already this morning.

"That you will be once I'm finish with you," grabbing her keys off the counter making her way out the front door only to run smack into'em." "Boy, you a mess," hanging up stepping to the side allowing him to enter her condo. "What's in the bag?" "Just a little somethin' to get our corporation off the ground," dropping his bag at his feet pulling Peaches in his arms. "I knew I wanted you the first time I saw you." "Hold it, playboy," sliding outta his embrace. "I haven't decided if I wanna fuck with you like that or not. You think coming over here with a duffle bag full of money suppose to impress me. Naw playboy, its already been written, a fool and his money will soon part, I don't need that in my life, I need someone that's about their business, to the point they can challenge me about mine."

"Dig, I already told you what it is witt me and how I get down. I might not know what an LLC is or what the difference between a C corporation and a S corporation, let alone why people chose to incorporate in Nevada versus the city they live in, all that's foreign to me, but I'm willing to learn, not only to better myself to better my situation." Peaches listened knowing he at least took the time to read the books she gave him.

"Okay Mr. Man, I see you trying and that's all I'm asking, cause if you know better, you'll do better", causing Maniac to crack smile. "So what type of corporation you think you should start off with?" "I'm thinking we, not me, should fuck witt the C being that's what the big boys fuckin witt." "True dat, but understand you must crawl before you walk. We look better messin' with the S cause we can start small and build, at the same time stay private keeping the SEC outta our business. Now dealing with the S we got 1000 non-par value stock, we need to turn into par value by selling each stock for a 1000 dollar a piece, you do the math," she said watchin Maniac do the math in his head. "That's a million dollars, playboy! That you can launder without them people doing anything about it, now play witt dat."

Maniac ears where burning and his mind wandering thinking of all the things he'll be able to put down. "Here," picking the bag off the floor. "There's a quarter mill in there, make it do what it do," kissin' her softly on her lips before telling her. "you really think I'm gonna let you get away, you better think again," smackin' dat ass on his way out leaving her smiling loving when a perfect plan comes together.

//

Face waited patiently for Ms. Lady to arrive cooking himself a small breakfast wondering if she posse the total package or just yo typical dime piece gettin' by on her looks alone, not able to think pass go. Either way Face had to have her throwing caution to the wind focusing on what position he was gonna hit dat.

KNOCK, KNOCK!

"Come on in," Face yelled from the kitchen. Coco entered cautiously not knowing what to expect hearing. This is no ordinary love playing softly in the back ground by Sade, catching the smell of somethin' cooking. "Hello," she called out closing the door behind her. "I'm in the kitchen," he replied adding cheese to his eggs never turning around to greet her.

Once he felt her presence he began to order her around. "Grab the OJ out the refrigerator, the glasses to yo left second cabinet." He wanted~ to see what type of female he was dealing witt, one you could boss around or one that spoke up for her self. "I didn't come here to serve you no orange juice, I came to deliver a message," she said with attitude. "I apologize Ms. Lady," turning to see her pouring two glasses of OJ in her hoodie short set. "But since you're my man peeps, I'll make it happen this time," turning to see the bulge in his pants handing him his glass.

"I bet my man love dat outfit?" "That he do but you need to focus more on what I came to say, rather than standing there eye fuckin me," following his eyes as they looked her up and down.

Face never expected Ms. lady to be so sassy and the thoughts of breaking her in made his dick just as hard. "Give it to me," he said nonchalant taking a seat to began eating his breakfast." Oh, he's an arrogant mutherfucka," she said to herself before relaying Noodles message. "All is good, belt up and drive safely cause there's speed traps waiting to trap a nigga, the game don't stop cause a nigga got popped, and the man in the closet will reveal himself. I hope I said it right" "Don't worry Ms. lady, tell'em I got it and that love is love. OH yea", going into his pocket. "Put this on his books," passing her a fist full of money. "Naw, he good, I got'em straight down there," refusing to accept his money."Well, you take it and buy yo self somethin' nice witt it," offering her the money again. "I'm good, but thanks anyway," leaving him with dat one look not believing she didn't take some free money.

Coco left realizing it wasn't that hard after all and by the look of that print in his pants, it was just a matter of time before she had her way, having Face eating out of her hands.

//

"J, what's the update," Unk asked reading his morning news paper. "It's too early to tell, the transition hasn't went as smoothly as expected. This Detective has not been playing fair keeping everything to himself, I've been pickin' up bits and pieces, but I haven't been able to put it all together yet."

"How's my lil niece doing' Unk wanted to know?" "She's doing fine other than the company she keeps." "What's that suppose to mean?" "She got involved with this street type of dude and from what I can tell, him and his crew are doing real good for themselves." "Hmm, that sound real interesting, you know I'm looking to reestablish my operation out there!" "I already know, but for right now it's best to hold off cause the same detective I mentioned early got some type of hard on for these boys. I don't know if it's true or not, but rumor has it that this detective set yo nieces lil friend up hoping to flip'em to turn on his boys for a body that hasn't even been found "Sound like my kinda people. How the young man holding Up?" "The way Coco breaking them doors down, I would say, he's holding." "Keep me posted and keep yo eyes on this detective, ain't no tellin' what he's capable of ." "You already know."

//

"Wasn't that Noodles girl I just seen rollin' outta here?" Max asked knowing it was. "Yea, that was Ms. Lady," Face responded lost within his own imagination. Max stood there not liking what seem to be so obvious."When yo dick starts to beat out yo hand, you'll starve." "What's that suppose to mean?" "It's not what that suppose to mean, it's what you thinking and before you comment know I've been around the world not once, but twice, Seen it all, heard it all! Now insult my intelligence if you want to. "Never dat, baby girl. I'm human and Ms. lady got it going on," Face said expressing his true feelings.

"Outta all the females in this city, you lusting over yo mans, dat ain't a good look, more dynasties been destroyed cause a man chose his dick over his hand, now ponder that while you're up here thinkin' about the next man bitch," storming out bumping into Tight-White and Dirt Bert.

"Man! What the fuck you done did to Max?" Dirt Bert asked.

"Don't trip, that's how a bitch gets when it's that time of the month, but she'll be good once we put this money play into motion." "That's what's up," Tight-White joined in saying. "So when we gonna get it poppin?" "Tomorrow!"

//

"I see you took my advice and allowed lil momma to earn her stripes." "You better believe it old school, but dig this since I got to be here might as well get this money, I already sent my kite out and shit should be poppin' sometime this week."

"Hold tight," Ethy said stoppin' Noodles from continuing. "I never said anything before cause wasn't nothings at stake, and this is no disrespect to you old school," turning to look at Noodles. "Can we trust'em?" "I respect you G cause most niggas would get blinded by the opportunity of gettin' at this money without weighing in the consequences of the people they decide to lay in bed witt, to make dat happen-?"

Ethy sat on Noodles bunk punch drunk trying to read between the lines to find the answer to his question while Noodles took'em on a ride without actually answering his question. "Yea, old school 100! After I found you and him posted up dat morning and the conversation you hit me witt, I had to make sure the company I keep is on the up and up." "Say no more, if you say all is good, then all is good, let's get back to the money," Ethy said feelin good about what was about to go down. "Like I was saying," Noodles continued puttin everything together.

CHAPTER 18

Tomorrow

"Good morning," Coco said to the female officer workin' the front desk as she signed in to go see her man. "Girl, you better than me." "Why you say that?" Coco replied wondering where the female officer was going witt it next. "I be damn if I start my day off every morning seeing a nigga that can't do nothing for me other than sell a bitch a dream," Laughing with her co-worker. "His ass be lucky if I come at all!" "That's the difference between a real bitch and a bitch dat wanna be real," lookin' back and forth between the two females gathering her things. "By the way, real bitches do real things and not only portray them," taking her sign in slip to the man behind the bubble.

Coco looked down at her ladies presidential Rolex seeing she still had 20 minutes to kill before visiting hours started taking a seat only to catch herself staring not believing her eyes.

"Outta all the places I coulda run into my girl it had to be here," she reasoned. "Then again I shoulda knew better cause if there was money to 'get, rather it be here or in the free world, my girl going to go get it. She's gonna be so surprised when I pull up on her crazy ass," waiting on her girl to come in.

"I bet dat bitch ain't beat us out today," Cheri said fillin' out their sign in sheet. "Mr. Boozer must be all of it," the female officer threw out there knowing they where gonna bump heads with his other visitor pointing in the direction they needed to go. Cheri and Peaches looked at each other, then at the tired lookin' female behind the desk. "You better believe he is," high fiving one another walking through' the waiting area not paying attention to any of the visitors only concerned about turning their slip in.

"Excuse me, Mr. Boozer already has a visiting slip in," the officer informed them. "I don't give a fuck what's already in, you need to be adding ours to it," Cheri barked at the officer while Peaches surveyed the room." I'm sorry I can't do that and you need to exit the premise," the officer ordered. "You think because you in dat wheel chair a mutherfucka won't get at dat ass, I'm hip to yo cripple ass and when I catch yo punk ass, I'ma tilt dat mutherfucka over," Cheri yelled taking her frustrations out on the man behind the bubble.

Within minutes officers came rushin' the waiting area. "Oh, yo punk ass had to call back up," She screamed, turning to' the small crowd of people waiting to see their loved ones. "Who the bitch that keep running her ass down here, so I can't see mine?" "It's okay, we can all go see'em", Coco said standing revealing her self.

The voice sounded so familiar it almost scared Peaches, but looking at the physical being in front of her it couldn't be. Cheri seeing the female from the picnic couldn't recall her name.

"Damn karate kid, give the nigga a chance to miss you, he'll love you more," causing everybody to laugh. Then it came to her."Ain't yo name Coco or something?" "I'm sorry to interrupt ya'll moment, but you got to exit the premises Ms. Lady," one of the officers said that rushed in. "You can come back tomorrow and see yo boy or you can come back when I get off, but you got to come back," he explained trying to get his mack on. Cheri smiled at'em seeing that he was a cutie, then turned to Coco. "Just tell'em his lawyer will be there to see'em next week and to call somebody," she said making her way out while Peaches followed close behind not believing how familiar both girls voices was and for them to have the same name, "What a coincidence," she mumbled to herself.

Coco shed a tear realizing she couldn't reveal herself knowing Peaches and Noodles knew one another and that had to be Cheri crazy ass, "I wonder which one he's fuckin' I hope it ain't my best friend, lord knows I hope it ain't her," wiping the tears from her eyes.

//

"Damn bitch, what you trying to do, kill a nigga," Det. Triggs asked Bull-Moose as she worked her magic suckin' the second nut out of'em within a 20 minute span. "You know I've been missing you, I don't know where you disappeared to, but bitch don't let it happen again," loving the way she handled a dick. "You act like you really missed a bitch or somethin', maybe I should get missing more often, You might appreciate me more," playing with the head of his dick with her tongue ."You got them boys shook; I can't wait until you lock all their asses up." "How you know," sittin' up stopping her from doing what she do best. "C'mon baby,let me-" grabbing at his dick.

"Fuck all dat, how you know I got them shook?" lookin' at Bull -Moose like she knew somethin' he needed to know.

"That's what the streets saying, they don't know what you capable of 'since you made that play at Noodles." "I figured that much, but dat fuckin' Noodles ain't break like I thought he would, then again it's still early in the game." "That it is," crawling her way between his legs." "You just keep yo ears to the streets and let daddy handle these boys." "Hmm, hmm," she replied with a mouth full before lookin' up to'em. "I can't wait to feel you inside me," diving head first back on the dick. "Ooh yea, that's it girl, show me why I fuck witt yo trifflin' ass."

//

"Where you at," Maniac asked pullin' in front of Peaches condo. "Where you want me to be" she, asked on her way to work."Girl, quit playin' witt me, where you at?" "If you haven't forgotten, I do have a job" "Fuck all dat, once we get this thang off the ground, I need you to trash dat bull shit and run the corporation." Peaches listened becoming frustrated with the way he was trying to dictate shit all of a sudden.

."Boy, don't make me exercise my right- "Yo right to what?" wondering what the hell she was talking about. "Hang up on yo simple ass." CLICK! Maniac looked at his phone saying to himself. "No she didn't," pushin' redial."Hold on lil tiger, I got somethin' I'm trying to shoot at you, so miss me witt that hanging up shit." Peaches smiled knowing she had'em right where she wanted him. "The worst. thing you can do is try and take my independence away from me, I love my job and my job plays an important role in what we trying to accomplish. I get the heads up on pieces of property going into foreclosure before they actually do, not to mention the commission ' I get off each sell that I'm throwing back into the corporation and you want me to quit, nigga please!"

"You right, I see how everything plays together, I can't wait until we start making shit happening." "What you mean start? I don't know what you take me for, but I don't play, I'm about my business. The day you gave me dat is the day I put everything into motion, we're incorporated in Nevada under PMC incorporated we have five single family houses that I spent 100k to acquire and once we fix them up each one good to go for no less than 60 apiece and soon as I get to my office I'm gonna take another 100k and invest into some offshore utility which will bring us 43% return on our money." "That's what I'm talkin' about but dig love, I'm 50 short on what I gave you the other day and I ain't trying to ride around all day waiting on yo sexy ass to get off, so what I need to do?"

"Just bring whatever you got to my job and I'll handle everything from there," she said not believing how smoothly things were going and she hadn't even hit'em off witt dat wet, wet yet

///

"Pull right into the driveway," Face instructed. "We already went over the plan, just stick to it and we gonna leave outta here richer that what we came." "I ain't never did anything like this", Seal (AKA), Apples replied having second thoughts about her involvement in all this. "Bitch, man up and let's get this money", Tight-White added ."You shoulda thought about dat before yo ass got behind the wheel. Fuck it, I'll delivery the box." "Chill Tight," Face said through clenched teeth. "Apples got it, don't you?", trying to smooth things out while Dirt bert sat back observing things telling himself," if she show any signs of weakness like she can't hold water, Maniac mother won't be the only body left behind.

"I got it ",she responded gettin' out the van with her clip broad and the small box addressed to Maniac mother. "Testing 1,2,3. Can ya'll hear me," Apples asked speaking through her wireless walkie talkie. "Yea, we hear you loud and clear," Face informed her. "Just act like you normally do when you deliver a package."

Apples walked to the door knees knockin' aware things will never be the same once she rang that door bell, somehow throughout the uncertainty and unknown a calmness came over her hearing her sister say, "You can do this, he never: gave a fuck about me or my family, so why the fuck you giving a fuck about his!"

The voice was so real to her ears she had to turn around only to find no one standing there, looking toward the sky as a single tear escaped her eye whispering, "I love you" before turning to push the door bell. "Who is it?" Ms. Louise yelled from the kitchen making her way to the front door seeing a FedEx truck parked in her drive way.

She reasoned it had to be the 14kt. gold plated silverware set she ordered on the home shopping' network. "Damn, ya'll people don't play, I just placed my order a couple of days ago," she said opening the door seeing a familiar face she hadn't seen in years. "Ms. Louise," Apples said before she could say anything ."I knew this name looked familiar, but I had no idea you moved." "Child, if you don't get in here and give me a hug," opening the door wide open. "Look at you, got yo self a job and everything. Ya'll Foggie girls always had a bright future even doe it's all behind you," motioning to all dat ass stuffed in them FedEx shorts causing Apples to chuckle. "Leave that box where it is and come share a cup of coffee with me," walking back to the kitchen leaving the door unlocked.

To the sound of that Face, Dirt Bert, and Tight-White exit the van all dressed in FedEx attire while Apples and Ms. Louise where in deep conversation when she heard a beep indicating someone had entered her home.

"That must be Maniac right there, Maniac baby," she called walking toward the front door when three men appeared outta nowhere. "Oh my," she said grabbing her heart until realizing they where dressed in the same attire Apples was in. "Damn, ya'll almost caused yo girl to fall out," turning to say somethin' to Apples when Face smacked her ass over the head witt the butt of his gun tellin' her fallin' body.

"You just shoulda," ordering Dirt Bert and Tight-White to search the house for any unexpected guest while he attended to Ms. Louise.   Within minutes Face had Louise buck naked, duck taped to one of her dining room chairs that he placed in the center of the kitchen, he disappeared for a moment returning with a wire coat hanger straightening to his liking placin' it on top of the stove turning the eye on high.

Everybody looked on observing Face at work, he opened the refrigerator and without warning threw a pitcher of ice cold water onto Louise body waking her up instantly and to add insult to injury smacked the shit outta her ass.

"Nap times over," grabbing a hand full of hair snappin' her neck back to look up at'em."Louise, I'm not gonna play games witt you," he whispered in her ear. "Tell me what I want to know and I'll leave just as fast as I appeared, but play games and you'll wish I never stepped foot through them doors," ending his sentence with a vicious back hand causing her to go semi unconscious. "Now Louise, what's the combination?"   "I-I-don't have it," she was able to say recovering from a blow that had her whole face stinging. "Wrong answer," Face replied taking her left titty and being that her back was to the stove she never saw the fire red hanger coming until it was placed on her erect nipple.

She was able to get off a short scream before Dirt Bert's instinct kicked in grabbing a towel off the counter top muffle' her screams. You could hear and smell her flesh burning and see the tears begin to fall. ". "What's the combination?" he asked again. "Fuck you mutherfucka!" Louise yelled through the towel.

"Have it yo way," placing the hanger back on the stove long enough to get it red hot applying it to her other nipple, but still no combination. For the next ten minutes Face touched almost every part of her body and Ms. Louise still held strong.

"She's a tough little cookie," Dirt Bert said looking at the work they put in. "That she is, but the best is yet to come," placing the hanger on the stove. "Get her outta dat chair and lay her ass on dat cold tile floor ,I wanna see how she really get down."

Dirt Bert and Tight-White did as they were told and put Maniac mother on the floor unsure of what was about to go down next, but with that big ass safe in the basement they really didn't give a fuck as long as the ending results got dat combination.

"Spread her legs, put'em in the air," Face commanded. "You think she like it in the ass or should I do dat little man in the boat", grabbing the hanger off the stove. "Burn dat bitch clit off," Tight-White suggested spreading her lips apart exposing the little man.

The closer Face got the harder Maniac mother tried to fight, she was tired and her will to hold on had its limits."I give, I give," she yelled."Ya'll can have it all, the combination 36-2-34,36-2-34. I'll move back to the projects," she cried hoping the worst was over.

Dirt Bert and Tight-White took to the basement rushing to a 6ft tall safe imagining the contents within, they were so hyped it took them a couple of tries before they got it right.

"See Louise that wasn't so hard, you took yo self through some unnecessary problems that coulda been avoided." Apples get Louise something to cover herself". "Why, why Seal, why you bring this to my home, I never once-" "Bitch, shut the fuck up, I ain't trying to hear none of that, when yo bitch ass son killed my sister-"

"Hot damn Face, we done hit the mutherfuckin' jack pot", DB said through his wireless walkie talkie. "No need to get side tracked, wrap the gift and get ready to exit", Face responded. "My son did no such thing ,he loved that girl." "Maybe he did, maybe he didn't, but one thang for sure he love his self more", turning to see Dirt Bert and Tight-White coming outta the basement carrying two duffle bags a piece signaling they were ready.

Face reached behind his back grabbing his silencer while reaching to his side holster with his other hand pullin' out his 9mm attaching both about to send Louise to another world where they said the grass is greener and free of pain. As he raise his arm Dirt Bert stopped'em.

"Let her finish it".

Apples witnessed everything unfold in slow motion ,her mind at full speed tellin' her, don't think just do it and without any hesitation she grabbed Face gun turned to see Ms. Louise screaming, but couldn't hear a sound lettin' off four quick shots, pop, pop, pop, pop!!!

"That's what I'm talkin' about, shoot dat bitch again" ,Tight-White yelled lovin' how she handled her business knowing if she didn't, her ass woulda been lying right next to oh girl.

"Take this bag, Dirt Bert said dropping the two bags he had in his hand taking the one wrapped around his shoulder giving it to her. "We leaving out first

They exit the house surveying their surroundings as they made their way to the van.

"It's all clear for the birds to fly," Dirt Bert relayed to his boys. "Hold tight, did ya'll get the tape from the security cameras?" Face asked. "Got'em tucked away," Dirt Bert responded gettin' situated in the back of the van.

Face rushed back into the kitchen with a pillow in hand causing Tight-White to wonder what the hell only to hear a small caliber hand gun discharge. "What the fuck?" And before he could continue Face responded through his wireless walkie talkie. "Just a little somethin' for our friendly detective."

//

"What's wrong with you?" Noodles asked after a couple minutes into the visit seeing she wasn't her usual self. "Which one you fuckin'? "Hoping it wasn't her best friend.   "Which one I'm fuckin, he repeated not knowing who or what the fuck she was talking about. "Yea, I ran into some of yo bitches down stairs," "Pump yo breaks, if somebody came down here to see me, it's because they wanted to, not because I ask them. Far as which one I'm fuckin', you shoulda asked them cause I have no clue who the fuck you're talkin' about," Noodles snapped! "Matter of fact, I ain't on diss," slamming the phone into the glass window heading down stairs.

"Go ahead, go ahead and run," Coco jumped up screaming. "Tell the bitch she can have you, I be damn if I keep on coming down here and mutherfucka don't appreciate it," she mumbled gathering her things.   "Bitch!" Noodles yelled reappearing in the window taking her by surprise. "You tell the bitch the next time ya'll cross paths." "I'm not even gonna waste my breath," she replied glad he chose to return instead of ending their visit.

So for the next ten minutes they traded snide remarks back and forth until Noodles asked. "What these ho's look like since I'm being falsely accused of fuckin' one of them?" "One of'em look like oh girl Rocis on 106 an Park and the other-" "You talkin' about Cheri and Peaches," Noodles said cuttin' her off. "You thought me and them was-," Bust out laughing again pointing at Coco. "Stupid ass girl, that's my people," making her feel that one way. "You got us arguing over some bull shit, you need yo ass whipped," Laughing so hard tears began to fall.

For the next hour or so they laughed and enjoyed each other's company until the officer signaled for them to start wrapping things up. "Did you give my man dat message?"Gettin' down to business before his visit ended."I did and he said he got you and Love is Love. Oh yea, yo girl told me to tell you, yo lawyer be to see you next week." "That's what's up," Noodles said lookin' into his girls eyes before saying. "I love you."   "You better," hittin' the glass with her hand. "But guess what, I love you more." Coco exited the Justice Center at a quarter to nine looking one way, but feelin' another, she knew deep down in her heart it was just a matter of time before shit hit the fan, she just hoped when it did she'll be able to control which way it flew and who it hit.

///

"Take off everything and throw that shit into a pile," Face ordered leading by example strippin' down to his boxers. "It's some sweat pants or what have you over there. Apples I got you another uniform once you get cleaned up," turning to Dirt Bert. "Max and the wonder twins should be here before long, take these clothes out back and set that shit ablaze," pausing to take a look at Apple ass as he hit the stairs. "What you lookin' at Tight-White?" Apples asked taking her uniform off. "You act like you never seen a bitch get naked before." "I'm just wondering can a nigga get hit off before Max and them show up," lookin' at all that ass squeezing outta them shorts. "Boy, you a mess and no you can't get hit off," making her way up the stairs after, you already know.

Face took them to the house out in Kings Mills instead of the Pj's, he wasn't taking any chances with the wrong people seeing too much or running into Det. Triggs especially the way he's been playin' shit lately. Everybody got the chance to clean up before Max and them reached the honey cone hide out.

"Bitch, what you keep smiling about?" Tight-White asked knowing the answer to his question. "Don't hate cause a bitch didn't chose you," causing everybody to bust out laughing as Max and the wonder twins entered the house." "What's so important I had to drop what I was doing?" Max asked still a little hot about the other day. " C'mon baby girl ,you still trippin about that old shit, plus we don't get down like that, not in front of company" Face replied gettin' up to give her a hug. "You know I love you," kissing her all over her neck. "Boy, you better quit before I make you kiss more than my neck," pushing pass him to see five duffle bags sittin' off to the side. She quickly turned to a smiling Face. "No you didn't," not believing he finally brought a play at dat nigga. "About time," turning to check the contents in the bag and grab the counting machine.

Face filled Cheri and Peaches in on what had transpired walking straight up on Cheri placing his hands under her chin looking directly into her eyes."This is only 1 of 3 plays I'm gonna shoot at this nigga and believe me it ain't gonna be nothing nice. Don't shed no tears," wiping the tears away.

"It's roughly 1.7",Max stated gaining everybody attention. "How you count all that," Tight-White said knowing she couldn't have, not that fast.

"When you get as old as me and just as wise, you work smarter not harder. Anybody gettin' money dat one way, rubber band their shit to where they can count it without having to recount it, rather it be 5,10,15,or 20 thousand dollar stacks, this so happen to be 10's,dropping a jewel for anyone wanting to pick it up stepping toward the mini bar to grab somethin' to sip on.

"Dig, everybody" ,Face said making his way to the center of the room. "Everybody got 200 coming-." "Wait a minute Face, I might not be the smartest person in the room, but its only 7 of us here and two apiece can't be nothing, but 1.4." Face started clappin' his hands taking everybody by surprise. "Bravo, I knew I couldn't get nothing pass you, now sit yo ten dollar ass down," giving her a look lettin' her know he was dead serious. "There might be 7 of us present ,but theirs 8 of us in this together, just because Noodles ain't here doesn't mean he don't get his just do," Face continued while Max surveyed the room checking out everybody facial expression and body language. She wanted to get a feel for some type of connection with each individual especially Dirt Bert and Tight-White cause little did they know she was ready to take them under her wing exposing them to a game they had yet to explore.

Max realized Face had out grown her and was on the verge of self destruction destroying a beautiful thang they secretly calculated and built from the ground up. He was naive to think she was only capable of seeing the things directly in front of her versus seeing the things to come before they actually came.

"There's 20 bricks we got on this lick too, but only me and the guys gonna see the proceeds." That statement alone caused Apples and Cheri to speak out while Peaches fell back not really giving a fuck knowing she had her own thang in the making and until the grim reaper came knockin', she was gonna milk dat nigga till his well ran dry.

"Why, we ain't gettin' cut in," they both asked lookin' at Face like you can't be serious. "Women been gettin' beat since the beginning of time and shit ain't about to change now! "Stopping that conversation before it grew wings. Outta the whole crew Max noticed Dirt Bert and Peaches wasn't excited like the rest, as if the money wouldn't make'em or break'em.

"Separate mine from ya'lls," Tight-White said rubbing his hands together spending his before he actually got it. "What's the rush," Max intervened puttin' the spot light on'em."You make me think yo pockets ain't right, I can see the girls being in a rush, but you, naw I ain't feelin' dat," making her way toward him. "you been puttin' in work for a minute ,matter of fact, what dat bank roll lookin' like?" Seeing him hesitate she already knew what it was. "Dirt Bert what you workin' witt?" "I'm half way there on my million dollar grind," taking even Face by surprise.

"I'm not saying add this to yo bank roll." "Who said I was," lettin' it be known what time it really was with him. "I don't expect you to have that much" Max said turning back to Tight-White. "Hell, I didn't expect Dirt Bret to be workin' wit those type of ends. So the way you be trickin' and carrying on, You can't be workin with no more than a bill and a half."

"What!" Apples said not believing her ears. "You tricked off 350 thousand on pussy! Shit nigga, the next time you trying to get on make sure yo girl be a part of dat," causing the whole room to burst out laughing.

"Don't worry, I be damn if he spend one dime of this money on some pussy," Max guarantee. "And not only dat, I'm taking yours too." "Hold on Max, you can't do that to the boys like dat."

"Don't tell me what I can't do,"lookin' Face straight into his eyes. "If I let yo ass do what you wanted to do back in the day, you wouldn't have the shit you have now," Max stated causing a silence in the house seeing the real being revealed. "Now 'listen Dirt Bert and Tight-White, there's two things in this world you don't never have to worry about me doing to ya'll," pausing to make sure she had their undivided attention. "Lying to you or trying to take something from you, it just ain't in my genetic makeup. I got big plans for ya'll and if ya'll just trust me, come harvest time we'll have a feast suited for kings. I say dat to say this, I'm gonna invest ya'11 share into a car dealer ship ,this way ya'll always have somethin' and not just them lil ends ya'll ,workin' witt now."

"Damn Max," Tight-White said sounding disappointed. "I feel you, but a nigga had plans for dat money." "l bet you did with yo trick ass, but don't trip once we get finish witt oh boy I got a lick in the making that's gonna make this look like monopoly money."

On the other side of the room Apples was trying to get Face's attention pointing at her watch indicating she had to go. "What up sexy," Face said pullin' her to the side. "Its 11:30, I need to be gettin' to work." "I already know, but dig. here's the situation. Just like Max handling the guys, I'm gonna do the same witt the girls cause never could I send them outta here with close to a half mill to do as they please, picture dat! But with you I can't govern yours, the game I'm puttin down is by choice, not by force."

Apples stood there listening with her mind already made up, she knew going home with all that money wasn't an option especially with J-rock nosey ass at home.

"Pimp nigga pimp", she said stopping him from continuing ."I'm not trying to be left out. Shit, from what I've seen and heard I'll be a fool to hit and run knowing there's a lot more to be made, just invest mine with theirs and let's get this money", kissing him gently on the lips before making her exit.

"Where's Apples headed?" Tight-White asked seeing the door close behind her. "That's yo problem always chasing behind a bitch, when the bitch should be chasing behind you", Face responded walking back into the living room. "Cheri, Peaches, ain't no easy way to say this, other than coming straight out and say it. Ya'll ain't leaving here witt nothing either, I'm throwing mine, Apples, and ya'll into Max hands to invest not only into the car dealer ship, but a clothes store and a hair salon."

Cheri couldn't believe her ears, outta everybody she was the only one still depending on a mutherfucka. "I'm cool with that, but the next time you decide to make a decision for me without asking me first, we gonna have problems," gathering her things tellin' Peaches, "Let's ride before I get to acting a fool up in here," looking Face up and down on her way out the door. "I can't believe this shit," she shouted opening the door to Peaches SUV.

"Trick calm down," pullin' outta the drive way. "I got everything under control." "How you got everything under control when we ain't leaving witt shit?" "Bitch, fuck dat lil money, I told you what it was back in Mexico," turning to look at Cheri as they drove down the street ."What I look like lettin' a mutherfucka think for me when I can think for myself. I'm milkin' dat nigga for more than he realize. Shit, a bitch already a half in." "A half of what?" knowing her girl could squeeze water outta a rock and pass it off as lemonade. "Half on our million dollar grind," she responded stealing a line from Dirt Bert.

//

"About time you answered yo phone, got a bitch thinking you screening shit."

"Raytonya, Raytonya," Maniac yelled trying to cut her off before she got winded ."Look, I've never been the one to carry a bitch, let alone miss lead one. I enjoyed what we had, but I found someone who completes me." "Nigga please, I ain't trying to hear none of dat, especially about another bitch and how she completes."

Maniac hung up realizing Raytonya will always be Raytonya as he pulled into his mothers drive way. He exited his truck just as his cell phone began to ring and without looking he tossed it back inside his truck knowing it had to be Raytonya."Fuck dat bitch", he mumbled opening the screen door. "How many times I gotta tell this lady not to leave the damn doors unlocked," making his way through the living' room headed toward the kitchen. The first thing he noticed was his mother laid across the floor. "What the fuck," rushing to the one person he loved more than anything. "Noooo," he screamed seeing her butt naked with multi gunshot wounds with blood oozing outta them.

The shock of seeing her in such a way he never noticed the burn marks or the .22 laying beside her. "Mom, I'm sorry, I'm sorry," he screamed knowing she would never hear him again or the words he spoke, the images of all the lives he took came full circle at that moment revealing it's self person by person, face by face ending the whole episode with the face of his mother."Noooo," screaming louder than the first time realizing his actions and decisions where the cause of his mother death and not of her own. "I can't believe I killed her, I can't believe I killed my mother," he kept telling' himself pacing back and forth not knowing what to do. "All for the love of money."

The mention of money snapped'em outta his trans causing him to rush to the basement only to see the worst of it.

//

"What! "Det. Triggs said puttin' his disco lights on top of his hood and sounding off his siren speeding through traffic. "I'll be on location within 15." "Do you want me to dispatch any cruisers in the area to that location?" "No! I'll radio in once I'm on location."

Det. Triggs arrived at 1244 Madison St in Madisonville within 10 minutes noticing Maniac SUV parked in the drive way."This is Det. Triggs requesting back up at 1244 Madison St", removing his side arm as he exited his vehicle. "Hello, hello," he yelled out entering the house. The sound of his voice startled Maniac sittin' on the basement steps causing him to turn and make his way up the stairs only to run smack into Det. Triggs.

"Nigga, you almost got yo fuckin' head blown off," puttin' his gun away. "Who called you?" Maniac asked knowing he didn't call the police. "Someone placed an anonymous call claiming they had a surprise for me."

"Det .Triggs, are you in there?" his fellow officers called out arriving on location. "I'm in the kitchen," he responded. "I need ya'll to secure the perimeter until the corner people get here and take Mr. Maniac downtown." "Take me down town for what," lookin' at Triggs as if he was insane. "I don't have time for yo shit, get'em outta here turning to observe Maniac mother while he cussed and fussed being drug outta there.

Det. Triggs instantly started surveying the crime scene noticing the wire hanger, the burn marks, and the multi gunshot wounds, to the different shell casin' scattered all over the floor."What the hell," finding the .22 laid beside her body, it didn't register at first then it came to him. The anonymous call, the surprise, and now the .22, he couldn't get outta there fast enough bustin' through the screen door jumping into his car and sped off causing the on lookers to wonder what the fuck!!

//

"Face you're slippin' and don't even realize it," Max said nonchalant seeing the way Cheri acted up. "I ain't fell yet, so I can't be slippin' dat much," smiling weaving in and outta traffic headed down 1-75. "Maybe not, but eventually you will if you continue to look out the window instead of lookin' in the mirror."

Face wasn't trying to hear none of dat, let alone trying to entertain her conversation, his mind was preoccupied with thoughts of Coco while she chose to shoot half ass riddles instead of speaking her mind.

"Baby girl, it's too much at stake to be coming at me with this five and dime ass conversation, if you got somethin' to say, say it, if not keep dat shit to yo self."

Max glanced over at'em for a second shaking her head before turning to stare out the window half laughing to herself. "I'll do just dat." she replied realizing what needed to be done.

///

"Mr. Boozer report to the sally port, you have a visit", the officer called over the loud speaker.

"Damn play boy, you pulled a Houdini catching two visit in one day." "What can I say once you become a boss on the streets, you don't stop being one cause you locked up," Noodles said entering the sally-port and before he could hit the door leading to the visitin' area, the officer stopped'em.

"You need to go with these two deputies." "What two deputies?" Noodles asked looking around like oh boy done lost his mind, only to answer his own question seeing two deputy's standing in the hallway once the sliding doors open.

"Let's ride young gun," the deputy said motioning for him to enter the hallway. "Man, I ain't going nowhere witt ya'll, I don't know what type time ya'll on, but ya'll got me fucked up." "Dig playboy," one of the black deputies said. "They say you got an attorney visit down stairs ,if you ain't trying to go so be it, I'll just radio in and continue doing what I was doing. "Oh! That's all ya'll had to say, but what's up with the hand cuffs and shackles?"

"Just a precaution when we taking somebody down stairs."

Wthin minutes Noodles was entering a room where he was suppose to meet his lawyer all handcuffed and shackled. "This ain't my lawyer! What the fuck you want," Noodles barked. "Dont worry deputies, I got this from here," closin' the door behind them. "Don't ya'll go too far, this won't be long at all", Noodles yelled as the door closed." What! You come to apologize for puttin' dat bull - shit in my whip, don't even waste yo breath, I'm good," settling into his seat feelin' himself.

Det. Triggs stood there watchin' every gesture, facial expression, and body movement Noodles gave off trying to read into any inclination he knew about what had transpired.

"Ya'll think, ya'll real slick?" pausing to come off the wall. "Taking innocent people lives." Noodles sat there lookin' at Det. Triggs gettin' closer and closer seein' the look in his eyes."Dig Triggs, I ain't trying to hear dat," standing before he got to close. "Matter of fact, I been in here to."

Det. Triggs didn't give him a chance to finish his sentence grabbin' him around the neck driving him against the wall pullin' back to take his head off when Noodles ducked pushin' him away. "Nigga, what the fuck wrong with you?" trying to get around the table and out the door, but couldn't move fast enough due to the shackles around his ankles.

"You thought you where gonna get away, young punk" catchin him witt a series of blows knockin' him off his feet. "I shoulda beat dat ass ,when I locked yo ass up the first time" ,kickin' him in the small of his back turning him over catchin' him straight in the eye.

The commotion could be heard down the hallway causing the deputies to come running."Hell naw!" one of the deputies yelled tackling Triggs off'em."You alright?" the other one asked Noodles. "What the fuck it look like," feelin ' his eye swell and the taste of blood inside his mouth. "Bitch ass nigga, you done fucked up", he yelled at Triggs gettin' to his feet. "Not only am I gonna beat this case, I'm gonna have yo badge, pussy mutherfucka," being escorted out the room, while Det. Triggs yelled back.

"Tell Face I found his surprise, I found his surprise."

With Det. Triggs not showing up, Det. Jones had to take on the duty of interrogating Maniac until late into the night mostly about who could commit such an act and what was in the safe. Maniac held to his guns not saying a word only staring off into space wanting to mourn his loss .After finally lettin' him go Maniac caught a cab across the bridge to cop'em a bottle to help ease the pain.

"Where to now?" the taxi driver asked. "Just get me back across the bridge and drive," he replied turning his bottle up.

A hour or so later the small rain turned into a huge thunder storm making it impossible for anyone to see.

"Look sir, I love yo company, but I love my family even more. it's rainin' cats and dogs out here, to the point 1'm ready to take it in before I kill us both out here", lookin' at Maniac through his rear view mirror. "Drop me off at 3636 Hyde park," taking' the rest' of his bottle to the head. No more than 20 minutes the taxi driver was pulling over. "Here you are sir and that will be 139,"reading the amount off the meter.

Maniac focused on his surroundings before diggin' in his pockets throwing two one hundred dollars bills through the glass partition. "Keep the change," staggering outta the cab into a down pour of rain and no sooner than he closed the door, the taxi driver pulled off leaving him to fiend for himself.

For the next ten minutes he just stood there gettin' soaking wet unsure why he even came here, but the thought of being alone wasn't an option.   Nevertheless, he made his way to her front door lying on the door bell until someone came to pull him off.

Peaches and Cheri was sound asleep in each other's arms when the sound of the door bell woke them up instantly. "Who the fuck is dat," Cheri asked lookin' at her girl then at the clock. "It's damn near 3 in the morning." "It's show time," Peaches informed her puttin' a t-shirt over her naked body. Within minutes she was at her front door while Cheri took refuge in the guest room. Peaches took a deep breath before swinging the door wide open.

"Nigga, get the fuck off my door bell," pullin' him inside. "Don't you know what time it is?" Watchin' him struggle to walk." Uuh, uh! Don't you sit yo wet ass on my couch," catchin' him before he sat down. "you gonna have to come' up outta them clothes before you catch a cold. Damn!" Smellin' the alcohol on his breathe. "You a mess, what you drive yo drop top over here," feelin' how wet he was as she undressed him.

"I killed her," he slurred fallin' back onto her couch as Peaches worked his pants off of'em. "Boy,quit playin', you ain't killed nobody."

"I killed her," he screamed grabbing Peaches by her shoulders before fallin' back allowing the tears to fall. Peaches seein' his pain up close knelt down between his legs. "Who you kill Maniac," pushin' him back in order to straddle'em moving his hands away from his face. "Talk to me baby, you're scaring me wiping' the tears from his eyes.

"My mother," opening his eyes to catch Peaches reaction. "No Maniac, please don't tell me you-.""NO! But the decisions I made in life did," closing his eyes lettin' the tears fall freely.

"All baby, I'm sorry," giving, him a hug where his face rested between her breast causing him to smell her scent and feel the warmness her body provided making his man hood come alive, as he roamed her body realizing she had on nothing, but a t-shirt.

She released him as his hands began to travel, touchin her bare skin. No words were needed ,as their lips touched. Things started to 'happen in slow motion as she raised her arms allowing him to take her t-shirt off pausing to admire her flawless body.

"I wanted you the first time I laid eyes-." "Shh! Don't spoil the moment with words, make love to me", standing on the couch placing one leg on the back of it giving him a view of the goodies a nigga would kill for grabbing the back of his head anticipating the touch of his tongue.

Maniac feasted on her forbidden fruit making her cum within minutes swallowing every last drop before guiding her slowly down to her awaiting saddle spreading her folds with the head of his dick.

"You're so fuckin' wet and so tight." "Shh! It's been a minute and you're so big," blowing his head up releasing her pussy muscles a little allowing him to enter a little further. "Oh, I feel in my stomach," she screamed causing Maniac to respond by pickin' her up still knee deep in dat shit carrying her around pounding dat ass feelin' his balls swelling, he had to find a wall for more leverage and support before he let loose

.Peaches was loving the way he was handling his business seeing the look in his eyes she knew he was damn near there as he buried his face into her chest pounding away.

"Look at me," she yelled taking one of her hands from around his neck diggin' his head outta her chest. "I want to see the look on yo face when you cum." As much as he wanted to and tried, he just couldn't as he let loose becoming weak in the knees.

"You cheated," hittin' him playfully in the chest as he slowly let her down.

"Ya'll nasty," Cheri said entering the living room wearing noth-ing, but some white satin panties and a half of shirt covering only her breast. "The way she was screaming, you might be workin' witt some-thing,' lookin' between Maniac legs. "You could at least put some clothes on." "Maybe I wanted him to know he got options," Lookin' him up and down headed toward the kitchen. "Maybe he do, but he'll chose me every time," Peaches responded walking her bow legged ass to her bed room with Maniac close behind watchin' what he had in front of'em and peepin' at what he thought he could get on the side.

CHAPTER 19

The After Math

" Oh baby, what happen," Coco asked touching the glass as if she could actually touch'em. "It's nothing-." "What you mean it ain't nothing?" "Calm down love, this punk ass detective touch me up the other day. "It look more like he assaulted you to me." "That he did, that he did, but dig, I need you to go holla at my man and see what the fuck going on cause this mutherfuck coming at me talkin' about he found his little surprise. Tell'em I don't know what type of games he got me caught up in, but I ain't witt diss shit." "Don't worry baby, I'm going to get at that, soon as I leave," lookin' at how swollen his eye was.

//

"Peaches, I need you to go get dat money so I can go get on." "It's not that easy-." "What you mean it ain't that easy?" sittin' up in bed. "Nigga you better lower yo tone and like I said it ain't that easy. You got to understand it's not like I got dat shit under my mattress or stashed in the closet somewhere, I got to dismantle a corporation and that shit gonna take time, it ain't nothin' that's gonna happen over night."

"Damn!" he said fallin' back on his pillow. "I know you didn't have all yo eggs in one basket," Peaches inquired trying to see if he was really broke or not. "I got close to 300 at my spot outside of what I got invested into the corporation." "Okay, now answer this. How long you been fuckin' witt yo people?" "A couple of years", he replied thinking about how he was gonna make it happen.

"Listen baby," sittin' Indian style in the bed. "If you gonna fuck witt me, You gonna have to trust me and know I got yo best interest at heart. Now, I haven't always been about my business, I use to be dat chick living in the streets fuckin' witt street type niggas until I woke up realizing I deserve better and can do better and stopped depending on the next mutherfucka to do for me. So don't think what I'm about to say is some bull shit," lookin' Maniac dead into his eyes. Yo connect needs you more than you realize they' have grown accustom to you buying X amount from them however you shop witt'em, they still got them thangs on hand regardless if you got the money or not and who else to give'em to than the person they belong to in the first place, if not I'll dismantle the corporation and get you what's yours; but understand this, I didn't get away from all that to fall back into it," making her eyes water as she turned to get off the bed.

"Peaches!" Grabbing hold of her arm before she could get away. "What's wrong baby? don't do dat," kissin' her tears away. "I made a mistake, but it's cool, I'll get over it," pullin away from him. "I can't have you in my life continuing this destructive life style, that shit only ends two ways, behind bars or in somebody grave yard. I can't go through that again and I won't," snatchin' away from him slipping on her robe as she exited the room.

Maniac was at a cross road in his life knowing if he didn't make the right decision his chance's of keeping her was slim to none.

"Okay love," catchin' up to her. "We gonna keep everything in tact with the corporation." "You think this is about a fuckin' corporation, you don't have a clue," turning away from him again on her way to the bathroom. "What is it Peaches, I've already lost my mother, I'm not trying to lose you too," he said whole heartily.

"Maniac," she said catchin' her breath before turning around. "I have genuine feelings for you, if not what we shared woulda never happened last night. I'm not trying to be in a relationship that can end whenever them people feel like ending it by coming and snatching you away from me or even~ worse them jealous ass nigga doing somethin' to me, to get at you, I won't put myself in that predicament again and I won't force you to choose, I'll make dat choice for you," Peaches said allowing the tears to fall.

"Look baby," puttin' his arms around her. "Give me four months and I'll fold my hand witt this shit," digging her head outta his chest to look at'em."I'm gonna invest into our future, not take away from it. After I see my people, I'm a drop you off somethin' ,now go wash yo pretty face and know the last thing I wanna see is yo eyes full of tears again," smackin' dat ass as she went into the bathroom.

Maniac turned around to catch Cheri standing in her door way lookin' sexy as hell suckin' on her two middle fingers. "You want some papi," she said in her most seductive voice. "Excuse me, you want some." "Who me?" he responded lookin' dumb founded as she move her panties to the side taking her fingers outta her mouth inserting them inside her wound.

Maniac was so lost in the show he never heard Peaches exit the bathroom. "She'll jumped on one foot and barked like a dog too, if you stand there long enough," passin' them both headed to her bedroom laughing to herself seeing thc look on his face being caught watching somethin' he had no business watching.

///

Max woke up early as usual making the necessary phone calls, to get things moving. No one knew she was more of a shrewd business lady as she was planning a niggas demise, either way she was going to get the job done. She invested 1.4 into Thompson McConnell Cadillac in Walnut Hills,150k into the 513 clothing stores that was poppin' up through out the city, now she needed to find a place to open their hair salon knowing they could launder a little somethin' through it without causing any suspicion from them people. It was almost 6pm when she finally took a break from the madness dealing with accountants, lawyers, and the people she chose to invest witt.

Knock, knock, knock!

"Who is it", she yelled from her office/bedroom. "Face, I ain't trying to talk to you right now," opening the door to see Dirt Bert standing there with a duffle bag in hand.

"I'm sorry to disappoint you, but I hope you got time to holla at yo boy," smiling entering her apartment. "Don't be silly, I'll always have time for a nigga about his business, speaking of which, what you got in the bag?" "Just a little somethin' somethin' I need you to invest for me. I was listening when you checked Face and realized who's the real brains around here and I'm trying to put myself in position to be alright for years to come and not just for the moment.”

Max listened realizing she found her next student and she didn't have to presaude'em, he volunteered making it that much beautiful.

"How much you bring me? "Wanting to know how serious he was. ” 500 thousand!!" "You dead serious about this," Max responded knowing he was willing to give up his whole bank roll to better his situation. "Do you have any suggestions about what you would like to invest in?"

"My job is to get this money, I'm a leave dat up to you, baby girl," giving her a kiss on the cheek as he exited running into Cheri on his way out. "Max, what you done did to dat boy, got'em smiling like dat.

"Wouldn't you wanna know," puttin his bag under the table. "Listen baby, I got a lot of shit I need to attend to, so I'm glad you got over here when you did." "I woulda got here sooner if I had some type of transportation." "That's my reason for callin' you over. I know the reason behind yo frustrations and why you blew up yesterday." "That wasn't nothing," Cheri commented trying to down play the situation.

"I'm not Face and that's not a jab at him, I love dat nigga like-cooked food and you know how I love to eat," bringing a soft laughter between them." I'll be the first to admit he's not playin fair when it comes to you, not saying he don't have yo best interests at heart cause he do! It's just that he's so occupied with everything around him he's not paying attention to the things and people close to'em.

I recognize outta everybody you the only one that don't have their own puttin' you in a situation to depend on the next mutherfucka and that ain't what it is, especially fuckin' witt me." Cheri stood there wondering how she knew the exact things she's been feeling, when all she wanted was her own.

"I'm good." "Don't you play witt me! Now take yo narrow ass on up to Thompson McConnell and grab whatever yo heart desire, later on today I'll have the keys to yo new house and the information to yo bank account, plus I enrolled yo little hot ass into Cinti Community College, I picked personal finance as yo major. I be damn if I raise a dumb bitch."

"Who you callin' dumb," Cheri playfully asked huggin' Max thanking her for everything. "I won't let you down." "I know you won't cause I'll beat dat ass first"!!

///

"I don't give a fuck where you work at, come through and pick this shit up", Face yelled at the deputy working at the Justice center as he answered his door surprised to see the most beautiful female he ever laid eyes on standing at his front door. "Matter of fact," motioning Co-co to enter. "Write this number down, 371-2542 ask for Dirt Bert and tell'em to handle it," hanging up before the deputy had a chance to respond. "So what brings you to my door step, besides wanting to see a nigga like me?"

"Don't flatter yo self, I'm just delivering a message my man can't deliver himself." "What's dat," grabbing Coco so fast by her small waist pulling her so close to'em, he could smell the head and shoulders shampoo she used to wash her hair, at the same time feel her breast rise up and down as she fought to catch the rhythm of her breathing."Dat's right, don't be afraid," he whispered.

"Do you act like this toward all yo boys females companion or is it just me? "Breaking from his embrace circling him as he stood still loving the mystery of it all. "How would Noodles feel if he knew the man he looked up to, the man he admired, was the same man trying to fuck his girl," stopping directly in front of'em to catch his million dollar response.   Face stood there dick so hard it hurt knowing his answer had to be truthful if he wanted shorty to respect him.

"He'll be hurt-".

"My point exactly! Now whatever going on out here that got this detective rushing down there assaulting my man claiming he found yo little surprise ain't what time it is."

"That's cute, but tell'em I just save his ass from having to do hard time and his lawyer will be down there tomorrow to fill him in about it, but back to you Ms. Lady," pullin' her even closer. "You don't have to take yo panties off, just pull'em to the side."

"That's even cuter, but if I ever decide to give you just a little bit, I'll have to kill you afterwards cause you wouldn't know how to act," turning on her heels leaving him standing there with dat one look on his face. .

///

Maniac started his day off with a lot of shit on his mind, he had to make funeral arrangements for his mother as he pulled in front of Ice Mike spot playin' the Ghetto boys, My mind playin' tricks on me.

Within minutes after going through the necessary precautions he stood in front of Ice telling him his situation. "I'm fucked up right now, I got to bury my mother and find the bitches responsible, at the same time, get my money right."

"I'm sorry to hear about moms and if you need any help witt dat situation, you already know. As far as yo money situation, I got you. I can't have you running around fucked up, that's a bad reflection on me and how I treat my people. I seen dat big as safe in the morning paper, I'm not even gonna ask what they got you for I just hope you learned from yo mistakes and patch them holes up in yo game cause now, it's all eyes on you," Ice Mike explained lettin' him know not only the police, but every robbery boy trying to come up. "But at the end of the day, let's get this money!!"

///

Det. Jones been at Maniac mother house going over different scenarios about how everything went down when Det. Triggs showed up.

"I'll be out yo way in a minute," looking around one last time. "Don't rush, I'd like to get some insight on this one," opening the door for them to finally work together.

"First of all, this was his stash house regardless if he won't admit it or not. From the big ass safe in the basement, to the electric box being place inside, to all the cameras mounted outside the house, not to mention the backup generator stored in the garage set up to come alive if the electric was ever to go out."

"Okay, okay, you made yo point, but how did they gain entrance?"

"I don't know especially when she had a intercom system in place meaning it had to be someone she knew or felt comfortable opening the door for", Det. Jones reasoned seeing a FedEx truck pull into the drive way. "Can I help you," Det. Jones said meeting the delivery man out front?" "I have a package for a Ms. Louise, the FedEx man replied. "I'm sorry, but Ms. Louise is no longer with us ."

"I'm sorry to hear that, but she already prepaid for the package so can you make sure her family get this," the delivery man said handing the detective the box before returning to his truck.

Det. Jones returned to the house trying to sort things out when he noticed a similar box by the front door with Ms. Louise name on it.

"I know dat look, what you got detective?"" I know how they gained entrance without causing any suspicion," Det. Jones responded lookin' up at Det. Triggs."But first we need to discuss what you got regarding those three double homicides before I continue to expose my hand

"You what!" Face yelled lookin at Max not believing the half of it. "You stepped off into somethin' you had no business doing."

"I had no business doing! Nigga please. Let it woulda been me" "What the fuck dat's suppose to mean?" Standing over her.

Max couldn't believe her eyes as Face stood over her, so before things got outta control and shit was said that couldn't be taken,' back, she soften her approach.

"Look Face, I didn't come to fight or tell you what you shoulda done or shouldn't, all I'm saying we need everybody to be happy and on the same page verse a person unhappy and workin' against us, it ain't in our best interest." Face listen realizing he was'nt mad at her for what she did, but more or less, mad at himself for not doing it first.

"More importantly, I need you to get focused and start planning how we gonna get at Fat Jeff," changing the subject to somethin' more meaningful cause at the end of the day, if it don't make dollars, it don't make sense. "This is childs play dealing wit Manica, our shit gotta be tighter than fish pussy if we gonna stand a chance at getting' at dis nigga. The bull shit aint nothin' Face smiled, even laughed a little. "Tighter than fish pusssy?" "Yea nigga,tighter than fish pussy."

CHAPTER 20

It's all good

In the days to come Noodles lawyer finally got down there to see'em.

"I apologize Noodles, but the murder trial took a lot outta me. "Did you win?" Noodles interrupted wanting to know the outcome. "It wasn't easy, but I pulled a rabbit outta the hat," Bobo responded real smooth. "But yo case ain't nothing' compared to that, thanks to Det. Triggs and his inability to keep his hands to himself."

"My girl was tellin' me the other day what Face had told her- "Don't even sweat it, I'll have you outta here by the beginning of the year, I'm workin' on gettin' yo probation squashed, due to the fact you'll have done close to six months county time before I can make anything happen. "That's what's up", Feelin' good about his situation ."That way I can pull outta here free and clear." "That you can, so until then I'm gonna file some motions in yo behalf just some routine stuff, motion to suppress, motion of discovery, and things of that nature to get the ball rolling. If you have any questions or concerns feel free to call."

Noodles lawyer left as he returned to his pod giving Ethy a head nod to meet'em upstairs. "What's good Screwed up? "C'mon witt dat screwed up shit," Noodles said getting down to business. "Where's old school? "Probably gettin' at them ends, every since dat thang came through, you already know. "That's what's up, but dig, my lawyer just told me I'll be here until, the first of the year, then I'm outta here."

"What about yo case? "Nigga, fuck dat case, I told you I'm a boss," Noodles said feelin' himself."But regardless where I'm at, you and old school gonna be good and when you touch down, get at me!!"

//

True to form Max did everything she said she would and no one was more happy than Cheri herself.

"About time they broke bread", Peaches said laying across Cheri's king size bed watchin a rerun of I love New York. "And bitch when you gonna let me push dat escalade?" "When you let me fuck dat nigga", strappin' on her 10' dildo. " "Girl ,he ain't gonna be able to han-dle all of that, you gotta build'em up for dat one, unless his ass been tamper witt," causing both girls to burst out laughing.

"Seriously, how far away we from hittin' dat nigga for that mill?"   "About two somethin', but I'll get that and some before its all over witt, especially when he find out I'm pregnant," poking her stomach out making it look bigger than it actually was. Trick, you done fell and bump yo head or somethin', I was just witt ass when you went to the clinic to get dat shot." "I know that, but he don't," Giving Cheri dat one look.

"Girl, you one grimy little bitch," high fiving her girl when the sound of the door bell took'em by surprise. "Bitch, who you done gave the address to? Let me find out you giving my pussy away," stealing a kiss before sending her off to answer the door.

"Look at you, driving big trucks, got a nice three bedroom house on a quite little street in Bond hill, Max did real good and I'm happy for you", Face said sincerely. "I just want to apologize for not making it happen for you myself."

Even doe she was secretly mad at Face, she no longer could be seeing the look in his eyes and hearing the tone in his voice. "Love is love," she replied giving him a hug.

"Hell naw," Peaches yelled from the top of the stairs."Ain't no fun if yo girl can't have none," running down the stairs joining in on the love."   "Dig, I really just shot through to hollar at you, check out the spot and give you these." Cheri looked at the two keys dangling from his hand seeing the BMW emblem imprinted on them realizing Face brought her another truck or somethin' moving him outta the way to look outside. "Oh my god, I can't take dat," seeing her brothers white on white 745Li BMW.

"Yes you can, he woulda wanted you to have it," puttin' the keys in her hand. "Now will somebody please give yo boy a ride back to the hood, I got shit I need to attend to."

They all jump in Mello 745Li ready to roll when Cheri paused for a moment to reflect on how much Mello loved this car and the memories it brought back.

"I love you big bra," she whispered out loud searching for his favorite song as she began to shed a tear. "There it is right there", getting animated as the song began to play. "Back in elementary, I cried out of misery", she rapped. "But in due time, grew up amongst a dying breed", lookin' over at Face puttin' the car in gear backin' outta the drive way. "Inside my mind couldn't find a place to rest, until I got that thug life tatted on my chest."

Face and Peaches watched as she went into her own zone hittin verse after verse, then all of a sudden hitting the gas causing them to fall back into their seats, they didn't want to disturb her groove knowing she was living for her brother.

"Is there a heaven for a G remember me, so many homies in a cemetery, shed so many tears. That's dat shit" wiping the tears outta her eyes stoppin' at the stop light. "You alright?" Face asked hoping' he didn't cause more harm than good giving her Mello car. "Couldn't be better," lookin' both ways before running the red light screaming, "Thug life mutherfuckas!!"

//

From the time Ice Mike hit'em off witt them 50 joints Maniac been doing the damn thang hittin' the streets dat one way taking 20 of those thangs to water coming outta there with 30 of-them, sellin' OZ at 5.50 a pop causing a stir amongst the little men in the streets, but Maniac didn't give a fuck even rubbing some of the big boys the wrong way sellin' birds for 22.5 still in the wrapper causing them to drop their prices in a market where niggas could get'em off for 25 easily.

It's been a week since his mother's death and it was time to make the necessary arrangements and lay her to rest in style. He spent 100k on her head stone alone, a marble statue of a angle wit wings wanting her to fly amongst the dead in heaven knowing she wouldn't be able to walk amongst the living on earth.

"Hey baby, you know I'm still mad at you." "Don't be like dat, I told you last night funerals ain't for me, I had a bad experience when I was younger." "I know, but I need you to be there for me-."

"And I will baby," touchin' Cheri to turn down the music. "Once you return home, I'm not even going to work tomorrow I'm dedicating my whole day to pleasing my king the way he needs and deserve to be." "That's what I'm talkin' about," thinking how each time was better than the last. "I'm leaving 50 in the bedroom and I'll see you later on tonight." "Okay love," CLICK!

Maniac had taken refuge at Peaches condo making it his own, she had'em so far gone he was ready to propose, but the only thing preventing him from doing so, he wanted to get his money right first.

///

"Baby girl," Dirt Bert yelled out trying to catch Max attention before she entered the building. "Boy, I know you got better manners than that screaming my name across the projects like you crazy, get on in here," playfully smackin' him across the head. "I got some papers I need you to sign." "What kinda papers?" he inquired following Max into her apartment. "I just bought you somethin' that's gonna earn you money for years to come and then some," turning to catch his reaction as she pulled the paper work from her brief case.

"That's what I'm talkin' about," grabbing the papers outta her hands to read. "God damn! "He yelled not believing what he was reading. "No you didn't," lookin' down at Max. "Tell me it ain't so," rushing Max lifting her off her feet spinning her around not giving her a chance to respond. "Boy, put me down, a simple hug and thank you woulda been good enough."
"Max, you just don't know how much I appreciate this," Finally puttin' her down. "I didn't know I coulda bought a McDonalds for a half mill." "You can't," causing him to look at them papers again then back at her not fully understanding. "It cost you 1 .5,"she explained. "I loaned you a mill to close the deal." "You loaned me what," Not believing her bank roll was like dat. "Hold tight, baby girl, where you get a mill from?" "That's not important, what is, I haven't given you shit I loaned it to you at a 10% interest," gettin' down to business taking Dirt Bert by surprise.

"Now take yo time and read everything carefully. As you can see I've formed a LLC making myself majority owner which will give us a five year tax break due to me-.being a minority, basically a woman. A lot of this I don't expect you to understand, so I'm gonna set up a meeting with my lawyer which I would love for you to take on also-'!

"Look Max, where do I sign, you loaned me a mill, what reason do I have not to believe what you're tellin' me?" Max listened smiling that Dirt Bert not only trusted her, but believed in her just the same.

"Sign right here, here, and here. Don't forget to date it also and since I got you here, you need to sign these as well," pullin' some more papers out dealing with the car dealer ship, the clothing store, and the hair salon. "Damn Max, You puttin' us in a nice position," signing his name on everything whispering to his self. "It's all good!!!"

CHAPTER 21

I'll always love you

Maniac buried his mother at Spring Grove cemetery where all her close friends and a few spectators paid their last respects to a lady most will miss dearly, as they lowered her into the ground.

You could hear the whispers in the back ground commenting on how lovely her head stone was and how everything was set up to send her out in style releasing 100 doves into the sky as the first drop of dirt hit her casket.

Maniac stood there full of emotions and pain while the choirs began to sing; "We'll always love Ms. Louise, we'll always love Ms. Louise," over and over again signaling the end of a beautiful ceremony.

The crowd began to disperse one by one dropping a single rose on top of her grave stopping in front of Maniac giving their last condolence. Raytonya appeared outta the shadows lying her rose on top of Ms. Louise grave turning to catch Maniac lost within his own thoughts.

"I miss you," she said snapping him outta his trans. "Shh!,"stopping him from responding. "Regardless how things turned out between us, I'll always love you and I give you my deepest condolence and if you ever need a ear, you got the number," kissing him softly on the cheek before steppin' off to leave.

"Raytonya! "He called out causing her to turn around. "Thank you," realizing what they had was more than a fuck thang!!!

"Baby, I can't wait until the first of the year, you got some hellva making up to do." "That I do, but until then what's keepin' my baby right through the night?" "A lot of cold showers and many lonely nights, but don't worry yo shit under lock and key," pokin' her tongue at'em as someone climbed the stairs interrupting their visit whispering in his ear.

What she witnessed next caused her to spaz out. "I know you ain't playin' witt yo freedom like that?" "Lil momma, fall back and let me do me," puttin his pack back between his ass crack surveying the area making sure all was good.

"You playin' Russian roulette witt yo freedom, You don't give a fuck about me or coming home, you got to be the stupidest mutherfucka." "Bitch!" standing up. "Who the fuck you callin stupid? You knew what it was when you started fuckin witt a nigga, matter of fact, I'm gonna take my stupid ass on back down stairs," throwing the phone against the window leaving her sittin' there with tears in her eyes.

Noodles didn't want his visit to end but he be damn if he let a bitch disrespect him and not stand on it.

"Screwed up!" Old school called out seeing Noodles exit the visit room with a depressing look on his face. "Not right now, old school," by passing him entering the pod hittin' Ethy to follow him up stairs. "Man this bitch got me fucked up," pacing back and forth.

"Dig screwed up, you my nigga and all, but I ain't on this soap opera ass shit, you and oh girl be on every other week, press yo buck and lil- momma be back tomorrow," gettin' up to go check his traps leaving his man to deal with his own domestic problems!!!

Coco exited the Justice Center eyes full of tears mad at herself for callin' her man stupid as she answered her cell phone almost knockin' someone over passing them.

"How you get this number?" "It doesn't matter how I got it, I got it! I'm just wondering when you gonna make time for a nigga and stop fakin!" Coco stopped to wipe the tears from her eyes knowing she had to fight fire with fire and get down for hers. "Meet me at Queen Ann's, need a drink," hanging up without gettin' a response.

If it wasn't for Det. Triggs damn near gettin' ran over, he woulda never witnessed the transition Coco went through from tears to someone on a mission causing him to alter his plans and follow suit.

Within minutes; Coco was sittin' at the bar taking shots of patron for about 20 minutes when Face smoothly walked in taking a seat next to her.

"I didn't think you where gonna make it," sliding off her bar stool to hit the juke box going through the selection until finding the right song to set her bait, Already knowing he'll bite a naked hook let-tin' Keisha Cole I shoulda cheated filled the room.

Coco was fillin' dat patron dat one way throwing her hands in the air singing alone with the song, I might as well have lied to you, as much as you accused me of lying," swinging her hips from side to side gettin' into the song.

The temptation was too much just to sit there and be a specta-tor; he had to be a part of dat not now, but right now. "Let's skip the side show and go to my place," taking her within his arms. She looked into his brown eyes and continued to sing.

"I might as well have, gone to the club, as much as you accused me of clubbing," turning her backside on'em. Face closed his eyes al-lowing her to do her. "I might as well have, given away: my love, as much as you accused me of doing it," turning pointing at his print. "What you gonna do witt dat?" smiling going to grab her things at the bar with Face close behind. "I shoulda cheated," she confessed on her way out the door almost falling if it wasn't for Face quick hands.

"You're a little to tipsy to be driving," holding her up lookin' down into her hazel eyes." I know, that's why I'm not," breaking away from him to flag down a cab. "Why you tell me to meet you here," fol-lowing her into the middle of the street. "Just to see if you'll come," kissing him seductively on the lips before jumping into her cab not knowing pictures where being taken' of the whole episode!!

//

"Unk, Its going down out here, mutherfuckas playin' for keeps." "That's how it's supposed to go if a nigga trying to have lon-gevity in this game, you can't second guess yo decision right or wrong."

"True dat, I guess the game is universal regardless where you at! Anyway, the detective I was tellin' you about the last time finally came around and put me inside the loop making it possible for us to work together, hopefully I can start connecting the dots and come up witt something."

"That would be lovely, but more importantly, how my lil-niece doing, she hasn't called oh Unk in a while making me feel love don't live there no more."

"You know that girl love you more than anything, she just got so much of her mother in her it ain't funny, and you know how Annaca could be, bless her soul."

"Yea my sister was a hand full, I can't deny dat, just stay on top of thangs and report back sooner than Later!", ending their conversation thinking about his beloved sister whispering unto the skis, "I'll always love you"!!!

///

"Shit girl, let a nigga pull the sheets outta his ass," complimenting her on the way she handle a dick. "You'll make a nigga fall in love off yo face game alone." "I can't tell, you ain't made no honest woman outta me yet." "And I wont! That shit would go against the grain trying to turn a bitch into a house wife," smiling how she tried her hand. "I ain't mad at chat, but I'll be settin' myself up for failure," Triggs told her trying to recoup from their session.

"So why ain't the rest of them mutherfuckas locked up," she inquired as she began to suck on his toes. "Ooh shit, you know what that do to me, come here and lay in my arms, you know I need a little rest before we jump this thang off again. I'm workin' a hellva case right now and I got them boys right in the middle of it." It's kinda complicated, but peep game. The guys that killed and robbed Mello, one of them was his girlfriend ex-boyfriend-." "Get the fuck outta here," turning around in his arms to see if he was serious or not.

"The tricky part about it all somethin' went wrong in dat apartment where dude ex-girlfriend or possibly still girlfriend got killed, either way the bitch dead and after a while dude gets mad that somebody killed her and turned on his whole crew killing everybody involved."

"Where does my baby come into play?" "I haven't come up with that part yet, but somehow Face and them found out who killed Mello and laid on their man finding out where his stash house was at, making it do what it do killin' the dudes mother in the process."

Bull-Moose laid in his arms visualizing everything he was tellin' her, even doe he never mentioned any names only referring to dude this and dude that, his last information not only put a name to'em, but also a face remembering seeing the news about somebody killing a lady then showing that big ass safe.

"I got enough evidence to bring dude in on multiple charges, but I'm waiting on Face and them to slip, so I can nail their asses to da wall.", Det. Triggs said feelin' his man coming alive thinking about puttin' Face and them behind bars.

"Let me find out, all we gotta do is talk about yo work and shit on and poppin,"positioning herself to ride dat dick. "Damn bitch, I love the way you work yo pussy muscles," laying back allowing her to do what she do best!!!

///

"How long his punk ass been over there," Tight-White asked seeing Det. Triggs car parked outside Bull-Moose apartment building. "He came through around one somethin' and its going on three now," Dirt Bert responded looking down at his watch.

"That bitch must got dat fire, got a nigga laid up in the middle of the day. I got to shoot through there later on and see what that thang workin' witt" ,rubbin' his hands together. "Since ya'll wouldn't let me kill the bitch, might as well kill the bitch, you know what I'm talkin' about," Tight-White said smiling ear to ear.

"That's yo problem, always trying to stick yo dick in something," Shakin' his head walking down the strip. "Oh yea, did you sign them papers?" "Yea, I sign'em, Apples and the wonder twins signing theirs now, matter of fact, I'm waiting on Apples to see what's poppin'- ."

"Ain't nothing poppin', witt yo broke ass," Apples said coming outta the building with the wonder twins right behind her laughing lookin' at the expression on Tight-White face. "Oh, it's like dat when a nigga been out here trappin' all day," pullin' a fist full of money focusing his attention dead on Apples.

"Then again, the way you like paying I might need to hit you off," causing everybody to laugh even harder.

Dirt Bert had his eyes on Peaches the whole time as she hung up her cell phone."Where you going sexy," Dirt Bert asked taking her by surprise grabbing hold of her hand. "I wish somewhere with you," speakin' from her heart as they locked eyes. "But I got to go entertain this nigga, so we all can bear fruit from my labor," easing outta his grip waving bye to everybody jumping into her SUV.

"Let me find out you trying to hollar at my girl," Cheri said snappin' him outta his daze. "Naw Cheri, I'm just recognizing her swag and seeing her come into her own watching Tight-White' ran across the street. "What the fuck!" Causing Cheri to turn around seeing Tight-White pissing on Det. Triggs door handle.

"He's a hot mess," Apples jumped in saying not believing he actually did it. "You did all dat for a hug, I can just image what you'll do for a shot of this pussy," giving him what he wanted.

Tight-White took full advantage of his hug, grippin' dat ass with both hands gettin' his grind on whispering in her ear. "I know you want this dick." "Boy, if you don't let me go, witt yo nasty ass," playfully hittin' him on the shoulder as Det. Triggs finally exited the building.

Bull-Moose had'em so spent all he wanted to do was get some where, pullin' on his door handle fillin' a wet substance.

"What the fuck," looking at his hand then down at his car door seeing the whole thing wet up turning to see Tight-White holding the front of his pants giving him a replay of how he sprayed his car pointing and laughing at'em. Det. Triggs was so hot he had to catch himself before doing somethin' that would cost'em his job later.

"Fuck you pussy mutherfucka," he yelled knowing once he got them pictures developed and sent off, he'll have the last laugh jumping in his car tellin' himself. "I love this shit!!"

Face looked outta his window seeing the whole scene play out, but really wasn't paying attention as his mind wandered thinking about Coco and how she seduced him without even taking her clothes off. Everything about her excited him and the thoughts of nailing her ass to the bed post excited him even more."I'm sorry playboy, but I got to get this one," hoping Noodles understood when he didn't understand his mutherfuckin' self!!!

CHAPTER 22

I'm Sorry

For the last three weeks Noodles refused every visit from Coco, not wanting to face the fact the picture he received implicated. He was hurting deeply not even reading the letters she sent over the last couple of weeks, but today he refused to hurt anymore gettin' in touch witt Ebony the night before expressing his wishes to see her, and of course she accepted not knowing she was nothing more than a pawn being played in a massive chess game.

"Mr. Boozer, you have a visit," the officer yelled over the intercom. "You going up," Ethy asked sliding into Noodles cell. "Or you still playin' duck, duck, goose?" half laughing at his own statement.

"You got jokes now?" "Naw, but I seen you finally broke down and picked the phone up last night." "That I did, but it was to call this other little somethin' to come hollar at yo boy," leaving his room eager to see the look on Coco face after three weeks of denying her visits. "Who I got up there?" Noodles asked the officer in the bubble.

"The number one stunna", he replied lookin' at his monitor. "Call down-stairs and let'em know-I'm refusing this one. 'Man!'" The officer said lookin' back at Noodles. "I don't know what ya'll youngster be on, but I be damn if I let that One get away," picking' up the phone.

"Dig, I'll go hollar at shorty and let her know ain't no sense in keep running down here," he said as the officer waved'em on.

Noodles took a deep breath before opening the door to hit the stairs, Coco walked back and forth patiently waiting to see if he would at least show his face after three weeks, she sent countless letters apologizing and explaining how much she loved him and how the thoughts of losing him was driving her crazy.

The wait was no longer as she turned to see him standing there. "OH baby," rushing to his window pickin' up the receiver. "I'm sorry baby, I'm so sorry, I'll never accuse you of being-." "I ain't trying to hear dat bull shit," he said through clenched teeth reliving the pain he first felt.

"Please baby, I don't wanna fight, I just wanna get pass this and move on with our lives."

"Ain't dat funny, I can see you done moved on, not giving a dam about us." "What are you talkin' about?" Blown away by his response. "I don't know what's going on or why you're acting this way, but please baby don't push me away-."

"Push you away, naw shorty, don't put dat one on me, You look good wearing that one all bye yo self. Anyway, I didn't come up here to tongue wrestle, I just wanna let you know ya'll look good together and ain't no sense in keep running down here when it's obvious you wanna be somewhere else-."

Coco listened knowing her little rendezvous had been exposed, but how she wondered and before she could dig further he was tellin' her. "Give shorty the phone," as Ebony stepped off the elevator.

"You choosin' this bitch over me," Coco screamed as Ebony quickly turned around only for the elevator to betray her closing in her face.

"Damn!" Ebony whispered pushing the elevator button not wanting no problems turning to see Noodles waving her over.

"You can have this one," Standing to gather her things. "But you got me fucked up," Coco yelled loud enough for Ebony to hear. "Cause come tomorrow or any other day I catch diss bitch down here or any other bitch, I'ma beat dat ass," throwing the phone against the glass. "Now, bring yo ass back down here if you want to," warning Ebony as she caught the elevator before it closed.

"Fuck dat bitch, what's up shorty," seeing the look in her eyes that let'em know she was scared to death!!

///

"Bitch, why you stoppin' here," Cheri asked rollin' up a blunt. "I need to go pick up a little somethin' something", jumping outta her SUV to enter the neighborhood clinic. "Let me find out yo pussy on fire", Cheri screamed out the window. "Imagine dat," entering the clinic quickly and finding what she wanted just as quickly approaching a young lady with several children around her and one in the oven. "Excuse me, I got 200,if you piss in this pill bottle for me." The young lady didn't even hesitate grabbing the pill bottle outta her hand.

"Shit, for 200 I'll fill this up and any other bottle you need filled, just keep an eye on my kids," disappearing inside the clinic's restroom to make it do what it do.

"Here you go," the lady said handing Peaches the bottle wrapped up in paper towels. "Thank you," handing the lady what she had coming.

"Damn bitch, dat was fast, they must've had yo shit on deck," sparkin' the blunt as they pulled off "That they did," holding up the pill bottle full of piss!!

//

With Face spending so much time catering to Coco over the last couple of weeks, he knew it was just a matter of time before he bust dat sweet little pee hole, so instead of sweatin' her he began to refocus on the things he needed to in order to make sure his team pulled off this caper successfully cause one thing for sure Fat JEFF wasn't the type of nigga you could half ass play witt and expect to live."Hey sexy", Face said answering his cell phone.

"Don't hey sexy me, witt yo good tellin' ass-." "Pump. yo breaks, what the fuck you talkin' about?" "Do'nt get absent minded now, yo boy know we-." "We what," stopping whatever she was about to say. "Cause we haven't done anything other than went out a couple of times and let a nigga feel dat ass." "Ha, Ha, Ha, ain't dat amusing, but it still don't explain how he found that out."

"Dig Coco, its bad enough I'm at you the way that I am, but to think I'm the one lacing his ears with that bull shit, you barkin' up the wrong tree. Make no mistake about it, I'm trying to knock fire out dat pussy verse trying to cause friction between you and my man, it's just not in my best interest, you feel me?"

Coco was driving down Liberty St. trying to make sense of it all, as she pulled into Shell gas station. "I don't know, I think it's best we slow-It. CLICK!

Face wasn't trying to hear none of that as he hung up, plus he just witnessed the money man from Fat Jeff operation exiting the building from his low key position in the woods.

"I'm sorry Ms. Lady", apologizing to Coco for hanging up on her ass. "But I need to follow this duck and see what type of pond he lead me to!!"

//

Maniac SUV made a wild u-turn on Reading Rd. as if it owned the street, the urgency in Peaches voice tellin' him to come home caused him to think the worse.

"Talk to me baby," he demanded running red light after red light. "I can't," and the phone went dead.

Maniac looked at his phone realizing she wasn't on the other end quickly pressed redial only for the phone to keep on ringing before going straight to voice mail, gettin' frustrated not gettin' an answer he threw the phone out the window focusing on pushin' his truck to the limit.

Within 10 minutes he came to a sudden stop in front of her condo flying' from his truck like his life depended on it storming through the door with gun in hand only to find Peaches sittin' on the couch bent over holding a pregnancy test in her hand.

"Baby, you alright," looking around for anything outta the norm as he approached her. "I-I-I'm pregnant," holding up the pregnancy test for him to see the result. "I'm not ready for this-."

"Hold on love," gently puttin' his arms around her wiping the tears from her eyes thinking how the lord take a life only to give one seeing this as a blessin' from the man above. "Look at me, all I ever wanted was a family of my own, I'm ready to be all you need me to be-."

"That's just it," breaking away from him. "It's not what I need you to be, it's what you wanna be. I've witnessed it many times before, ya'll say this, that, and the other, but soon as a bitch body begin to spread and ain't lookin' appealing, ya'll out the door chasing dat other bitch that could care less about yo simple ass," throwing the pregnancy test at'em escaping to her bedroom. "I'm not about to go through that," she yelled over her shoulder.

Maniac wasted no time catching up to her hugging her from behind. "Just give me a chance," he whispered. "Just give me a chance."

After everything settled down she persuaded him to go buy

another test to make sure the first one was accurate. She went into the bathroom for a couple of minutes returning with the test where they waited patiently for the results.

"You look at it first," Peaches said giving him the test. "What it say, what it say?" Maniac looked seeing the plus sign feelin' a sense of father hood coming over him. "It say we gonna be a family," meeting her tears with his own!

///

"Ice, what the hell been going on?" Self asked lookin' at his partner in crime. "Dig Self, I'm not even gonna fake it to make it,I made a decision that was in our best interest, I know you wanna pull dat niggas cap back, but-." "But nothing," Self said cutting Ice off. "I come back from up top ready to put them goons on'em and they tellin' me you done red lighted'em," not believing his man would do such a thing.

"Self, don't look at me like dat, my decision was a business one. We got 500 of them thangs coming every month, rain, sleet, or snow! It's already fucked up TS gone leaving us witt 200 of them thangs on hand and you tellin' me to knock a nigga in the head adding another 50 to it, naw Self, that don't even make sense."

"Maybe it don't, but it will if his loyalty is ever tested," leaving Ice to ponder his last statement, whispering. "I'm sorry you feel dat way!"

///

"Baby girl, what's really good? "Face said sneakin' up on Max. "Don't make that a habit strapping her bay nine back to the inside of her thigh. Face already knowing how she carried it. "You where gonna hit yo boy?" "I just should, maybe it'll knock some sense into yo ass, you think I don't know," lookin' up at'em for the first time.

"C'mon Max," avoiding eye contact picking up the papers she was reading in front of her. "I can't help it I'm attracted to someone, long as I don't cross dat forbidden line, it's all good," glancing over the papers seeing Max and Dirt Bert was the owners of a McDonalds.

"It's not about you being attracted to someone, It's about you acting on it and betraying the one person who will never betray you," Max expressed gettin' up to retrieve her papers. "Thank you," taking her seat again." "Think what you want, say what you must, I love dat lil-nigga and I don't give a fuck about dat bitch, if she back door'em to fuck me, he don't need that ho no way," Face vented really mad at what he just read concerning Max and Dirt Bert.

"Now that you got dat- off yo chest, tell me somethin' that's gonna get us paid and not laid," Max said referring to Fat Jeff ."Cause if you keep on touchin' dat stove when I done told yo ass it's hot don't blame nobody, but yo self when you get burned!!"

//

"What the fuck you mean you quittin' yo job," J-rock demanded chasing behind his girl?"

"Like I said, I'm quittin' dat bull shit FedEx gig to run this Beauty salon Face and them about to open." "You think I'm about to let you quit a good paying job, to go work at some hood shit. Bitch, you done lost yo fuckinl mind?"

"Look baby," ,Turning around to look at her man cause he was trippin. "They giving me part ownership and paying me 15 dollars an hour to sit on my ass, You damn right I'm quittin dat bull shit! Now if you just wanna argue for the sake of arguing, not right now," pickin up her keys headed for the door.

"Bitch, let me find out you fuckin one of them niggas, I'm a go up side yo head," J-rock yelled at her on her way out the door. "I'm sorry it gotta go down like dat," she said sliding inside her BMW. "Cause a bitch gotta do what a bitch gotta do!!!" smiling as she pulled off.

//

Maniac was puttin' dat work in dat one way thinking about nothing more than providing for his family and securing their future. He already cashed out the first corporation with a mill that they decided to form another one flying so much money at her she thought a nigga stop sellin' drugs and started robbing banks.

It didn't take long for him to get back right thanks to Ice and willingness to let'em have his way. "Nigga, when you gonna let up off the gas pedal cause you're around here speeding", Ice Mike said counting close to 9 hundred thousand for the 50 joins he hit'em off witt.

"Ice, I ain't trying to see these niggas, but in my rear view mirror, I'm just trying to make it do what it do." "Trying! Nigga you done went from 40 a month to 50 a week, you're pass trying," Ice revealed half laughing. "And these niggas can't stand it" 'Like you told me before at the end of the day, if it don't make dollars it don't make sense and I feel sorry for any nigga that don't feel dat way!!"

//

"Screwed up, when you get as old as me you start to look at things differently, the things that use to be important ain't that important anymore versus the things a person thought wasn't, but really is."

"What you gettin' at old school?" "What's important, lil-momma continues to come down here despite you denying her visits and what's not important is what you think she did." "She's fuckin' witt my nigga old school, you can't right the wrong with this bull shit you throwing at me!"

"I'm not trying to right no wrong or wrong no right, but beware of the dog that brought you the bone, even doe a picture tells a story it never reveals the story behind it or the true story within it, you're lying here with half of a story refusing to get it all-."

"Mr. Boozer, you have a visit," the officer called over the intercom." "Keep lettin' yo pride dictates yo actions and over riding yo heart, you'll be one lonely mutherfucka in the end," leaving Noodles to decide and think about what he wanted to do next.

He stood there watching his girl sitting on the bench reading the latest Sister to Sister while listening to her iPod, she was use to'em not showing up her attention wasn't on the window, but on the things in front of her, if it wasn't for the little girl almost running over her feet she probably woulda never looked up until finishing her article.

They locked eyes for a moment before she slowly made her way to'em, he place his hand on the glass, she quickly followed suit as she took her seat not saying a word only staring into each others eyes until he finally reached for the receiver.

"Why you keep coming down here?" "Cause I refuse to let go, I refuse to think it's over when the best has yet to come", rubbing the glass as if she could actually feel the inside of his hand.

"The best is yet to come, how can we get to that when the worst is smackin' me in the face, to the point I'm hurting on the left side?" Coco could feel his pain and needed to say something that could comfort him through these times.

"Do you remember when I told you there may come a time where you might question what we have and my love for you, this is that time, just believe in me, believe in us and let nothing or no one come in between that." "It's easy for you to say, when you're not 'the one gettin' the short end of the stick!"

" I know baby, but please just hold on cause for me, lettin' go is not an option, I'm gonna continue to come down here regardless if you come up those stairs or not and when it's all over I'll be the one waiting to take you home and I promise I'll reveal everything and leave no rock unturned." Noodles listen seeing the look in her eyes and hearing how sincere she sounded wanting to go all in and allow his heart to lead the way despite his mind tellin' him, fuck dat bitch!

"Dig love, don't play me for no fool and string me along if this ain't where you wanna be, cause it's all fun and games until somebody gets hurt"!!!

CHAPTER 23

Never Saw it coming

"I'm tellin' you, just wait another week or so we can get more out of'em." "I don't have time, I got too much on my plate already and its time to put this nigga behind us," Face explained talkin' to Peaches and Cheri. "I need you to get dat nigga to go home, so I don't have to worry about moving a body."

"When you want me to make this happen," Peaches asked upset that she wouldn't have enough time to work'em for that last bit of change she wanted to get out of'em.

"Tonight!"

"How the fuck I'm suppose to make dat happen when I never been to his place before, shit, the nigga act like he's homeless shacking up with me every night-."

"I would too," Face responded lickin' his lips. "Fuck you Face," she barked. "I'll make it happen for you one of these days, but until then, do what you gotta do," leaving them in Cheri's living room as he exited planning his next move.

"You act like you done fell in love with this nigga or some-thing." "Bitch please, I could care less about dat nigga. I'm trying to work'em for another 300 to bring our total to 1.5, then they can have his ass."

"Trick, you been puttin' dat work in, I say we make it happen for ourselves and knock dat nigga off. "It sound good and it would sound even better if I knew you wouldn't freeze up on a bitch." "Freeze up!" " Yea freeze up, cause it's one thing to say what you'll do, but it's another to actually do it. I love us to much not to put you in a situation not knowing."

"Bitch, I can't believe you, but it's cool," not even gettin' mad. "I'll just have to show and prove then next time don't pump fake, let's make it happen!!!"

//

Maniac was extremely pleased with himself being he bounced back the way that he did and having one of the Baddest chicks in the city about to bear his child, what else could a man possibly want.

Just as he exited the studio on Elm and Green about to jump into his SUV Det. Triggs appeared outta nowhere.

"What the fuck you want," Maniac barked closing his door puttin' the key in the ignition. "I know somethin' you would love to know." Det. Triggs responded with a devilish smile on his face. "Don't we all," turning the ignition seeing all eyes on them from the people standing out and about.

"It use to be a time we shared all types of information with each other without the politics in the way, but since you're fuckin' witt certain people, you done put a fence up acting like you never played both side before," smiling as Maniac nervously fought to put his truck in gear.

"Dig Triggs, this ain't a good look for us to be out here like this, answer yo phone I'll hit you in 10," pullin' off catchin' the look of a few spectators as he drove down Green St.

//

"Ya'll be careful tonight," Max said taking a seat across from Dirt Bert. "I talked with Bull-Moose and she informed me, Det. Triggs is watching and trying to catch ya'll slippin'-." "Damn baby girl, you got yo hands into everything and everyone", Dirt Bert said recognizing how tight her game was. "It gotta be like dat if you expect to survive in this game! You know anything about chess?" "Naw Max, I can't say that I do. I always thought it was a old man game."

"Oh no Dirt Bert, it's much more than dat, more than you can ever imagine," just as she was about to go into greater depth a small commotion erupted outside her window with Tight-White in the thick of things.

"You gonna give me this little money when you owe me more. Naw play boy-." "I got you tomorrow, I promise you Tight." "Hell naw, don't got me, get me," Tight-White demanded about to snatch quarters outta shorty when Dirt Bert intervened.

"Tight-White, let dat shit be!"

For that split second he turned to respond oh boy took off running yellin' over his shoulder. "I got you, I promise, I got you."

"You better or I'm a beat dat ass," Tight-White yelled back turning to Dirt Bert. "You saved his ass this time ,but let'em come through here tomorrow without mine!!"

///

"It took you long enough, I was beginning to think you didn't fuck with me no more," Det. Triggs said driving up Vine St.

"Cut the small talk! What you know that you think I wanna know?" "Slow down pimpin', what I got to say believe me you wanna know, so miss me with the tough man act and listen up. You done made some people very unhappy touching their love ones that the only way they could hurt you back was to touch yours in return." Maniac almost crashed hearing what Triggs just told'em "I don't know what these boys agenda is or what they got in the mix for yo ass, but I do know these boys don't play fair and probably got the up's on you and you don't even know it, so my advice to you, change everything up from yo living arrangements, to the truck you drive, all the way down to the way you move around in these streets."

"I owe you for this one," pausing to clear his thoughts before asking. "You think they responsible for my mother's death?" "I'm quite sure of it, but trying to prove it is something totally different." "I feel dat, but if it ain't asking too much, who them boys be?"

Det. Triggs laughed to himself. "Damn Maniac, you touched that many people you can't narrow it down, that's crazy, but for what it's worth, dem E-town boys are watchin, ending their conversation allowing Maniac to deal with his own demons!!

Self pulled up just as Maniac truck bent the corner, he couldn't stand seeing him sharing the same air he breathed and the thought of him double clutching and playin' both sides of the fence boiled his skin more ways than one.

"I'ma have dat ass before it's all said and done," Self told himself entering the building. "I see yo partner just left."

"C'mon Self, witt dat bull shit, the only partner I got is standing in this room witt me. You know the deal with oh boy, it's all about the paper." "You losing sight of what's real and what's not, all about some paper allowing this nigga to continue to eat off our plate when you know in yo heart he ain't right."

Ice sat back knowing he couldn't argue the truth, let alone debate it. "Okay Self, do you, but I just hit'em witt 50 joints-."

"Don't even trip, I'ma let'em knock dat off, but once he drop them ends off, it'll be the last drop he make in this life time," smiling lookin' across at his man happy he finally saw the light and puttin' a end to this foolishness!!

Maniac rushed home after his conversation with Det. Triggs realizing the threat of someone harming his girl and unborn child was realer than real.

He never took into account the love Mello people had for'em or the extent they would go to revenge his death as he pushed his SUV to the limits weaving through traffic staying in his rear view mirror making sure he wasn't being followed.

Peaches heard his truck pull into the drive way while lying on the couch plottin' how she could kill two birds with one stone not knowing one of them was about to be handed to her.

"Baby! grab yo shit and let's roll," he ordered pullin' his 9mm makin' sure one was in the chamber. "Do it sound like I'm speaking French! Go get yo shit!"

Peaches stood there seeing the look of fear in his eyes wondering to herself what the hell done happened watchin' him move from window to window lookin' outta them. "Baby stop, you scaring me! "Running to'em allowing him to comfort her.

"Peaches," Digging her head outta his chest. "It's not safe for us to be here, the sooner we leave the better-." "Where will we go, where will we stay," she asked hysterical lookin' up at'em? "Don't worry, I got us"!!

///

"Screwed up, what got you laid back in chill mode?" old school inquired entering Noodles cell. "I'm just lying here trying to put it all together wondering if my man would really betray me like dat." "If he betray you, he wasn't yo man." "My point exactly, but this the same man who raised me, put me on my feet and guided me through mostly all my trials and tribulations, even with this bogus ass case I got now, he put a play in motion and caused a chain reaction to where I'm about to beat this shit. Its crazy old school, I can't explain it." "What's understood don't need to be explained," old school adviced'em.

"That's a prime example of what I'm talkin' about and what I'm going through right now. My man used to hit me witt all sorts of clichés' and me not knowing the true meaning or understanding behind them just took'em as some slick shit to say, and the one that's keeps coming to mind the most, believe nothing of what you hear and only half of what you see! How the fuck is that possible and I'm staring at a picture of my man kissin' my girl," Noodles ranted and raved lookin' at old school for some type of magical response.

"All I can tell you, is stop staring at a picture hoping it talk back cause it ain't gonna happen and one thing for sure, what ever happens in the dark will come to light, just be willing to accept it good or bad!!"

//

Peaches felt lady luck was on her side entering Maniac house from the garage, she had accomplished one obstacle, but her greatest challenge yet was gettin' dat 300k before them boys came.

"We keepin' sercets," she said with a little attitude trying not to touch anything that would leave any finger prints.

"Go ahead witt dat bull shit," dropping his duffle bag in front of the couch turning to watch Peaches pullin' her suit case on wheels. "Damn you sexy when you mad," trying to ease the tension between them. "Boy, don't play with me, either you tell me what's going on or watch me jump into my truck and take my ass home."

Maniac leaned against the edge of his couch knowing he had to reveal something cause lettin' her go back home wasn't an option.

"Come here girl," holding his arms out. "I did some things in my life I'm not proud of, but its somethin' I did nevertheless. The people I caused harm to and brought a black cloud into their world founded out, I was behind it and now they want to return the favor."

Peaches listened realizing things where unraveling and somewhere along the way a nigga slipped and woke up the dead.

"So what you need me to do?" giving him the impression she was down for whatever "Just continue to love me and give me a chance to get at these niggas!!!", kissing her softly on the lips grabbing her suit case alone with his bag heading toward the bedroom.

///

"What you smiling about," Det. Jones asked taking a seat across from his coworker.

"Sometimes you got to let nature run its course and if that don't work, plant the seed and point'em in the right direction," Det. Triggs responded knowing the streets of Cinti was about to become a war zone. "What you gettin' at detective," hoping he wouldn't crawl back into, his shell and not reveal his hand."Just say, I'm a about to allow justice to be served the old fashion way." "How is that?" seeing that far out look in his eyes. "A eye for a eye, and those left standing _at the end we gonna lock their asses up, you know what I'm talkin' about," laughing at the sight he envisioned in his mind.

///

"Its show time," Face yelled gettin' everybody attention. "I just got Peaches text message, we out in five."

Everybody began to dress accordingly for their mission when Cheri approached Face. "I wanna be the one to send his ass away from here." "I wouldn't have it any other way," seeing somethin' in her no one else has yet to see in her watchin' Max watch him.

They all climbed inside a utility van with Apples driving and Cheri riding shot gun with the guys posted in the back discussing how everything was suppose to go down. Within 20 minutes they where hittin' the Forest Park exit.

"Okay Apples, once we hit his street circle the block and once you feel the coast is clear let us out and keep it moving, I'll radio you in once all is good," Face said puttin' shit in motion.

The guys exited the van swiftly running to the back of the house checkin' their surroundings before pickin' the lock. The sound of H-town filled the house lettin them know Peaches had his undivided attention, they quietly creep up the stairs allowing the music to lead them to their destination, they peeped inside the room. what they witnessed caused them to pause and appreciate the song being played.

"Cause tonight baby/I wanna get freaky witt you/let me lick you up and down/til you say stop, let me play witt yo body baby/til you get hot." "Surprise mutherfucka," Face yelled causing Maniac to suddenly look up from eatin' Peaches forbidden fruit only to feel the impact of his 9mm across the top of his head and being snatched from between her legs to the floor. "Nigga move, I'll end this shit now," placing the gun to the back of his head.

Maniac laid there motionless on the floor as blood soaked into the carpet from the open wound on his head. Dirt Bert. and Tight-White stared at Peaches nakedness as she laid on her back legs wide open placing two fingers inside her pussy whispering, "you want some", causing them to almost lose sight of what was going on.

"Please, just don't harm my wife and unborn child," Maniac pleaded finally finding his voice.

"That's the least of yo worries," Face said as Dirt Bert and Tight-White appeared securing his arms and legs while Face laid dat cool steel on his neck.

All types of things were running through his mind, he knew the game all to well knowing if he cooperated and gave his intruders what they wanted 9 outta 10 his family would be spared.

As they drug his ass from the bedroom he tried to peek back at his girl before his life on earth was no more.

"Nigga, what the fuck you lookin' at," Face yelled striking him instantly across the head sending him to a room of total darkness.

While the guys attended to their business Peaches attended to hers, grabbing Maniac duffle bag taking 10 of those thangs outta there trying to stuff them in her suit case."Damn it! "She mumbled realizing some- thing gotta go in order to pull this off.

"Little red riding hood, the big bad wolf is secured," Face spoke through his wireless walkie talkie. Apples pulled right into the drive way after receiving his message, they quickly began the clean up job from top to bottom making sure their wasn't any physical evidence of Peaches ever being there.

"Girl, what you up to," Cheri asked seein' Peaches taking the sheets off the bed wrapping some of clothes inside. "Here you go," grabbing Maniac duffle bag. "I found this under the bed," giving Cheri the signal to shut the fuck up knowing their conversation was being heard. "My bad," covering her mic. "I had to make room in my suit case to put 10 of them- thangs in there. Shit, I couldn't get dat 300k, but you better believe I was gonna get somethin'."

"I ain't mad at you, but here," taking her hand off her mic tossing her the all black outfit with her wireless walkie talkie.

Maniac was finally coming around hearing the noise of a vacuum running wondering what was going on as he began to open his eyes realizing he was face down on the couch tied the fuck up.

Face was sittin' across from him noticing his movement. "We got a live one," Speaking through his walkie talkie. "Little riding hood, come get yo big bad wolf."

Cheri exited the bedroom with duffle bag in hand coming down the stairs tossing the bag at Face's feet before snatchin' Maniac off the couch. "What's the combination," puttin her foot on his neck. Maniac fought to breathe realizing the foot on his neck was to small to be a mans.

"Little red riding hood, he's not gonna be able to tell you anything unless you take some pressure off his neck," Face calmly stated.

Cheri was so caught up in finally gettin' the chance to revenge her brother's death, she needed Face voice in her ear to bring her back to the agenda at hand. "What's the combination," she asked again takin' her foot completely off, his neck. "18-33-3," he said not giving a fuck about nothing, but saving his girl and the baby she was carrying. "Please! Don't harm my wife. Ya'll can have it all, I got close to 900k in the safe and 50 joints."

Cheri quickly put her foot on his neck tellin' him. "Shut the fuck up! Duck tape this bitch," calling Tight-White for his assistance while Dirt Bert got at the safe.

"Punk ass nigga," Tight-White said kickin' the shit outta his ass. "Yo momma gave up a harder fight than this," causing Maniac to relive the pain of losing her 'all over again.

"You coward mutherfucka, let me loose,I'll kill all you mutherfuckas," not caring one or the other about dying, he just wanted to get at somebody. "Yea right," Tight-White said kickin' him again before duck taping his ass.

"The nest is empty, ready to ride," Dirt Bert informed them through his walkie talkie. Everybody received it including Peaches making her way down the stairs carrying her suit case and dragging the bed linen behind her. "Bring his ass over here," Cheri demanded seeing everything packed and ready to roll.

Tight-White snatched his ass off the floor and the first thing he noticed was his girl dressed in all black standing alone with no restraints when Cheri took off her mask.

Maniac couldn't believe his eyes lookin' back and forth between them cussin' and screaming as tears began to fall dreading the day he laid eyes on dat bitch.

"That's right mutherfucka, you been played," Cheri informed him waving Peaches over. "You thought you where gonna fuck my brother, my bitch, and fuck me too," grabbing the picture outta her pocket lettin' him get a good look before rubbin' it in his face while her and Peaches shared an intimate kiss in front of everybody. "And I wasn't going to do nothin'! You got the game fucked up! Turning his ass around and bending'em over the couch."

Everybody thought they had seen it all, heard it all, but from what Cheri indicating the best was yet to be seen. Cheri roughly pulled his boxers down as she dropped her pants revealing a 10" strap on.

"Hold up ."Dirt Bert said lookin' at her like she was crazy. "What you about to do with dat?" "I'm about to show this nigga what it feel like to get fucked with no Vaseline", spreading his butt cheeks as she forced the head up his ass.

Maniac fought like crazy to no avail feelin' every inch entered his rectum as he screamed, hollered, and everything else he could think of to block out the pain from Cheri banging his guts out.

"That's right mutherfucka take this dick," She said violating him to the highest degree until his bowels let loose causing Cheri to pullout of'em.

"I told you," Peaches said seeing her girl covered in blood and feces. "You had to build'em up for dat one," high fiving her girl for a job well done. Nevertheless, Maniac was just as happy now the whole ordeal was over with his ass still in the air.

"Lets wrap this up, little red riding hood, you put on a hellva show," Face spoke through the wireless walkie talkie.

"Give me five more minutes and we out," walking around the couch positioning herself in front of him grabbing a hand full of hair lifting his head just as Apples appeared snatchin' her ski mask off revealing her identity.

"Yea mutherfucka, I'm the last person you thought you'd ever see," smackin' the shit outta his ass before Cheri started rubbin' her bloody and shitty strap-on in his face. Seeing Seal he realized she was the one that connected the dots and the cause of his down fall.

"How do it feel to get fucked by a girl," Cheri whispered in his ear breakin his train of thought. "I should blow yo brains out," reaching back for Face's gun with the silencer placing it to his temple. "But that would mean you had one," pulling back and walking away, taking everybody by surprise. "You need to die for who you are and not what you betrayed to be, bitch ass nigga," jammin' the silencer up his ass lettin' off six quick shots. "What the fuck," everybody in the room said not believing what they just witnessing!

Then she turned him over and hit'em twice in the heart for good measure. "That's my kinda girl," Tight-White yelled seeing Cheri differently as everybody exited the house with Peaches still shocked headed toward the garage with suit case in tow.

30 minutes or so they were pulling into the drive way to the honey cone hide out and just like before Face lead by example stripping down to his boxers laying everything in the center of the room. One by one everybody followed suit leaving the crew in their under wear, but this time around Tight-White wasn't staring at Apples." "Shorty, what's happening?"

"What the fuck you mean what's happening?" Cheri said lookin' at the way Tight-White was lookin' her up and down. "Don't make me beat yo ass Tight-White," causing everybody to burst out laughing.

"You better leave my baby alone," Max jumped in saying gettin' at the money bag. "Dirt Bert handle this," pointing at the clothes in the middle of the floor. "And don't forget the linen in the van," Face said going to clean up. Within an hour the crew was cleaned up talkin' about the events that had taken place while Max and Face where puttin' together their next course of moves.

"Excuse me, excuse me," Max yelled gettin' everybody attention. "To night wasn't about the money, but more or less to revenge one of our own that was taken away before his time-." "And tonight," Face said passin' out bottles of ace of spade. "We will celebrate his life of today and his life of tomorrow," raising his bottle high in the air before pouring some out saying "R.I.P, my little soldier," allowing a moment of silence to pass. "We got close to 900k meaning everybody got a buck and some change coming. What ya'll trying to do witt it? "Max asked.

"Invest mine," Dirt Bert said leading the way for everybody else to follow suit leaving Tight-White as the only one not to respond.

"Fuck what ya'll talkin' about, let me get dat change and invest dat dollar," causing the whole room to laugh including Max. It was only one somethin' in the morning everybody sippin' and drinkin' doing them when Face cell phone vibrated.

"What's up?" he said not recognizing the number. "You hang up on me and I'm callin' you back," the female responded makin' Face smile. "Dig love, let's stop playin' games and make this happen cause once our boy touchdown we gonna have to break up like Ben and J-Lo", gettin' into his mack mode.

"Let's get a room at the Embassy suites-" "Never dat, meet me at my spot in 20 and use the back entrance." "Don't want nobody seeing me coming or leaving?" "I don't know about you leaving, but best believe you'll be cuming.

Max noticed Face in his mack mode and instantly knew who it was on the other end without having to ask. "Dig ya'll, I would love to stay, but I got something I need to attend to, so ya'll continue to enjoy ya'll selves and I'll see ya'll when I see ya, unless ya'll see me first," making his exit quickly to go make it do what it do!!!

//

Coco was sittin' in her car making sure she had everything in her overnight bag when Face pulled up in a utility van, had he not pulled directly beside her she woulda never known.

"Let me find out you got a 9 to 5!" "I'ma do whatever it take to get at them ends," he responded helping her outta her car. Within minutes they were inside his apartment settin' the mood for what was about to go down.

"Here put this in," giving Face a CD outta her bag. "You came prepared, what else you got in the bag?" Face inquired. "Everything we need to make our night as special as I can especially when you know we dead wrong," lookin' at Face sideways. "But you only live once," pullin' a oz of dat white widow out. "Here daddy," tossing him the bag while she disappeared to put something more comfortable on. Face fell back grabbing his cherry wraps puttin' one in the air instantly making himself a drink and Coco one as well. As the music began to play softly in the back ground Coco appeared wearing a red hot negligee with red stockings and garter belt to match workin' the shit outta some 6" stilettos. "You like what you see," turning around allowing him to see the whole package.

Face could only shake his head up and down tellin' himself to calm down as she began to give him a show many people would pay to see through a glass window man or woman, but here he was living out a fantasy he had the moment he laid eyes on her.

After he finished his blunt and half of his drink he was ready to fuck, the bull shit wasn't nothing glancing at his watch seeing that it was damn near 2 remembering he needed to make an important phone call.

"I don't excite you enough, you need to make a phone call," taking the time to down her drink calming her nerves.

"Naw love, just a little somethin' I needed to handle", grabbing Coco hand leading her toward his bedroom not wanting to waste another minute!!

"Det. Triggs, someone just called claiming yo biggest surprise can be found at 3232 Beresford in Forest Park. What would you like me to do?" the dispatcher asked. "Send the nearest patrol car in the area to that address, I'll be there in 20 placing his disco lights on top of his car and hit it.

Det. Triggs pulled up to a circus every TV station in the city was on location with 20 or so police cars parked up and down the street. "Seal this area off, this is a fuckin' crime scene," he yelled at a couple officers standing around doing nothing.

"It's crazy in there," Det. Jones said as they entered the house and true enough you had unbelievable people walking in and out peepin' at the horrible scene in side.

"What we got," Det. Triggs asked the coroner? "Black male, 6ft, 230, no older than 28, multiple gunshot wounds up the rectum and two to the heart-."

Det. Triggs looked around puttin' on his gloves grabbing a hand full of hair to get a good look at his suspect instantly recognizing Maniac. "Get out, get the fuck out," he yelled and for those who wasn't moving fast enough he began pushing them out.

"What's wrong?" Det. Jones asked seeing the tears in his eyes. "Nothing!" Turning grabbing his handkerchief outta his pocket placing it over Maniac heart allowing the blood to soak into it knowing what he had to do.

"Man, what the fuck you doing," seeing a foul play being put in motion. "Somethin' I shoulda done a long time ago," allowing the circus back in while he sped off on some Mark Foreman shit!!!

///

Face woke up to a warm feeling between his legs seeing Coco washing her juices from his dick.

"Yea shorty, you got dat work," attempting to reach out to her only to find himself tied the fuck up. "Okay shorty untie yo boy I ain't into dat S&M shit, you can have yo way without all this", laying back seeing both of his hands tied to the bed post as well as feet.

"Calm down tiger," shaddle'em fully clothed. "Do you remember what I told you?" "Quit playin' and untie me before I get mad!" "I don't give a fuck about you gettin' mad, get mad! "Smackin' the shit outta his ass. "Now, do you remember what I told you?"

Face was in his body. "Bitch, you better keep yo hands to yo self before I-." "Before you what," smackin the shit outta his ass again causing him to raise off the bed attempting to put hands on her only for his restraints to stop'em. "Ooh bitch, you wanna play like dat," tasting the blood inside his mouth. "That's right, I'm running this," muggin' his ass asking him again. "Do you remember what I told you?"

"We had so many conversation, you tell me what the fuck you said!" "Wrong answer mutherfucka," back handing his ass this time. "Look bitch!" Face yelled. "I don't know what type of games yo crazy ass on, but I'm a beat dat ass when you untie me!"

"Ain't that cute, but you don't have a clue do you?"

Face laid there struggling with his restraints realizing she had the upper hand deciding to play a softer angle.

"Okay, okay shorty, you win-." "I know," punching him straight in his eye. Ahh!"he yelled feelin' his eye swell up instantly. "Bitch, what the hell done got into you," lookin' into her eyes seeing somethin' that wasn't right.

"You don't remember me tellin' you always look a person in the eyes before you kill'em?"

Just then Faces memory went back in time standing there lookin' at that 10 or 11 year old after killin' both her parents raising his gun about to lay her young ass to rest when outta no where she said. "Before you kill me, let me see yo face".

The picture and that conversation was so real and clear in his mind he continued to let it play out. "Why the fuck you wanna see my face when it will be the the last face you'll see in this life time"? "I was taught you look a person in the eyes before you kill'em and I wanna give you dat opportunity, plus see the face I need to look for once you cross over to the other side on judgment day, so I can revenge the murder of my mother, my father, and myself-."

"That can't be you," looking' at Coco in disbelief not seeing any resemblance from that little girl except her eyes. "How did you survive?" knowing he hit her twice to the dome.

"I had a real bad accident when I was younger that the doctors inserted a metal plate in my head not knowing it would be the reason I'm still alive today. You have no idea all the things I went through, the different surgeries, the sleepless nights, the nightmare of yo fuckin' face, the face that brought me so much pain, you fucking coward", hittin' him with two quick jabs swelling his other eye.

"00h bitch! "Face screamed wishing one of his restraints came loose!

"Shut the fuck up! I just wanna know was it Dirt Bert or Tight-White with you dat night?"

"Wouldn't you wanna know," smiling not giving a fuck. "It's crazy the man you sucked and fucked is the same man who watched yo mother give me the best." Coco smacked the shit outta his ass preventing him from finishing his sentence remembering how her mother degraded herself trying to save her family.

"It's cool," gettin' control of her emotions. "I'll tell'em both how you toyed with their lives when you coulda saved one of them.

Face saw the end coming and wanted to take as many people witt'em as he could, but his pride and what he stood for wouldn't let'em staring down at Death before dishonor tatted over his heart.

"It was Mello, Cheri brother," he whispered.

At first she didn't know if to believe him or not, but seeing the look in his eyes, she knew it was the truth pullin' her 9mm with the silencer already attached.

"Damn bitch, you came prepared ", accepting his fate.

"That I did," placing the 9mm to his temple as he closed his eyes. "No Face, don't cheat me from the way I was raised," pokin' him with the gun until he opened his eyes.

She stared deeply into his eyes. "I can't do you like you did me," pullin' the gun slowly away from his temple at the same time reachin' into her pocket with the other hand producing a straight razor and in one swift motion sliced him across his throat hittin' his jugular as blood squirted everywhere.

Coco sat on top of' him as his life slowly slipped away tellin' her parents to rest in peace. She quickly began cleaning up taking the sheets from beneath'em placing them into a bag, then removing his restraints throwing them in there too walking through his apartment collecting any physical evidence of her being there tossing them items in the bag as well.

She stood in the living room making one last sweep when she remembered the CD, just as she hit the eject button she heard the sound of sirens then the sound of tires coming to a sudden stop, car doors opening and closing.

She didn't hesitate running to Face's third floor window seeing what she already knew turning quickly grabbing the things she needed hittin' the lights as she rushed down the hallway leading to the back door when suddenly the front door flew open taking her by surprise, she spent around dropping everything firing from one knee, the first shot missed badly, but the next three didn't!!!!

TO BE CONTINUE ...

YO best asset is using yo eyes and ears!!!!!!!

Vincent Boozer

December 15, 1961 - February 11, 2011

The last of a dying breed.

You'll never be forgotten UNK...

Carl Anderson

Known as Face. This young and very talented story-teller is showcasing his skills in his first debut novel, The Forbidden Fruit. Reppin' E-Town, he gives you the life he was exposed to :living within the inner city. Determined not to fall victim of his environment, he stayed focused never losing sight of his dreams and ambitions. Now he's able to reap the rewards of his sacrifices!!!

Hit up Carl Anderson at bigfacecarl@yahoo.com

Look out for his follow up novel

Never Seen It Coming

November 1st, 2014

Ms. Khadijah

Known as Dede, this beautiful young lady has seen her share of trails and tribulations. Digging deep within her own life experiences, she is able to give her readers an up close look into her world.

Labeling her debut novel, The Forbidden Fruit, her testimony!!!

Hit up Khadijah at kabhulaziz0002@gmail.com

allnpublishing.com

allnpublishing@gmail.com

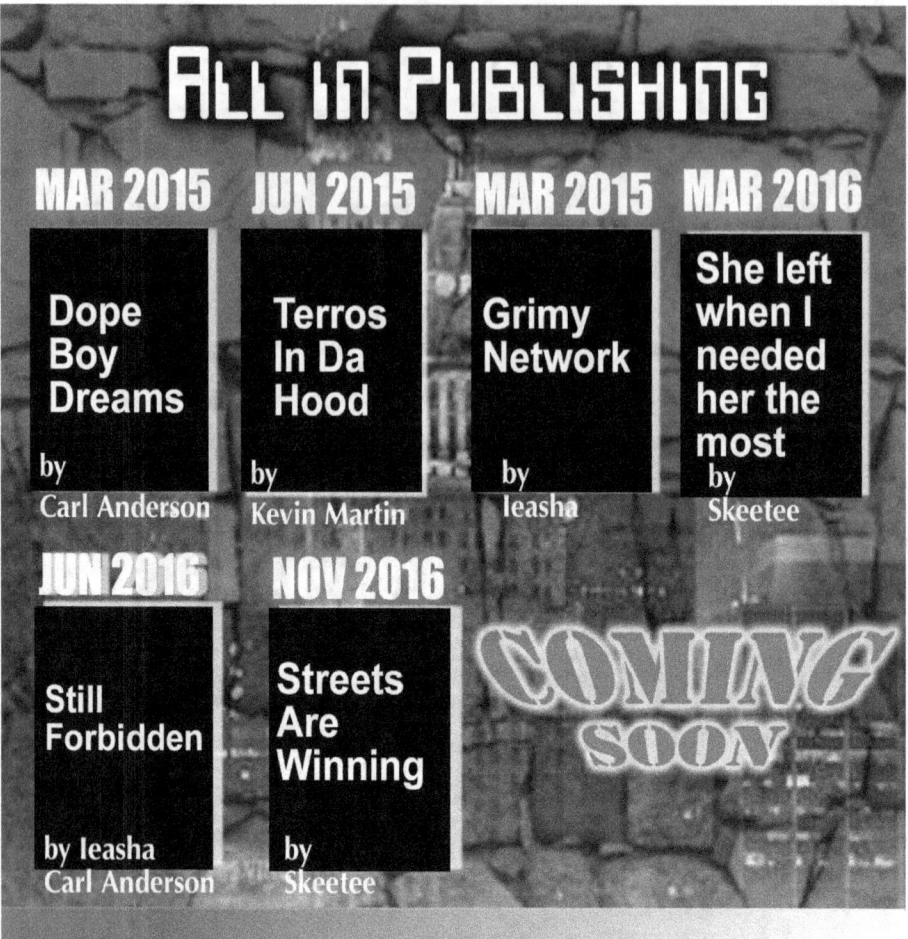

A'Milli Monroe
Model, Dancer, MC, Entertainer

The *Elusive Model* of
All in Publishing
Bookamilli@gmail.com   **PH: 305-726-1192**

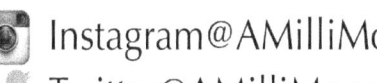

Instagram@AMilliMonroe
Twitter@AMilliMonroe
FaceBook AMilliMonroe

www.ingramcontent.com/pod-product-compliance
Lightning Source LLC
Chambersburg PA
CBHW070117260626
47160CB00004B/1511